"Beautifully ... ... unexpected in the best o... ...n McGuire, *New York ... ...ling author of Ashes of Honor*, on *Wisp of a Thing*

PRAISE FOR *THE HUM AND THE SHIVER*

"With a deep love for the mountains embedded in his language, Bledsoe crafts a deceptively simple story of family and community, laced throughout with the music and beliefs of a magical reality. Elegantly told."
—*Library Journal* (starred review)

"This powerful, character-driven drama, set forth in superbly lucid prose, occurs against an utterly convincing backdrop and owns complications enough to keep everyone compulsively turning the pages. A sheer delight."
—*Kirkus Reviews* (starred review)

"Bledsoe's rich, nearly poetic prose . . . captured me at page one and didn't let me go 'til the end. If you are a fan of urban fantasy, this is a book you need to add to your list today. There are secrets ancient and wild waiting for you to discover, and I enjoyed every minute."
—*Seattle Post-Intelligencer*

"Bledsoe turns standard urban fantasy tropes on their head. . . . The slowly unfolding mystery of the Tufa is a fascinating and absorbing masterpiece of world-building."
—*Publishers Weekly*

TOR BOOKS BY ALEX BLEDSOE

Blood Groove
The Girls with Games of Blood

The Sword-Edged Blonde
Burn Me Deadly
Dark Jenny
Wake of the Bloody Angel
He Drank, and Saw the Spider

The Hum and the Shiver
Wisp of a Thing

THE HUM
AND THE SHIVER

ALEX BLEDSOE

TOR®
fantasy

A TOM DOHERTY ASSOCIATES BOOK
NEW YORK

THE HUM AND THE SHIVER

Copyright © 2011 by Alex Bledsoe

A Tor Book
Published by Tom Doherty Associates, LLC
175 Fifth Avenue
New York, NY 10010

www.tor-forge.com

Tor® is a registered trademark of Tom Doherty Associates, LLC.

ISBN 978-0-7653-6590-3

Tor books may be purchased for educational, business, or promotional use. For information on bulk purchases, please contact Macmillan Corporate and Premium Sales Department at 1-800-221-7945, extension 5442, or write specialmarkets@macmillan.com.

First Edition: October 2011
First Mass Market Edition: December 2013

Printed in the United States of America

0 9 8 7 6 5 4 3 2 1

ACKNOWLEDGMENTS

Special thanks to Rev. Jacqueline Sharer Robertson, Dr. Elizabeth Perry, James Travis, Jen Cass, Kate Campbell, Sjolind's Chocolate House, Schubert's Diner, Marlene Stringer, Paul Stevens, and Valette, Jake, and Charlie.

THE HUM
AND THE SHIVER

1

A screech owl stood on the porch rail, its tiny talons scratching against the wood. The dawn light made the tufts of its wind-ruffled feathers look jagged and bloody. The bird had a voice far out of proportion to its size, and was intimately acquainted with the night winds that guided the Tufa destiny. It was also, when seen during the day, an omen of death.

So when Chloe Hyatt, a pureblood Tufa, saw it through the little window over the kitchen sink, she froze.

Water from the faucet ran heedlessly down the drain. She began to hum a secret tune for both calm and protection. The day's events were going to be difficult enough without adding this to it.

The owl's head turned almost 180 degrees to stare at her. The movement was so sudden, she jumped. For a moment the bird held her gaze; then it flew off into the trees.

She followed its flight and caught the haint's outline

as it faded into the dawn. As it had done for the last week, the apparition remained silent and watchful all night. When it first appeared, they'd all approached it, but it ignored entreaties from Chloe; her husband, Deacon; and their younger son, Aiden. Kell, her older son, would have sensed it and come home from Knoxville had it been meant for him. That left only one Hyatt ordained to receive its message: her wayward middle child and only daughter.

But though the haint wanted someone else, Chloe knew the owl was intended just for her. It wasn't the first death omen the night winds had recently blown her way.

The sun crested the side of the mountain, turning the ominous red dawn to gold. Midges and pollen hung sparkling in the air. Everything brought by the night wind vanished.

Deacon came up behind her and kissed her on the shoulder. He smelled of aftershave and that generic dandruff shampoo he liked. "Morning," he said quietly, not wanting to wake Aiden. The boy had been so excited about his big sister's impending return that he hadn't fallen asleep until midnight, after both Chloe and Deacon sang him their usually foolproof lullabies. Even Tufa children, it seemed, could hear the hum but resist the shiver.

"You haven't made the coffee," Deacon observed.

"Sorry," Chloe murmured. She put the carafe under the faucet.

Deacon peered out the window. "Was the haint still out there this morning?"

Chloe nodded as she filled the coffeemaker. She did not mention the death owl. Deacon had been upset enough by the unseasonable blooms on her acacias.

"You'd think it'd know she ain't here yet," Deacon continued. Chloe dried her hands, hoping Deacon didn't notice the trembling. "Just 'cause they're from the other side don't mean they're any smarter than they were before. When it was alive, it might've been one of those people who were always early for things."

He nodded. "True enough. You sure it ain't for you or me? Maybe we should call in Bliss, see if she can talk to it."

"It won't speak to her, you know that. Aiden can't see it, and Kell would've been home from college by now if it was for him, sensitive as he is. That only leaves one of us."

Deacon nodded. He spoke the name with all the weight it carried: the name of his middle child, the one who caused him more sleepless nights and grief than the other two put together. It was a name the whole world now knew, the name of his only daughter.

"Bronwyn."

The Black Hawk military helicopter blew wispy fog from the treetops as it circled over Needsville, Tennessee. The rotors' throb bounced off the Smoky Mountains, echoing as if a herd of gigantic, apocalyptic horsemen were charging over Redford's Ridge.

The pilot dropped as low as he dared, twenty feet above the power lines, as he approached the town. He recalled his father's description of a similar approach to an Asian village, only instead of power lines, it had been palm trees, and the villagers had pointed guns and artillery instead of fingers and American flags.

"Your folks are sure glad to see you," he yelled over his shoulder to the young woman in the passenger seat behind him. She did not respond.

Needsville's main street—its *only* street—swarmed with people watching the helicopter as it passed overhead. But Bronwyn Hyatt, a private in the United States Army for at least the next thirty days, knew that the pilot's observation was wrong; these weren't "her" people packing the street below. Hell, the entire population of Needsville couldn't block its own traffic. Most of the crowd consisted of reporters and well-wishing strangers drawn to the circus her return home had become; the vehicles she saw were TV news vans and shiny SUVs, not the rusted-out pickups and old sedans of the natives. As she scanned the crowd, she saw very few heads with the same distinctive straight, jet-black Tufa hair that she wore neatly pulled back and tucked under her uniform's cap.

Her official minder, public relations liaison Major Dan Maitland, peered out the other window. "Jumping Jesus on a pogo stick, look at all that," he said. "Where the hell are they all going to stay? Didn't you say there's only one hotel in town?"

Bronwyn shifted her weight slightly to take the pressure off her leg. The metal rings and struts of the monstrous Ilizarov apparatus wrapped around her thigh and calf, sending bone-holding screws and pins through her pasty, tortured skin. She would've been more comfortable on a stretcher, but she'd been on her back quite enough these last nine weeks. And not, she reflected wryly, in the way her Needsville reputation always implied.

Maitland leaned close and shouted above the engine, "Can you see okay?"

Bronwyn shrugged. The engine's vibrations jingled the new medals on her chest. "Seen it all before," she said.

"Yeah, but from the air?"

Again she shrugged. Tufa flight was something she could never explain to someone like him.

Maitland patted her on the shoulder. He was a career officer, frighteningly good at his job, and exuded false sincerity with such skill that dozens of flash-in-the-pan media figures still counted him as a friend when he likely couldn't remember their names. Luckily Bronwyn had seen right through him at their first meeting and maintained a cool cordiality that ultimately perplexed him. He seemed unable to imagine anyone, male or female, immune to his charm. Watching him hide this confusion was one of the few things that still brought Bronwyn any pleasure.

Maitland said something to the pilot, and the helicopter passed back over the town, banking sharply so Bronwyn could be seen at the window. The harness that held her in the seat dug into her shoulder. When she placed her left palm against the glass to maintain her balance, she saw many of the hands below wave in response. The sun glinted off a thousand camera lenses. None of this was a surprise, but it disheartened her just the same. A hero's homecoming, and she couldn't even remember what she'd done to earn it. Or even if she'd done anything at all.

As the helicopter rose to continue on to the small county airport, she caught a glimpse of an old man seated in a rocking chair outside the post office. Rockhouse Hicks did not deign even to acknowledge the circus around him, or her passage overhead. It wasn't in his nature to admit, even for a moment, that someone else might be more significant than himself. That made her smile; some things in Needsville truly never changed.

But the smile faded almost at once. That was both Needsville's charm and its curse. Nothing of significance ever did change, or ever would. She herself was living proof of that. And she was too numb to feel either anger or sorrow at the realization, just the weight of its reality.

"We'll be landing in five minutes," the pilot told Bronwyn. "I just got the message that the motorcade's already there waiting for you."

Craig Chess watched the helicopter circle overhead as he lifted the box of plastic disposable silverware. He stood on the porch of the Catamount Corner, Needsville's only motel, and the cacophony in the street made him wince at its shrill, unnatural loudness. Needsville was a quiet town, both by disposition and logistics: Three hundred taciturn, mysterious people spread out over an entire valley simply didn't make much noise.

Now, thousands of people from all over the country brought the entire hamlet to a dead stop. And all, he reflected ironically, for the return of one local girl who, he'd been told, couldn't wait to leave.

"Makin' it okay, there, Reverend?" Marshall Goins asked from the storeroom.

Craig shifted the weight of the box in his hands. "Sorry, got distracted by all the commotion."

"Yeah, it's a sight, ain't it? I always figured Bronwyn Hyatt would cause a major ruckus one day, but I never thought it'd make the national news."

"It's *inter*national," Craig corrected. "I saw a German TV crew setting up."

Marshall emerged from the storeroom with another box. The label said NAPKINS, 3,000 COUNT. "Do you really need that many napkins?" Craig asked.

"Yankees are sloppy. Better to have too many than not enough." He also paused to look over the crowd. "You ever figure a town this little could hold this many people?"

"Never," Craig said. "Did you?"

Marshall shrugged. "Good for business, if nothing else. I'm selling parking places in the side yard, and we're booked to the gills. Hell, we even have some folks paying to camp out in the lobby." He paused. "I mean, 'heck.' Sorry, Reverend."

"I use the word myself sometimes," Craig said. "Does the fire code allow you to put people in the lobby, though?"

Marshall chuckled. "Not much worry about codes and such here in Needsville, Reverend."

Craig was eleven months shy of thirty, and had received his appointment as minister for the nearby Triple Springs Methodist Church just after graduating from Lambuth College in Jackson. He'd never met Bronwyn Hyatt, but had heard so many stories about her since he arrived six weeks earlier that he felt as if he knew her. "Ten feet tall and bulletproof," as the Travis Tritt song said, only she apparently never needed alcohol to feel that way. A full Tufa at a time when most families had diluted their heritage through intermarriage, she was as well known for her exploits as for her famously profane language. Needsville's extended Tufa "community"—essentially everyone—had more than its share of iconoclasts, but Bronwyn, though she was only twenty years old, was extreme even for them. He wondered how her horrific wartime experiences, now chronicled all over the world, had changed her. He hoped not much, because he secretly hated to think he'd never get to meet the girl once known as the "Bronwynator."

Marshall brought him back to the moment when he said, "I think these two boxes'll do us, Reverend. Just put yours inside the dining room entrance, and Peggy can sort 'em out. Thanks for the hand."

"Glad to help out, Marshall. You and Peggy have made me feel awfully welcome."

The older man went inside the motel, and Craig was about to follow when something caught his eye: a man with the distinctive black Tufa hair struggling to get his camera in position for a shot. That struck Craig as odd, and it took a moment to realize why: None of the other Tufa were taking pictures.

Craig watched more closely. The man also wore a lanyard with an ID tag that said PRESS. He managed to get his camera up above the heads of the crowd just in time for the helicopter's final pass. When he pulled it down and scanned back through the pictures, though, he frowned and muttered to himself.

Craig decided that, although this man had the general look of a Tufa, it must be a coincidence. His conduct was so different from the quiet, suspicious natives that he had to be simply a Yankee reporter who happened to have dark hair. After all, there wasn't a single newspaper in all of Cloud County, so no real Tufa journalist would have anywhere to work.

Craig went inside, threaded through the out-of-towners texting, talking on cell phones, and begging for accommodations, and deposited the last box by the dining room entrance. Normally the Catamount Corner used cloth napkins that matched the tablecloths in the dining room, but that wasn't practical, or appropriate, for this crowd. They treated the town like it existed solely for their benefit, and deserved no more than they got.

As he turned, he was knocked into the wall by a man with slick hair and a pin-striped suit talking into his Bluetooth as he muscled his suitcase across the lobby. "Come on, baby, you know I didn't mean it. Just score me some, and I'll pay you back when

I get back to town. I'll even take you out to dinner somewhere nice, what do you say?"

Craig sighed and pushed himself upright. *God loves everyone,* he reminded himself, *even Yankee jackasses.* He worked his way to the door and out into the street, hoping he still had time to get close enough to witness the main event.

Three burly MPs helped Bronwyn out of the helicopter and into her wheelchair. One of them accidentally brushed the curve of her breast with his hand and flushed bright red, although he said nothing: apologizing, after all, was for fags. She held on to her cap and the hem of her skirt, both of which threatened to fly askew under the idling rotors. She carefully arranged her injured leg on the upright footplate, the metal rings gleaming in the sun.

The one-hangar airport, with its lone runway and faded orange wind sock, served mainly crop dusters and charter sporting flights and was overwhelmed by the sudden military occupation. In addition to the huge Black Hawk delivering its human cargo, the local National Guard motor pool provided two staff cars and a jeep. Beyond them waited some sort of huge vehicle that did not, from the little bits Bronwyn could see around her escorts, appear to be military.

Maitland stepped behind her and took the chair's handles. "Are you comfortable?" Before she could answer, he continued, "We added a special seat to the motorcade to accommodate your leg."

"Don't forget the crutches," Bronwyn said. "I'm not making a speech sitting down." It was her only real demand, but she intended to stick to it. The people of Needsville were not about to see her unable to stand and face them after everything that had happened.

"All arranged," Maitland replied. And then Bronwyn saw the vehicle intended for her return home.

She grabbed the rubber wheel runner and brought the chair to a sudden halt. Maitland's stomach bumped into the back of her head. She stared for a long moment, then slowly turned as much as her injuries allowed. "Major Maitland, I know you outrank me, and I apologize in advance for my language, but there is *no . . . fucking . . . way* I am getting into, or onto, *that.*"

Maitland crouched beside the chair as if he'd expected this response all along. In his Teflon voice, he said, "I understand, Bronwyn, really. I thought it was tacky, too. But it was donated by the Ford dealership in Johnson City, and it might sow ill will in the community if we don't graciously accept it."

"I don't care if it sows black-eyed peas," she snapped. "I'll do this show, but not if I have to ride in that."

Maitland's voice grew softer, and he leaned so close, she could smell his aftershave. "Private Hyatt, this is not a 'show.' It's a hero's welcome. Perhaps you should be a bit more . . . gracious?"

Bronwyn turned her dark eyes on him. "Major, I'm as gracious as a possum at the Brickyard, but there's no way I'm going to ride through my hometown like some sort of trailer park beauty queen."

"I agree," Maitland said. "The thing is, it would make it much easier for all those people to see you. So it's really not for *you,* it's for *them.*"

There was no arguing with that. Left to her own preferences, Bronwyn would've returned home in the middle of the night wearing sunglasses and a blond wig. This carnival was for everyone *but* her.

The platform for her return consisted of an enormous Ford pickup truck jacked up on gigantic tires, towing a small yacht. The masts had been removed, and a sort of throne had been mounted high on the foredeck. The bow sported the now-ubiquitous high school moniker known far and wide since her rescue: THE BRONWYNATOR.

When she saw the name, she muttered, "Oh, God," and shook her head. "Do I get to keep it when we're done?" she asked sarcastically.

"Ah . . . no, I'm afraid not."

Bronwyn managed a knowing smile. "You're very good at your job, sir."

"I'm just grease for the gears of necessity," he said with absolutely no irony.

Craig threaded through the crowd lining the street until he reached the incongruously new post office building. Rockhouse Hicks sat in a rocking chair on the porch. Something about the old man stopped strangers from approaching him, and even other locals gave him plenty of space, inside an invisible circle that kept everyone else away. The effect was almost tribal, as if Hicks were a chief or medicine man. Craig's research on the Tufa, though, insisted they were all fervent individualists with no hierarchy, so he couldn't be any sort of leader. Unless Hicks's peculiar birth defect—six working fingers on each hand—fulfilled some unknown community superstition, Craig could only work with the idea that people avoided the old man because, simply, he was a shit-head.

But with the Tufa, you could never be sure. Dark haired and dark skinned, yet not white, black, or Native American (although often content to be mistaken for any of the above if it meant they'd be left alone), the Tufa kept their secrets so close that, to Craig's knowledge, no one even knew how they'd turned up deep in Appalachia. Yet when the first official Europeans had reached this valley three centuries earlier, the Tufa were already here, living quietly in the hills and minding their own business.

Craig, however, was determined to reach out to everyone, even (or especially) the ones no one else would accept. One of the first things he learned was that no one in Cloud County really liked Rockhouse, and he sympathized with the mean old man's isolation. So he leaned against the wall beside him and asked, "Ever seen a helicopter over Needsville before, Mr. Hicks?"

Hicks slowly turned. He had sun-narrowed eyes that made his expression impossible to read, but the hint of malevolence shone through. Craig imagined that as a younger man, Hicks had been serious trouble.

"Reverend Checkers," he said.

"Chess," Craig corrected with a smile.

Hicks continued to glare at him. Then just as slowly, he returned his gaze to whatever he'd been contemplating before. Craig knew this counted as a dismissal, but he wasn't giving up that easily. "She's getting quite a welcome. Can you see okay from here? I bet they'd let you sit up on the podium if you asked."

"Seen that girl since she was knee-high to a wet fart. Don't reckon she looks that different now."

"Now she's a *hero*, though."

Hicks said nothing, but spit out onto the tiny lawn at the base of the post office flagpole.

"You don't think so?" Craig persisted. "She killed ten enemy soldiers single-handed."

"They say."

"You don't believe it?"

Hicks spit again and shrugged. "Wasn't there. Don't trust stories about killings unless I see the corpse myself. Been burned that way."

The hint of mystery piqued Craig's interest, and the annoyance in Hicks's voice felt like as big a triumph as a whole congregation answering the call to salvation at the end of a service. *Any* reaction Craig got from the old man was a step forward, a break in the isolation. "Well, I'm going to see if I can find a better spot to watch from. Y'all have a good day, Mr. Hicks."

As he worked his way back along the road, he bumped into the man he'd seen earlier, the Tufa reporter. He said, "Excuse me," and tried to catch a glimpse of the name on the press pass. It read SWAYBACK.

The yellow ribbons tied to trees, fence posts, and telephone poles, clichéd as they were, made Bronwyn feel surprisingly warm inside. She recalled tearing ribbons from some of the same trees when she was a kid, convinced they were too hokey to have any meaning. But now that they were displayed for *her,* she understood them in a new light, even if she still thought they were inane.

Like Cleopatra on her barge, she was towed slowly down into the valley toward Needsville. She sat in the ludicrous chair and gritted her teeth against the vibrations going through her shattered leg bones. Somehow they'd mounted a leather recliner to the foredeck, with a modified footrest to support her injured leg. It seemed solid enough, but did nothing to make her feel less ridiculous. She thought about waving with the back of her hand turned out, like Queen Elizabeth, or mouthing "This is so lame," as Nancy Kerrigan had at Disneyland. But at least for a little while longer, she was still a soldier; she'd do neither.

She wanted to stare straight ahead, at the fresh lines painted on the highway after the state repaved it earlier in the spring, but there was no resisting the pull of the mountains. At first she looked only with her eyes, cutting them enough to see the lush trees and rolling slopes visible past the MPs standing at the deck rails beside her. But like that first taste of liquor to an abstaining drunk, it only made it worse. The leaves sang to her, tunes blew through the breeze, and for a moment something that had been silent and still since she'd left this place vibrated deep in her chest. But it was only a moment; like everything else, it faded to numbness and left her aware of its presence but unable to actually feel it.

Except somehow, she sensed danger. Not the immediate kind as she'd known in Iraq, but real nonetheless. It was like a shadowy animal glimpsed over the tall grass that ducked out of sight the instant before she turned to look directly at it.

It took twenty minutes to drive the half mile from the city limits to the bandstand and podium set up outside City Hall. The crowd's response was every bit as loud as the helicopter's engine. Bronwyn saw few heads of straight black hair or dark sullen eyes among the throng; and, as she expected, Rockhouse Hicks had not moved from the post office porch. It was okay, though; she'd have plenty of time to see the locals. These strangers weren't here to see *her*, anyway; they wanted the Bronwynator.

Two MPs carefully carried her to the stage, where Maitland provided the promised crutches. Her injured arm could barely do its job, but it was a matter of pride that she stand before these people. She reached the podium and waited patiently while the applause continued and the cameras fired away.

As the cheering died down, Major Maitland eased up to the microphone. "Private Hyatt will make a statement, but as you can see, she's not up to any questions. We ask that you respect her courage, and her injuries."

Bronwyn unfolded the two pages of typing with the word APPROVED stamped in red near one corner. She blew into the microphone to check her distance from it. Then she cleared her throat and said, "Thank y'all for being here. It's great to be back in Needsville." She stopped for renewed applause. Her voice sounded thin and weak in the loudspeakers, certainly not strong enough to belong to a First Daughter of the Tufa.

"I'd like to thank everyone who hoped and prayed for my rescue and recovery," she continued. "For a long time, I had no idea anyone even knew or cared about what had happened to me. Now, believe me, I know that to be false. I feel blessed, honored, and grateful beyond words for the love my home community has given me so freely."

She felt herself turn red. Intellectually she understood, and even agreed with, the need for these words to be spoken aloud. But having to say them still incited those old rebellious feelings. They weren't as strong as they'd once been, though; it was like the shadow of something that used to be gigantic.

"I'd like to thank the staff of the VA hospital for the excellent care they gave me. I'm also grateful to several Iraqi medical personnel who helped save my life while I was in their care. And of course, to the brave Marines who rescued me.

"I'm proud to be a soldier in the United States Army. I'm relieved that some of the soldiers I served with made it home alive, and it hurts that some did not. I'll miss them. And now . . . *I'm* going home."

She quickly folded the speech, turned, and this time did not resist when the MPs moved in to aid her. As they carried her down the steps, she made eye contact with a woman in the crowd who had straight black hair and soft, tender eyes. The woman held out her right hand in a fist, wrapped her thumb over the back of her index finger and then turned her wrist and spread all her fingers wide.

Bronwyn said nothing. It wasn't normal sign language, although it *was* a sign and she knew the language. But she couldn't find the strength to respond, and her hands were busy making sure she wasn't accidentally dropped onto the sidewalk. She was placed in the passenger seat of a shiny Town & Country for her trip to her family's home, and as the door closed she looked for the woman in the crowd. But, not surprisingly, she'd vanished.

The sense of danger momentarily returned. Certainly it didn't come from the woman in the crowd, whom Bronwyn would trust with her life and song. But the woman knew about it, Bronwyn was certain. And it explained her serious, even grim expression when everyone around her was cheering.

By the time Bronwyn finished her speech, Craig had maneuvered close enough to get a good look at her face. He'd seen photographs, but he was surprised by how beautiful she was in real life. Mountain girls' faces tended to have hard edges, sharp planes, and leathery skin; Bronwyn had the high cheekbones and strong chin, but her complexion was smooth and unlined, and still had the softness of youth. Her dark eyes were large and hinted at self-aware intelligence.

Craig scolded himself. He tried to avoid thinking about people, especially women, that way. It was unprofessional for a minister, and unkind for a human being. What mattered was what was inside, not the surface they presented to the world.

Someone jostled him from behind, and when he turned, a camera's flash blinded him. "Whoa!" he cried, putting up his hand to shield his eyes.

"Sorry," the photographer said without looking up from his camera's screen.

As his eyes recovered, Craig realized the photographer was Swayback, the reporter who looked like a Tufa. "Hey, who do you work for?" Craig asked before he could stop himself.

Swayback looked up, alarmed. "Wait a minute, you're not gonna complain to my editor just because a flash went off in your face, are you? Good grief, there's a million photographers here, it could've happened to anybody. I said I was sorry."

"No, I just—"

"Tell you what: I work for the *Daily Planet*. My editor's Perry White. You tell him all about it." Then Swayback turned and disappeared into the crowd.

By the time Craig turned back toward the podium, Bronwyn Hyatt was gone and everyone began to disperse.

2

The trip in the Town & Country was as bone jangling as Bronwyn expected. She sat with her broken leg across the folded-down middle passenger seat, padded with pillows that kept it elevated and immobile. Cloud County's secondary roads were not maintained by the state, and once you left the main highway, they quickly became little more than paired gravel ruts with a grass strip between them. Most Tufas drove vehicles suited to these conditions; perhaps the army should've delivered her home in a tank.

Behind them—*far* behind them, since the last military vehicle was instructed to go very slowly—came the press. Nothing could stop them completely, and a news-channel helicopter even shadowed Bronwyn's progress. But as Maitland said, it was part of America now to want to know everything about a celebrity, especially a fifteen-minute one. Better to give them something than to stonewall and have them start digging.

The scenery was so familiar that for a moment Bronwyn forgot everything around her and believed she was riding home in Dwayne's pickup; the slight haze from her pain medication could easily be the low buzz of homegrown pot. It lasted only an instant, but it was disconcerting all the same. She took a deep breath and forced herself to concentrate on the fence posts and barbed wire passing in undulating waves.

As they neared her home, people stood along the fence, scowling into the dust raised by the cars. She could not discern particular faces, but their dark hair and presence here identified them. They would never be caught dead in the madness currently possessing Needsville, yet neither would they allow Bronwyn to return home without acknowledging it. It had nothing to do with the war or patriotism; or, rather, it sprang from a kind of loyalty tied to no physical location. It was a concept of "family" unique to this place and to these people, those with the truest Tufa blood in their veins.

"I don't see any cars or trucks," Maitland observed. "How'd all these people get here?"

Bronwyn smiled. "Not much is far away from anything else in these hills, if you're willing to climb up and down a lot."

"Are these friends of yours? Do you need crowd control?"

"No, Major, these are my people. It's okay."

Bronwyn's family lived in a long single-story home set into the slope leading up to Hyatt's Ridge behind it. The yard slanted down to a flat area, where the family parked its vehicles in the shade of a huge pecan tree. Other trees hung over the house, hiding it from the scalding Tennessee sun. A wooden fence blocked off the front yard from the surrounding woods, and a metal gate could be closed at the end of the driveway. It was open now, though, and decorated with an enormous yellow ribbon.

Chloe Hyatt sat in a straight-backed chair on the wooden deck porch, her hands in her lap. She watched the approaching dust cloud over the tops of the trees. "Here they come," she said.

Chloe wore a simple summer dress with a muted flower pattern, colorful but not gaudy. The spaghetti straps emphasized the strong, straight shoulders she had passed on to her only daughter. Her black hair hung to the middle of her back, held in place with a white ribbon. She had deep smile lines and a hint of crow's-feet, but otherwise looked like she might be Bronwyn's older sister rather than her mother. Despite her air of reserve, she radiated health and energy the way all true Tufa women did. It was part of what made them so desirable—and so dangerous.

Deacon stood beside Chloe, dressed in his funeral suit. It was the only one he owned, and it seemed silly to purchase a new one for something as simple as his daughter coming home. Deacon was a tall, hard-bodied man with a set to his jaw that spoke of the determination of Orpheus, while the twinkle in his eye was more Dionysian. Like Chloe, there was something about him that was both immensely attractive and subtly dangerous, although in his case it was mixed with humor so dry, it blew over most people like dust from the road.

Both Chloe and Deacon were full-blooded Tufas. That meant they looked as much like brother and sister as they did husband and wife, even though they were related only tangentially, as people tended to be in small communities. Outsiders often jumped to conclusions that embraced old clichés of mountain-family inbreeding; Needsville, though, paid the Hyatts the respect their bloodlines inspired, and that their conduct reinforced.

Eight-year-old Aiden watched the trucks approach up the narrow road. He was lanky, his black hair long and unkempt, and he squirmed uncomfortably in his button-down shirt and khakis. He stood at the bottom of the porch steps, practically vibrating with excitement as the first vehicle made the turn into their driveway. Two more pulled in on either side. "Holy shit," he said.

"You want me to wash that tongue with lye soap, boy, keep up that language," Deacon said without looking at him. But he agreed with the assessment. They'd watched the parade and speech on television, glad they decided not to meet Bronwyn in town. "You knew it was going to be a big deal."

"Yessir," he said, and pointed at the TV news trucks traveling in bumper-touching eagerness behind the final vehicle. "And I also told you we'd need the shotgun."

Deacon smiled. "Go get it, then. Shut the gate once the army gets through, then keep them TV peckerheads out."

"Yessir," Aiden said eagerly, and rushed into the house.

"You sure it's a good idea to let him use a real gun?" Chloe said.

Deacon shrugged. "He'll only be shooting reporters. No real loss, far as I can tell. Besides, for every one you shoot, I bet two more pop up."

"You're thinking of lawyers," Chloe deadpanned. Deacon grinned.

Aiden returned with a 16-gauge side-by-side double barrel slung breech-open over his shoulder. His shirttail was already untucked. He rushed down the hill into the dust. Vague shapes moved through it, but none of them seemed to be Bronwyn. Finally four big men emerged onto the yard, pushing something between them.

Chloe stood. "My baby girl," she said very softly, and hummed a tune only Tufa mothers knew.

Bronwyn gazed around at the familiar yard, with its old swing set and basketball goal off to the side. Eighteen years of her life had been spent here, yet it seemed far less substantial than the events of the past two. She had to struggle to connect the memories with actual emotions. She remembered using the rented Bobcat to level enough ground so she and her friends could actually play ball; then she'd taken off down the road, intending to clear a new path across the hill to her favorite swimming hole. She'd been eleven then, and it must've been exciting. Her father had used his belt on her behind seventeen times that day. Had she been angry about that? Or hurt? She couldn't recall.

"Bronwyn!" Aiden cried as he bounced down the yard toward her. One of the MPs went for his pistol when he saw Aiden's shotgun, but Bronwyn said quickly, "It's all right, he's my little brother."

Ignoring the big men around her, Aiden was about to jump in her lap and give her a hug when he saw the metal rings and pins on her leg. He skidded to a stop, eyes wide. *"Wow,"* he gasped. "Does that hurt?"

"It sure don't feel good," she said with a laugh. "But it's better than it was. Come here, you little muskrat." They hugged as much as the chair allowed.

"Dad wants me to keep out the reporters," he said breathlessly. "Gave me a shell for each barrel."

"What a big, strong boy," Major Maitland said. "You must be Aiden. You can just run on back up to the house, we have men assigned to guard the gate while your sister's getting settled."

"And now you have one more," Bronwyn said when she saw Aiden's disappointment. "He can help. The squirrels around here tremble at his name. Right?"

Aiden grinned. Maitland bit back his protest and simply nodded.

"See ya," Aiden said, and dashed past her toward the gate. Reporters, seeing the end of the line, leaped from their vehicles while they were still moving. They were torn between the certainty of speaking to the people along the road, or the chance of possibly catching a glimpse of their quarry. Many opted to dash for the now-closed gate at the end of the drive. Some looked ready to jump the fence, but the stern Tufa faces looking back at them quickly changed their minds.

Bronwyn turned her attention to the house. It looked exactly as she remembered it, as it probably always would. Along the porch awning hung wind chimes that looked like the tacky ones found in a Pigeon Forge tourist gift shop. When the wind touched them and played their tunes, though, any Tufa instantly knew better.

"Bronwyn!" a reporter screamed behind her.

"Private Hyatt!" another demanded. The voices quickly became a cacophony.

"Take me to the gate," Bronwyn said suddenly, and tried to turn the chair herself.

Maitland used his foot to block the wheel, knelt, and said, "I think you'd be better off ignoring them."

"I plan to, but I want to say something to them first." She met Maitland's gaze with her own resolute one. "Five minutes, sir, to suck up to the press. You surely can't object to that."

He sighed and nodded. The MPs pushed her across the grass, onto the gravel, and up to the gate.

Aiden sat astride the barrier, the gun across his knees. He tried to mimic the stoic stare of the soldiers. A dozen reporters, TV cameramen, and regular photographers battled to get close to Bronwyn. The gate rattled as they surged against it.

Bronwyn smiled into the flashes and held up her hands. "Hey! *Hey!* Y'all want me to talk, you have to shut up a minute!"

Gradually the media grew quiet except for the fake electronic shutter clicks of the digital cameras. When she had them as silent as they were likely to get, she said, "Y'all, please. I've been as nice as I could be to you, talking to you and answering your questions, but this—" She gestured behind her. "—is my family's home. Y'all wouldn't want me coming to your place and behaving like this, would you? So please, I'm asking nicely. And you, Tom Karpow, you know exactly what I mean. I talked to you for a solid hour on *Nightwatch,* you can't say I wasn't cooperative. Why are *you* acting like this?"

The anchorman she designated would not meet her eyes, and the other reporters began to look sheepish as well. It was not her brilliant oratory, she knew, but the combined presence of so many Tufas united in one cause.

In the silence a camera clicked, and some turned to glare at the offending photographer.

"Thank y'all for understanding," Bronwyn said. "As soon as I'm able, I'm sure the army will have me out stumping for the war. In the meantime, the more you let me rest, the faster I'll be available again." She turned to Maitland, who was speechless; even he couldn't handle the press with such ease. She said, "That's all, sir. The men can take me to the house now."

The slope up to the house was harder than it looked, and the soldiers pushing her began to breathe hard with the effort. They stopped below the porch steps, and Major Maitland said, "Hello. I bet you're Bronwyn's father, Deke. You must be very proud of your daughter, she's a real American hero."

Deacon nodded. No one called him Deke. "If I must be, good thing I am. And I'm proud of all my children."

If Maitland sensed the mockery, he didn't let it show. He turned to Chloe just as she raised her left hand, palm out, and touched her pinkie and middle finger with her thumb. The gesture was meant for Bronwyn, who felt a shiver of something stir in her numb heart. She raised her own left hand and responded, palm down, index finger curled.

Maitland said, "And this must be her mother. Ma'am, you two could be sisters."

"Flirt," Chloe said with no change of expression.

Bronwyn smiled a little more. Maitland was so far out of his depth, he didn't even realize he was in the swimming pool. "Well, she's certainly been an inspiration to all of us. Right, gentlemen?"

The MPs voiced a tight chorus of, "Yes *sir*." One of them, in fact, had spent five uncomfortable minutes trying to articulate how honored he was to accompany Bronwyn. She had finally thanked him with a kiss on the cheek just to end the awkwardness.

Maitland looked around the porch. "I, ah . . . thought you'd have made arrangements by now for her wheelchair."

"We have," Deacon said. "We moved the couch back so she can get around it, and put a runner down so it wouldn't track up the floor."

"Well, that's all important, of course, but I thought there might be a ramp out here to help her get in and out . . . ?"

Deacon nodded at the MPs. "Reckon them boys are strong enough to tote one girl up four steps. We'll manage after that."

Maitland continued to smile, but his confusion grew too great to hide. "I'm sure they can, but the government sent you money to—"

"Sent it back," Deacon said.

"Beg pardon?"

"We. Sent. It. Back. You can check. We'll take care of Bronwyn in our own way. In six months, you won't recognize her."

"I'm certain that's true, but—"

"Major," Bronwyn broke in. Deacon could string Maitland along for an hour without ever cracking a smile. "I'll be okay, really. If the fellas can just get me up onto the porch?"

Maitland sighed and motioned to the MPs. They easily lifted the wheelchair and placed it on the porch. Chloe stepped behind it and took the handles. "I appreciate y'all bringing my daughter home," she said. The gravity in her voice kept the others silent. "And for patching her up. You're welcome at our table anytime."

"Why, thank you, ma'am," Maitland said. A bystander would have thought his graciousness fully genuine.

From the porch Bronwyn could see to the end of the driveway, where the media waved and shouted to get her attention. Her nose itched, but she didn't want to scratch in case a photograph was taken at that exact instant. WAR HERO PICKS NOSE wouldn't do much for her dignity. The Tufas along the road moved toward the house, talking softly among themselves. Many of them carried musical instruments.

Chloe found Bronwyn's hand and threaded its fingers through her own. Bronwyn hadn't held her mother's hand in years, and it felt simultaneously alien and comforting. She looked up into the face, so similar to her own, and felt that same tingle in her chest again. It was stronger this time, but still didn't catch fire.

"When you boys get down to the fence, ask Aiden for permission to open the gate," Deacon said. "It'll make him feel big. Besides, if I know him, he's got them reporters eating out of his hand."

"Ain't heard the gun go off," Chloe said. "That's a good sign."

An MP handed over Bronwyn's crutches, and another deposited two bags of clothes and personal belongings on the porch. "This is all your gear, Private," he said with a wink.

At least she didn't intimidate *every* man she met. "Thanks," Bronwyn said. To Maitland she added, "And thank you for looking out for me, Major. Doubt we'll meet again, but I'll always appreciate what you've done."

He smiled. "I imagine that when the book deals and TV shows come along, you'll see me again."

Bronwyn bit back her snide comment; she'd already had innumerable offers for the rights to her life story, for absurd amounts of money. Turning them down had been easy, but of course, everyone around her, including Maitland, thought she was just holding out for more. She let them think so. The truth, *her* truth, would just confuse them.

She turned to the door. "You do know the wheelchair won't fit through there with me in it," she said to Deacon.

He handed her the crutches. "Your arms broke, too?"

"Mr. Hyatt!" Maitland exclaimed. "Look, I know she's your daughter, and I don't mean to be rude, but really, is that any way to treat her after all she's been through?"

Deacon remained impassive. "The bullet went right through her arm, missed the artery and the bone, and it's healing up fine. Or so the army doctors said."

"Dad doesn't believe in coddling, Major," Bronwyn said with a grin. She slipped the crutches beneath her arms and, with Deacon's help, pulled herself upright. The pin brace weighed a ton, and maneuvering it was exhausting, but just like the speech, she intended to walk through the door to her home under her own power.

As she crossed the threshold, Chloe hummed a melody older than the mountain they stood on. Like all the Tufa tunes, it was part prayer, part story, and part statement of intent. It signaled to the universe that Bronwyn was once again home, under the protection of the night wind and its riders.

Maitland came down the steps with the MPs behind him. He stopped, looked back at the house, and shook his head.

"Problem, Major?" one of the MPs asked.

"Yeah, there's a problem. That girl's wasted fourteen of her fifteen minutes of fame, and doesn't seem to care."

"I got family from Kentucky, Major. These mountain folks, they don't have the same priorities as the rest of the world. I mean, look at 'em—they'd just as soon shoot us as go fishing."

"Is that what they say in Kentucky?" Maitland asked wryly.

He shrugged. "The sentiment's pretty universal in these parts."

Maitland shook his head. "Well, another thirty days and she's no longer my problem, or Uncle Sam's. After that, she'll get her wish. The world will forget all about her. Then we'll see how she likes it."

The men in uniform made their way back to their vehicles and departed.

Inside, Deacon helped Bronwyn settle onto the couch. The living room, with its open-beam ceiling decorated with abstract designs, loomed like a protective hand cupping her. "Thanks, Daddy," she said. "That major is a real piece of work. You should've seen what they made me ride on in town."

"We did. Watched it on TV. They let you keep the boat?"

She smiled. "I asked them that very same thing."

Deacon went to the refrigerator and pulled out three bottles of beer. He handed one to Chloe and another to Bronwyn. Her doctors repeatedly instructed her not to mix alcohol with the Vicodin, but they didn't understand the effect simply being back home would have. No painkillers would be necessary from now on. "I also saw Bliss Overbay in town. She looked awful grim."

"We'll talk about that later," Chloe said.

Bronwyn clinked the neck of her bottle against her father's. "And ol' Rockhouse was still sitting on the porch at the post office."

"Suits me," Deacon said. "As long as he's there, everyone can keep an eye on him. It's when he's gone that I get antsy."

Bronwyn nodded and took a drink. One time Rockhouse caught her going down on his nephew Ripple, who was only slightly less handsome than his other nephew Stoney, the unanimously crowned love god of all the Tufa girls. Unlike Stoney, though, Ripple was smart enough to let her know when he was about to finish, which happened to be the exact moment Rockhouse slapped the car top and demanded to know what those goddamned kids were doing. The next few moments had been messy, and terrifying, and exciting, like most of her favorite experiences. But she never forgot the way Rockhouse looked at her as she scrambled to get her shirt back on. Something in that old man left her, and every other Tufa girl, vaguely queasy.

She was about to ask for more gossip when she heard a faint, regular tapping. She glanced at the front window and saw a sparrow perched on the outside sill, pecking against the glass.

Brownyn looked at her father; he'd seen it, too. They both knew what it meant: a family death in the near future.

"You think that's for me?" she asked softly. She should have been terrified, but she was too numb even for that. "Is that what Bliss was worried about?"

"Just a bird confused by all the ruckus, honey," Deacon said with all the laid-back certainty he could muster. "Sometimes it don't mean a thing."

"Yeah," she agreed. "Sometimes."

Aiden burst through the front door. He propped the shotgun against the wall just as Deacon said, "That gun best be unloaded, son."

The boy patted the pocket where he carried the shells. "Didn't have to shoot nobody, dang it." He saw Bronwyn, and his face lit up. "Hey, can I show her now?"

"Show me what?" Bronwyn asked.

Deacon nodded. "But make it fast. Bunch of people are here to see her."

"Show me what?" Bronwyn repeated.

Aiden grabbed her crutches. "Come on, you won't believe it."

"He's right," Deacon said. "You surely won't."

3

Bronwyn's bedroom door still squeaked at the halfway point. It had squeaked all her life, and betrayed her many times when she'd sneaked out, or in, late at night. She could've oiled it, but it had become a point of honor to face this devious hinge, to open and close it so slowly, the squeak did not give her away. And now it renewed its old challenge as she opened the door.

The immediate sight cut short any reverie, though. She balanced on her crutches, shoulder against the doorjamb, and stared.

"I fixed it up for you," Aiden said breathlessly behind her. "What do you think?"

American flags hung *everywhere.* The two windows sported flag-patterned curtains, small arrangements of flags and flowers rested on her desk and dresser, and flag banners crossed at the center of the ceiling. A pair of pillows, one with stars and the other stripes, rested on her bed. "Wow, Aiden," she said at last. "It looks real . . . patriotic."

He squeezed past her and stood in the center of the room, bouncing proudly. "Had to order them curtains off the Internet. Took all my 'lowance for a month. Was afraid they wouldn't get here in time. You really like it?"

"I am genuinely surprised," she assured him. She was also appalled, since that symbol now meant a whole lot of new things to her, most of them ambiguous, a few downright unpleasant. But Aiden didn't need to know that. If he'd convinced their parents to let him do this, he must've really had his heart set on it.

She put the crutches against the wall and carefully eased the two steps to her bed. The weight of the pin brace tried to pull her off balance. She sat heavily, and Aiden plopped down beside her. The bounce sent little needles of pain through her leg, but she held back the gasp.

"Shawn and Bruce say you're a hero," Aiden said. "I said you're a heroine, because that's what they call a girl hero, isn't it?"

"Heroin's what you shoot in your arm in the big city," she said.

"That's spelled different. I know, I came in third at the spelling bee."

"Yeah, well, I'm no hero *or* heroine. Just a soldier." The word felt odd in her mouth, and sounded alien now. What exactly did it mean anymore?

"Didn't you kill ten Iraqis before they captured you?"

She smiled and tousled his hair. "You think I could kill ten people, Aiden? That's sweet."

"Well, did you?"

She thought carefully about her words. Aiden had not visited her in the hospital in Virginia, so he hadn't seen her at her worst, hooked up to more machines than Anakin Skywalker.

He still thought of her as his daredevil big sister, and while she no longer wanted the role, she also didn't want to hurt him. "That's what they *say* I did. I got whacked upside the head real good. It makes a lot of things fuzzy. I don't remember it right now."

"But you will?"

"Don't know. Not sure I want to. Killing people for real ain't like it looks on TV. All that blood has a smell, did you know that? And them bullets, they're hot; makes the skin where they hit smell a little like cooking bacon." Her voice had grown soft and quiet. She was describing things she recalled as sensations rather than full-blown memories. She took a deep breath and continued. "Plus sometimes you have to kill someone sitting as close to you as I am. Think you could do that?"

Aiden shrugged. "If he was trying to kill me."

"So you could kill someone if he's trying to kill you because you're trying to kill him because . . ." She trailed off and waited.

His face scrunched up the way it had when he was a puzzled toddler. Affection for him swelled in her; then like every emotion, it found no real purchase and faded back to the numbness. "It sounds complicated," he said after a minute.

"It is. And it's supposed to be. It shouldn't be easy."

"But you did it."

She nodded. "*If* I did it, it was because I was trained to do it, and I gave my word I would."

He leaned against her, his own arms pressed tight to his side to keep from hurting her. "Glad you're back," he said simply.

"Me, too," she said, and kissed the top of his head.

"Your leg going to be okay?"

"Eventually."

"It's all hairy."

"Yeah, well, shaving around all this stuff is like mowing around the garden statues in Uncle Hamilton's yard. Hey, you see where these metal pins go into my skin? I have to put antibiotic cream on them or they'll get infected, but I can't reach all of 'em. Reckon you can help me out later?"

His eyes lit up the way a boy's do when presented with the chance to do something icky. "Heck yeah. How about your arm?"

"Oh, that was nothing. Bullet went right through. Want to see?"

He nodded eagerly. She undid her uniform blouse and pulled it off her shoulder. The gunshot wound was now a puckered, scabbed hole that would shortly fade to a scar. His eyes widened as he leaned around to see the back of her arm with its matching exit wound.

"Wow," he whispered. "Does it hurt?"

"Compared to my leg? No way. Now, can you do me a favor?"

"Sure."

"Get Magda out from under the bed for me."

He jumped up, which bounced the mattress again and sent a lightning bolt of pain through her leg, up her spine, and into her skull. She bit back the cry, but sweat broke out all over her. She grabbed the bedspread tight and clenched her teeth.

Oblivious, Aiden pulled the tattered case from beneath the bed. It had once been expensive, and even now only the outside showed signs of age and wear. The buckles were shiny, and when she placed it across her lap and unsnapped them, the green velvet lining was as rich and deep as it had been the day it was made.

But the mandolin inside held her attention. Magda had been built in Kalamazoo, Michigan, in 1914, according to the history Brownyn had been told when Granny Esme gave her the instrument. She was a Gibson A-5 model, with two sound holes that looked like calligraphied letter *f*'s parallel to the strings. She was polished to burnished perfection except in places where the finish was worn down to the wood grain, evidence of her nearly century-long use. This was no priceless heirloom to be locked away; Magda had been passed to Bronwyn so she could be used, so the songs embedded in her might grow and be shared.

Granny Esme first played Magda in one of the mandolin orchestras popular at the time the instrument was originally built. It had been something of a scam at first: traveling music peddlers put together small community groups, encouraging the purchase of their wares as a way to participate in the latest fad. But in Cloud County, among the Tufa, the mandolin's antecedents were already well known, and the merchant was surprised to find families who actually owned Italian *mandores*. He'd put together a brief tour, sold his entire traveling stock, and moved on. Among old-timers, talk of the Glittering Strings Mandolin Orchestra still passed in whispers, lest the fragile majesty be smirched.

An envelope had been tucked under the strings near the bridge. She opened it and pulled out the card. A generic get-well-soon message was printed on the front; when she opened it, a little speaker played a tinny version of "Another One Bites the Dust."

"That's from Kell," Aiden said.

"I figured," she said with a wry smile.

The handwritten message inside it read

I'm sorry I couldn't be there to meet you, but I'm sure everything went well. You've always been the toughest person I know; now you're the toughest person anyone *knows. I'm*

*so proud of you, not for joining the army, or for getting
shot up, or for killing ten people single-handed; I'm proud
of you for coming back to Magda after everything that's
happened. She's been waiting patiently, just like the night
wind.*

*Love you, baby sister. Now, stop chasing boys, put on
some shoes, and act like you've been to town before.*

Kell

She put the card back in its envelope and placed it aside on
the bed. Then she returned her attention to Magda.

She lifted the instrument carefully from its case. She felt its
weight in her fingertips. It was not fragile, but she hadn't touched
it, touched *her,* in two years. She no longer trusted herself.

"Mama tuned her for you, restrung her and everything," Aiden
said.

Bronwyn took the mandolin in her arms. She strummed her
thumb along the eight steel strings. The sound was pinched
and flat.

"Well, *that* ain't right," Aiden said.

"No," Bronwyn sighed. She stared at the neck, trying to recall
the fingering, *any* fingering, for *any* song. Nothing came to her.

"What's wrong?" Aiden asked.

"Maybe I don't feel like playing," she snapped.

His eyes opened wide. "For real?"

As always, she was unable to sustain any passion, even anger.
"I lost a lot of blood, Aiden. Between that and my skull getting
cracked, they said I might have some brain damage that could
affect my memory."

"You have . . ." And he whispered the last two words in
amazement. "Brain damage?"

She no longer had the patience to deal with him. "You will, too, if you don't stop being a shit. Now, get out of here and leave me alone."

Aiden made a face at her, then jumped up and ran out the door. He collided with her wheelchair, still blocking the hall, and tumbled over it. He lay still for a moment, then hollered, "I'm okay!"

Bronwyn burst out laughing, which sent jolts of pain through her whole body. Aiden stood up, put the chair upright, then scampered away.

Bronwyn shook her head. Aiden had always been impulsive, more like her than he was like their even-tempered older brother, Kell. But he never seemed to have her drive to tweak authority, to crush barriers, and seek out anything forbidden. He'd apparently gotten the best of both his siblings, without their bad qualities. Too bad it took her folks three tries to get it right.

She looked back down at Magda. The instrument felt awkward in her hands, and she couldn't recall at what angle she used to hold it, or the particular way she liked to place her fingers on the neck prior to playing. The images and feelings were there, but tantalizingly out of reach behind the same fog that mercifully hid the events of her ambush.

She carefully placed the instrument back in its case and closed the lid. Then she looked out the window. Down the hill, reporters still gathered at the gate, no doubt probing the family home with telephoto lenses and special microphones. She smiled; technology was all well and good, but nothing could penetrate a Tufa home without permission. And few homes in Needsville were as thoroughly Tufa as the Hyatts'.

Deacon appeared in the door. "Folks are starting to bring in the food. Hope being famous makes you hungry." His eyes narrowed. "Why is your uniform open?"

"I was showing Aiden my bullet hole," she said as she rebuttoned it.

"What did he think?"

"That it was cool."

"Well, he's just a boy."

"And he thinks I'm a hero."

"You're not," Deacon said definitively. "He'll figure that out. Come on when you're ready."

Bronwyn sat with her fingers on the top button of her uniform blouse, staring after her father. She agreed with her father's assessment, so why did his words sting so painfully? Hadn't she just told Aiden herself that she wasn't a hero?

Again something rose in her and faded. She got back on her crutches, hobbled to the wheelchair, and backed it clumsily down the hall.

The kitchen and living room were filled with people, all with identical jet-black hair. The buzz of conversation was offset by the idle plucking of stringed instruments, although no songs announced themselves. The little chips of music flitted through the words like butterflies among trees, with the same semi-magical effect. Delicious odors of thick, home-cooked foods filled the air, a striking change from the hospital and military slop she'd grown accustomed to eating.

"Excuse me," Bronwyn said to the big man blocking the hall. When he stepped aside, a cheer went up, and Bronwyn immediately put on what she called her *Meet the Press* smile. It wasn't insincere, but neither was it fully genuine; rather, it did the job the moment required, and she could only hope that it would grow more real with time.

She shook many hands and received many kisses on her cheeks and forehead as she worked her way to the kitchen. At last, exhausted and flanked by her parents, she listened blankly to the well-wishing and thankfulness. The one question she had, though, concerned her older brother, and when there was a break in the festivities, she asked Chloe, "So where *is* Kell, anyway?"

"He had finals this week," Chloe said. "He'll be here come the weekend. Said he might call tonight if he gets a study break."

Bronwyn smiled. Kell was the master of weighing alternatives, and had no doubt carefully considered all the angles before announcing his intent. Certainly at UT–Knoxville, he'd find it easier to avoid the media carnival in the driveway.

The festivities went on until past nightfall. People began to leave then, and again Bronwyn received many handshakes and kisses. At last Deacon closed the front door, leaving only the Hyatts in their home. "Whew," he said.

"Nice to be liked," Bronwyn said, "but it'll flat wear you out."

"It's important they see you," Chloe said. "You know that."

She nodded. "I'm a soldier, I'm used to doing what's good for the group."

"You're *not* a soldier anymore," her father said.

Bronwyn knew what he meant. The Tufa left Cloud County at their peril. Depending on how much true Tufa blood they had, all their protection, and all their strength, could be stripped away by distance and time. She knew her father believed that was why she'd been hurt, and for all she knew, he was right. But on this point he was also wrong. "I'm still in the army, Dad, I'm just on leave. My enlistment's not up for another month, and with all the stop-loss policies in effect, they may not let me out."

"You'll be let out," Chloe said. "If you want to be." She dropped an armload of beer bottles into the garbage and looked evenly at her daughter. "Do you?"

Bronwyn couldn't hold the gaze. Chloe, in that elliptical Tufa way, was asking about a lot more than her career plans. "I don't know, Mom."

"Will they let you fight again?" Aiden asked eagerly, then yawned.

At that moment the wind nudged one of the porch chimes. Its notes should have been random, but instead they were the first notes of a song every Tufa knew:

> *The moon shines bright*
> *And the winds alight*
> *On the rocky pinnacle of home*
> *Nowhere but here*
> *Is the wind so near*
> *To the song deep in my bones*

"I don't know," Bronwyn repeated.

In the twilight, Deacon and Aiden walked down the hill toward the gate. Three vans and a dozen people were still there, their huge lights drawing clouds of eager insects. All the camera lenses swung toward them as they approached, and questions flew at them.

"Is Bronwyn planning to return to the army?"

"Does she remember being shot?"

"Can she tell us how many people she remembers killing?"

Deacon calmly put up his hands. His left one curled his

pinkie and ring finger into his palm, making a variation of a peace sign. When the reporters paused to hear his answers, he said, "Y'all just calm down, we brought you some leftover brownies and we'd like to ask you to be a little quieter so Bronwyn can rest. It's been a heck of a day."

The bombardment began again instantly, and he simply stood there, hands up, smiling benignly. It took a moment, but one by one, the most persistent of the reporters fell silent, and looked away in something very much like shame. The big lights were switched off, and they were plunged into darkness while their eyes adjusted. The insects attracted to the glow flitted away into the night.

"Thank you," Deacon said. "Aiden, hand out them goodies, will you?"

Aiden took the pan of brownies to the fence and handed them across the aluminum gate to the reporters. As he did so, he hummed a tune his mother taught him, so softly, none of the reporters had any idea they were even hearing it. The first to sample the brownies responded with an enthusiastic "Mmmm!" and the others quickly followed suit. Once they'd all tasted them, Deacon dropped his left hand and held out his right with the thumb across the palm, as if indicating the number four.

"Hope y'all enjoy those," he said. "And please, let my daughter get some rest for the next few days. She won't be hard to find once she gets back on her feet, and if she remembers anything, I'm sure she'll want to tell about it."

The reporters all left within fifteen minutes. Many of them felt a combination of sudden, inexplicable guilt at their scavenger-like scrambling after the story; those without the moral capacity for such feelings, and because of that unprotected by the magic in the Tufa song, dealt with more prosaic digestive issues brought on by Chloe's brownies. Nothing so crude as poison had been used, merely the kind of intent a true Tufa could sing into *anything,* even cooking.

Chloe helped Bronwyn undress and use the bathroom, then bathed her with a sponge. Finally she helped her into a clean T-shirt with the Tennessee Titans logo across the front. "You've put on some weight," was her mother's only observation about her daughter's shattered, stitched, and scarred body.

"Yeah, well, hard to jog when you've got this cell phone tower wrapped around your leg," Bronwyn said as she leaned on Chloe's shoulder and maneuvered to the bed. She sat heavily, then reclined as her mother carefully positioned her leg. The ceiling above her was comforting and familiar, even with the flag banners dangling from it.

"You'll be out of that thing in a week, you know," Chloe said as she adjusted the pillows.

Bronwyn nodded. "I won't mind, believe me." She certainly looked forward to seeing the look on the doctors' faces when they saw how quickly she healed now that she was home.

"Aiden asked if you needed him to sleep on the floor in here. In case you had nightmares."

Bronwyn smiled. "Yeah, he's suddenly my bodyguard. Good thing you didn't bring him up to the hospital."

Chloe lit a candle on the bedside table. It was homemade, and laced with something that quickly filled the room with a softly pungent aroma. It took Bronwyn a moment to recognize it.

"That's heather," she said, frowning. "What's it for?"

"You'll have company later," Chloe said. "A haint."

Bronwyn sat up straight. She remembered Bliss in town, and the bird tapping at the window. "Now, wait a minute—"

"It is what it is," Chloe snapped. "Talking to me about it won't make any difference. Talk to *it*."

"Does it have anything to do with the death omen I saw today?"

"What death omen?" Chloe asked almost mockingly.

Bronwyn knew when her mother was hiding something behind sarcasm, and said, "Bird pecking at the window trying to get in."

"Birds can get confused just like anything else."

"Yeah, that's what Daddy said."

"He's a smart man." The two women looked into each other's eyes; finally Bronwyn sighed and turned away. Chloe placed the candle on the windowsill. "The candle should draw the haint here shortly."

Bronwyn flopped back on the pillow. "Not tonight. Hell, Mom, I'm exhausted."

Chloe chewed her lip thoughtfully. "Reckon you have a point. But you can't put it off too long. It's been coming around for a week already." She blew out the candle and took it with her as she turned off the light and went out the door.

Bronwyn lay in the dark, staring at the ceiling. The flag banners rippled slightly in the breeze through the open window. She glanced over and saw the ragged piece of blue glass on the sill, protection against the uninvited. No haint could pass that, even one summoned by the smell of heather. But haints, she knew, had all the time in the world.

Death omens didn't, though. They appeared only when the end of someone's life was in the near future. Chloe's harsh reaction told Bronwyn that this wasn't the first one, either. The question was always, whom were they meant for?

There was a song, a short little ditty that Tufa children used to make wishes on the night wind, hovering just beyond Bronwyn's consciousness. If she could've called it forth, she would ask the wind for clarity, and for an explanation. She closed her eyes and concentrated, trying to bring it forward.

She was asleep within moments.

4

Craig Chess watched some of the TV vans pull into the Catamount Corner parking lot while the rest continued on out of town. All the motel's rooms were booked, and Peggy Goins was making a small fortune with her special "media rates." As Craig sipped his coffee, the reporters rushed up the stairs to their rooms as if their feet were on fire. Some held their stomachs as if they might not make it to the bathroom.

The Fast Grab convenience store was new in town, built on a lot catty-corner across from the motel. Two picnic tables were set into the concrete patio outside. At the moment only Craig sat there, although earlier he'd had the pleasure of hearing two different men on cell phones explain to their wives how nothing was going on with their pretty young interns. He could've gone home hours ago, but he just couldn't tear himself away from the chance to encounter more examples of the worst humanity could offer. A minister, he reasoned, had to know the enemy in order to combat it.

That was the *other* reason he'd stayed in Needsville long after the parade. He needed to know these people by sight and name if they were ever to trust him. For the last two Saturdays, he'd hung out at the Fast Grab, speaking with the clerks and any willing customers. There had not been many.

He'd known coming into this assignment that he'd been given an almost impossible task: ministering to a people with no interest at all in his faith. It wasn't missionary work, because missionaries brought other things, food or medicine or money, to use as tangible spiritual bait. Craig could offer the Tufa nothing but his own sincerity.

The last person out of the news vans, a young man with a ponytail and a small bar through his septum, walked over to the store. He was clearly not an on-camera personality, but one of the myriad support staff who made sure the reporters looked their best. He sat down across the table from Craig and said without preliminaries, "Can I ask you something?"

"You just did," Craig said.

The man laughed and pointed at him. "Hey, good one. No, seriously, though. You live here, right?"

Craig nodded.

"What the fuck is *up* with this place? I mean, I spent some time in Europe when I was in college, and the people in this town are like freakin' Gypsies or something. Gypsies with great teeth, that is. Is that why they call them the Tootha?"

"Tufa," Craig corrected. "And it's a real mystery, all right. Nobody knows how they got here, but they've been in this area, mainly in this very valley, as long as anyone can remember. In fact, when the first white settlers came over the mountains headed west, the Tufa were already here."

"And they never left, is that it?"

Craig shrugged. Before accepting this position, he'd done lots of research, but the gaps and questions far outweighed the facts. The contemporary Tufa claimed no knowledge of their origins, and some of the stories other people told about them were too absurd to accept. Depending on whom you believed, they were a lost tribe of Israel, a relic population from Atlantis, or descendants of mutinous Portuguese sailors marooned off the Carolina coast by Columbus. These wilder theories kept away any serious researchers, and that seemed to suit the Tufa just fine. "Not too many leave, no. And from what I hear, most everyone who leaves eventually comes back."

"Like Bronwyn Hyatt?"

"Don't know her, so I can't say."

The man blatantly looked Craig over, noting his sandy brown hair. "Are you . . . one of them?"

"No, I'm from Arkansas. Just moved here about six weeks ago with my job."

"What do you do?"

"I'm a minister."

The man immediately looked down and away like a guilty child. Craig knew this reaction, had seen it often among Yankees or other people who spent little time in church. He couldn't imagine that a TV news technician knew much about religion except for what he saw on television, and that was enough to give anyone pause. The man said, "Really? Wow, that must be some job. I mean, with the souls and all. . . ."

Craig smiled. "Relax. I left my brimstone in my working pants."

"No, I mean, it's . . . well. Thanks for the info, padre." He offered his hand. "See ya around."

"And the Lord will see *you*," Craig said in a mock-ominous

voice. The man hurried back to the motel without looking over his shoulder to see Craig's grin.

Alone again, Craig drank the last of his coffee and considered heading home. The street was littered with debris from the parade; there were no real civic institutions, and each person was responsible for keeping up his or her own property. Since half the buildings along the highway were abandoned, the wrappers, plastic bottles, and cigarette butts might stay indefinitely. It made the place look especially pathetic, and even the mountains silhouetted against the fading sunset couldn't erase the sense that all the life had been leeched from the town.

Craig crumpled his cup and tossed it into the garbage can, then went inside. The girl behind the counter, Lassa Gwinn, was heavyset, dark eyed, and very clearly smitten with the handsome young minister. Just out of high school, with both the distinctive Tufa look and the heritage of her particularly nasty clan (sympathetic locals had warned Craig to avoid the Gwinns whenever they came to town), she seemed to Craig like a buttercup blooming from a manure pile. Because her crush on him was so obvious, he tried to walk the line between being a supportive clergyman and leading the poor girl on.

She hummed a tune and plucked on a crude, homemade autoharp. Since selling him the coffee, she'd pulled back her hair and applied eyeliner. When she saw him she immediately turned red. "Hey, preacher," she mumbled.

"I told you, Lassa, you can call me Craig." The melody was a minor-key ditty with one of those inevitable progressions that, even though he'd never heard it before, made it sound instantly familiar. "What song is that?"

She almost answered. Her mouth opened, she took a breath to speak, but then her lips clamped shut and she looked up at him with a mixture of shame and aching regret. Her blush intensified. "No song," she said. "Just me picking on strings."

"It sure was pretty."

"Well, I ain't no musician," Lassa said.

"You could've fooled me. Can you read music?"

Before she could reply, the front door slammed open, making Craig jump. A tall, lanky young man with a white cowboy hat strode through. He had the belligerent swagger of someone used to provoking fights, and the grin of someone who usually won them. He announced, "The night's got my name on it, baby."

"Hey, Dwayne," Lassa muttered without looking at him.

"How's things in Needsville tonight, Miss Lassa?" he called as he went to the beer cooler.

"Same as always," she replied.

The man pushed past Craig with neither apology nor acknowledgment. He was so broad-shouldered, Craig could've hidden behind him. He put a boxed twelve-pack on the counter. "And a pack of Marlboros, too," he said.

Lassa put the autoharp down and nudged a stepstool with her foot so she could reach the cigarettes. "Were you at the parade for your old girlfriend today?"

"Naw, I ain't into that shit. Bunch of fuckin' rubberneckers thinkin' they're seeing a goddamned hero." He tore open the cigarette pack, pulled one out, and lit it at once. "She ain't no hero. 'Scept when she's on her back," he added with an abrasive laugh.

Lassa blushed anew at his crudeness. She took his money, gave him his change, and watched him leave. He never even glanced at Craig. He climbed into a jacked-up ten-year-old Ford pickup and roared off, deliberately spinning tires so that loose gravel sprayed onto the store's concrete patio.

Craig breathed through his nose long enough to get his temper under control, then said casually, "And just who was that?"

"*That* was Dwayne Gitterman," Lassa said. "Bronwyn Hyatt's old boyfriend."

"No kidding. Didn't sound like they parted on good terms."

"She went off to the army without telling him." Then Lassa seemed to self-censor and added, "Or so I heard. Probably wrong, though."

"Why wouldn't she tell him? Was she afraid of him?"

Lassa laughed. "Not hardly. I guess she just didn't want the damn drama."

"Seems like an unpleasant young man."

"He's an asshole. And he knows it. But he's too tough for most anyone to do anything about it."

"Except Bronwyn Hyatt?"

"Yeah, 'scept her, that's for certain."

Craig smiled. "That's the thing about guys who think they're tough: Eventually they always meet someone tougher. If he didn't learn his lesson from Bronwyn, there'll be another on down the line."

As Dwayne's taillights dwindled in the night, a Tennessee State Police cruiser pulled up to the store. The trooper got out and gazed after Dwayne as if contemplating pursuit. Then he sauntered, in that distinctive lawman way, into the store.

He was a big square-headed man with short hair and a mustache shot through with gray. His eyes were cold, like an attack dog waiting for someone to cross some unseen line. He gave Craig an appraising look. "Evening."

Craig nodded. The trooper's little metal name tag said PAFFORD. "Evening."

"Don't believe I've seen you in town before. You with them reporters?"

"No, sir," Craig said, deliberately deferential. He'd met plenty of state troopers, and knew better than to get on their bad side. One minister in Cookeville got a ticket every Sunday for six weeks because he asked a trooper to stop cursing at his children in Walmart. "I'm Reverend Chess, of the Triple Springs Methodist Church."

Pafford's expression changed from intimidation to respect. He offered one huge hand. "Pleased to meet you, Reverend. My family and I attend the Methodist Church in Unicorn under Reverend Landers."

"I know him well," Craig said. "He's been a big help to me in getting started."

"Excuse me," Pafford said, and turned to Lassa. "Did Dwayne Gitterman seem drunk to you?"

She shook her head. "No, sir, he bought some beer, but I didn't smell any on him."

He nodded, although his frustration was evident. "That's still violating his parole, but I'd never catch him now. Dwayne never should've got out of the pen. He's just marking time until he goes back. Same thing for his girlfriend, that damn Hyatt girl."

"The war hero?" Craig asked, feigning ignorance.

"War hero." Pafford snorted. "Wouldn't surprise me if it turns out that her giving somebody a hand job was the real reason for that crash in Iraq in the first place. She's from a good family, but not all black sheep are boys. Do you know what they used to call her around here?"

Again Craig innocently shook his head.

"The Bronwynator. Because she tore up everything good

and decent anywhere around her. I used to think ol' Dwayne led her into it, but he's been pretty good since she's been gone. Now I reckon it was *her* prodding *him*."

"Well, she doesn't seem in any condition to be causing any trouble now, judging from what I saw on TV."

"Ah, them Tufas heal up faster than mud gets on new dress pants. No offense, Lassa, you know what I mean."

Lassa shrugged. "That's not really an insult."

"But mark my words, with Dwayne out of jail and Bronwyn home, it's just a matter of time before they get together again and start making trouble."

"What sort of trouble?" Craig asked.

"Dwayne deals pot and drives that damn truck like a maniac. He got sent up for robbing a convenience store a lot like this one. And before she went in the army, that Bronwyn spent more time on her knees than a preacher." He suddenly turned red along his neck and ears. "I mean, er . . . no offense, Reverend."

"None taken," Craig said, keeping his casual smile.

Pafford leaned close. "These Tufas, though . . . they're like some goddamn cult or something, if you ask me. Always shutting up just when they're about to let something slip. If they start coming to your church, you better watch that your collection plate doesn't come back lighter than it left."

"I'll do that." His smile was harder than ever to hold.

Pafford excused himself, went back to his car, and drove away. Lassa said, "There are days I wish somebody would just shoot him."

"Why is that?"

"He pulled over my cousin's family two years ago. They had a little pointer puppy with them that got out. He shot it. Claimed it was attacking him. With its milk teeth, I guess. Came in here laughing about how my cousins were all crying."

"Man like that must have a lot of pain inside."

"No, a man like that puts all his pain on the outside where people can see it. Like he's singing a song for everyone to hear, even though he knows he can't carry the tune, and dares someone to tell him to shut up." Then she began changing the paper in the credit card machine.

5

"Hey, Don, you're part Tufa, ain't you?"

Don Swayback looked up from his computer, quickly minimizing the Internet browser window he had open. He started each day with the blogs of a group of UT coeds; it was his own private sorority, and if he ever paused to think about it, he'd realize how pathetic it was for a man his age. But these days he wasn't much into thinking. "Beg your pardon?"

Sam Howell, owner and editor of the Unicorn, Tennessee, newspaper *The Weekly Horn,* stood up rather than repeat the question. The office, such as it was, was located in a small Main Street storefront between the antique mall and State Farm Insurance. It was cramped, hot, and surprisingly noisy, with the smell of thousands of cigarettes soaked into the ancient wood and carpet. A job at a paper like this meant you were just starting out in journalism, or your career was essentially over. Since Don was thirty-four, a little overweight, and a lot apathetic, his trajectory was obvious. Especially to Don.

"You're kin to those Cloud County Tufas in some way, aren't you?" Sam said as he walked around his desk. "Fifth cousin twice removed by marriage or something?"

Sam was a big man, a native of Michigan's Upper Peninsula with a slate gray crew cut and faded navy tattoos on his arms. He'd served in Viet Nam, and while there had freelanced for *Stars and Stripes*. This led him to journalism after his tour, and now he owned the paper he'd first started with back in the seventies. Not that there was much left to own, since circulation dropped regularly. Still, every week, Sam managed to squeeze out a new edition, often with all the copy written by him and Don.

"There's a Tufa in the woodpile of just about everyone between the Tennessee River and the Carolina border, Sam," Don said. "What about it?"

"Yeah, but you *look* like 'em. You got the hair and the teeth."

"Sam, it's seven o'clock in the morning and I haven't finished my first cup of coffee yet. Say what you mean."

Sam rolled one of the office chairs over to Don's desk and sat down. He leaned close in that paternal way that always set Don's teeth on edge. "I was just looking at your photographs from the parade over in Needsville yesterday. They weren't very good."

Don sighed and shrugged. "The national media had all the good spots, Sam. There were a lot of people there."

"I know, Don, that's why it was news. It looks to me like you were there for ten minutes, shot so many pictures you hoped one would turn out, then left."

Don said nothing; that was exactly what he had done.

"That's not really acceptable professional behavior, Don. This was a big deal, and now I have to pay to use a newswire photo. That doesn't make me happy."

"I'm really sorry," Don said, hoping it sounded genuine.

"I know you are, and that's why I'm giving you a chance to make up for it. I want an exclusive interview with Bronwyn Hyatt, and I want you to get it."

Don frowned. "Because I have black hair and good teeth."

"That's oversimplifying it, Don. You're a good reporter when you're interested in what you're covering, which ain't very often these days, let's face it. I'd like to think that a cute little war hero might be enough to get your attention."

"I don't know what's most insulting in that statement, Sam."

"Truth is truth, Donny-Boy. You're slacking, and you know it. We both know you didn't go to that softball game last week, you wrote the story from the postgame stats the coach gave you. Now *this* is something to get your teeth into. You want it or not?"

"If you're trying to charm my pants off, Sam, you better buy me dinner first. *You're* the veteran here; it makes more sense for you to go talk to her."

Sam shook his head. "Different world, different war. I was drafted and did my time; this girl signed up on her own. Now, I know you don't approve of the war, but I hope you can put that aside enough to see that there's a good story here."

"It's a story everyone in creation already knows. For a week she was on every channel at least once an hour. What could I possibly ask her that no one else has thought of?"

Sam spread his hands. "See? That's the challenge. Are you up to it?"

Don sighed. Once he'd been eager, and hungry, for a story like this. Then, over time, he'd understood that every story, even the good ones, was as transitory as a breath. But he was in debt up to his eyeballs, and needed insurance to cover his cholesterol medicine. "Sure, I'll give it a shot. You got any contact information?"

"None at all."

"So you haven't talked to her or her family, or anything?"

"Nothing." Sam put one big hand on Don's shoulder and shook him in what was meant to be brotherly camaraderie. "Show me what you got, Don. Seriously. Knoxville's got a big ol' school of journalism, and everyone that comes through it ends up looking for a job."

He gave him one last shake for emphasis, then went back to his desk.

Don sighed and opened a new browser window. He entered *Bronwyn Hyatt* into the search engine and began accumulating background information.

"*Who* wants to see me?" Bronwyn said, her mouth still full of half-chewed biscuit.

"The Right Reverend Craig Chess," Deacon repeated. He'd finished his own breakfast and was enjoying both his coffee, and his daughter's dismay. He wore overalls and a UT Volunteers baseball cap. "He's waiting on the porch."

"And who the hell is the Right Reverend Craig Chess?"

"He's the preacher at the new Methodist church."

Bronwyn's eyes opened wide. "There's a Methodist church in Cloud County?"

"Near as. Right over the county line on Highway 70 going toward Morristown."

She knew the location. It was the closest spot to Needsville where a church might be built, since no Christian churches would ever succeed in Cloud County. Still, who did this lunatic think would *attend* his church? Even across the border in Mackenzie County there were few people who weren't Baptist, certainly not enough to maintain a whole church.

And why on earth was he coming to see *her*? Did he want her autograph? Did he want her to speak to his congregation? "It's seven o'clock in the morning, Dad."

"Reckon he knows farmers get up early," Deacon said.

"That reminds me," Chloe said, then called out, "Aiden! School bus stop, *now*!"

"This is crazy," Bronwyn said to no one in particular.

"I can invite him in," Chloe said. She wore her hair loose, and it made her look particularly vital. She was clad in old jeans with the knees worn through and a gray army tank top Bronwyn had given her the previous Christmas. "Or I can send him on home. But you should make up your mind before the dirt daubers start building nests on him."

"Fucking hell," Bronwyn muttered. She laboriously hauled herself upright on her crutches, then hobbled to the front door. She emerged onto the porch and squinted into the morning sunlight. She saw no one to the left beneath the awning, then turned to the right.

She would've gasped out loud had her teeth not been clenched against the pain of movement.

The man standing there was just shy of six feet, with short brown hair and scholarly glasses. He had broad shoulders and a narrow waist that his jeans and polo shirt showed off to great effect. When he saw her he smiled, and she flashed back to Lyle Waggoner's teeth twinkling in the credits of the old *Wonder Woman* TV show. The morning sun outlined him like a saint in an icon painting.

"Ms. Hyatt," he said, and even his voice was a turn-on,

smooth and just deep enough. "I'm Craig Chess." He offered his hand. "It's an honor to meet you. Hope it's not too early to come visiting."

"Hi," she managed to squeak out. Her legs wobbled in a way that had nothing to do with her injuries. Suddenly she felt hugely self-conscious, with her unwashed hair pulled haphazardly back and a baggy T-shirt that hung to her knees. She awkwardly tugged the bottom hem down, tearing it free from where it had snagged on the leg pins, to hide the fact that she hadn't put on any shorts. And when was the last time she'd shaved her good leg?

"Thank you for seeing me. I know after yesterday you must be tired of all the attention."

She could only nod. Parts of her that had not responded to anything in months were waking up and announcing themselves.

"Do you need to sit down?" he asked, concerned.

She shook her head. Her mouth was too dry for words.

"I won't keep you, but I wanted to tell you, I'm available if you ever need anything before you get back on your feet. Or after, of course. I can drive you into town, pick things up for you, whatever."

This broke through her sex-deprived stupor. "Wait, you're offering to be my *chauffeur*?"

"Or run any errands you need."

"I'm not a Methodist, Reverend."

"No, but you're a person in my parish who might need some help. I'm not trying to convert you, I promise. It's just part of my job."

"How noble of you," she said dryly. Her physical responses couldn't entirely overwhelm her cynicism.

"Bronwyn," Deacon said softly, warningly. She hadn't realized he stood just inside the screen door watching them.

"Okay, I'm sorry, I'll take you at face value, then. Thank you. But really, I don't need anything. Mom and Dad can do my errands, and I'm getting more and more self-sufficient all the time. I'll have this getup off my leg so fast, you won't believe it."

Craig nodded. "That's fine. You're lucky to have such a supportive family around you. But may I ask you something a bit . . . esoteric?"

"Sure."

"What about your spirit?"

She blinked. "I beg your pardon?"

"You've been through a lot, to put it mildly. Things like that often make people reevaluate their relationship with God." He said this with no irony, and no trace of sarcasm. Perversely, this made him even hotter. "If you want to talk, I'll listen. And I won't offer advice unless you ask."

"We take care of our own," Deacon said to save Bronwyn the embarrassment. He spoke with no hostility, yet firmly enough to discourage any disagreement. "What we believe is private, and we worship in our own way."

Craig nodded. "I certainly respect that, Mr. Hyatt." He turned to Bronwyn. "But my offer to help, in *any* way, stands. I left my phone number with your father."

"Thanks," she said. "Really." The cynical side of her nature reflected that, once you've been on TV, everyone was your friend. Even smoking-hot young ministers. And the help she wanted from him at that precise moment was luckily made impossible, or at least prohibitively awkward, by her injured leg.

He smiled. "I figure you've been buried under enough platitudes, so I won't add to the pile. But it really is an honor and a pleasure to meet you. And—" There was just the slightest hesitation, as if he were debating adding the next comment. "—it would be a pleasure even without everything that's happened to you."

He nodded to Deacon and walked down the porch steps toward his car, an older-model Altima. It was, of course, white.

"Seems like a nice boy," Deacon said.

"Yeah," Bronwyn agreed, wondering if there was a special circle of the Christian hell for women who admired a preacher's ass.

She needed more coffee.

Craig turned onto the highway and headed toward Needsville, but his thoughts were nowhere near the road. They remained back at the old house built into the side of the hill, where he'd just met a girl who affected him more quickly and intensely than any he'd ever encountered. Even Lucy, his first love, had not struck him straight through the heart with the urgency of this black-haired young woman.

And yet he couldn't identify what about her had done it. She was almost ten years younger, from a completely different background, and entirely uninterested in the things that defined his life. She was *world famous,* for heaven's sake, and for the rest of her life would be "that girl rescued in Iraq." No doubt there was some young soldier out there just waiting for leave to come visit her, probably another Tufa or at least someone familiar with their ways and approved of by her family. If he didn't get himself under control, Craig might be fated for a backwoods beating by a bunch of angry Tufa cousins in the near future.

And yet . . .

Those eyes. That dark hair falling from its tie in wild, loose strands around her face. Those lips, unadorned yet still full and delicious. And that *voice* . . .

He sighed. There was a time and place for everything, and this was neither. Craig was not a virgin; he'd been called to the ministry as a young adult, so he'd sowed his share of wild oats, and knew any future sex would have to wait until he found a woman he truly wanted to be his wife. He'd dated several women since deciding to be a minister, and almost married one of them. He could acknowledge the attraction, accept it, and yet not let it control his life.

But he could not understand why it had to be a battered, barely grown war hero from an obscure ethnic group. What, he thought half-seriously, was the Good Lord smoking?

6

"That was weird," Bronwyn said as she settled in at the kitchen table and propped her crutches against it. "A preacher trying to save souls in Needsville." The weirdest part was that the intangible defenses that kept most outsiders at a distance, like those reporters, apparently hadn't impeded the young minister.

Her father put a fresh cup of coffee in front of her and sat down in the opposite chair. "Yeah, reckon it's a weird time. What with that Internet and all them cell phones, Needsville's almost part of the world these days."

"The world ain't ready for us, Daddy," she said with certainty. "I've been out there and seen it. We'd be like tulips in a windstorm."

He nodded. "Can't say I'd be sorry to go back to the way things were 'bout twenty years ago."

"Before I was born?" she teased. "Am I that bad?"

He looked at her evenly. "Might do it differently with you if I could start over."

"Daddy, you did fine. Some things are just born wild, and it takes a while for 'em to run it off."

"You run yours off yet?"

She looked down at the coffee. From this angle, it reflected her father's face. "I sure ain't feeling too wild these days. Don't know if it'll come back or not. Part of me hopes it does, the rest of me . . ." She trailed off with a shrug, then took another sip of her drink. "I don't even know where the rest of me is right now."

"You'll be fine," he said with certainty. "Although I'm worried to hear you paraphrasin' Ronald Reagan."

Bronwyn smiled, then looked around. "Hey, where's Mom?"

"She went out to check something in the garden. Said she'd be right back."

She looked out the window. Her mother was on her knees at the bottom of the yard, picking the beginnings of weeds from the dirt. Her autoharp rested on a folding chair nearby. A mockingbird flew down, perched on the chair, and pecked once at the instrument's strings.

Bronwyn couldn't hear the sound, but the scene made her smile. As a little girl she'd sat in that same chair plucking those same strings, aching for the day she could coax music from them and fly on the night wind.

"I can carry you out there," Deacon said. "Or push your wheelchair."

She shook her head. "No thanks. It ain't that. It's . . ."

"Couldn't play Magda?"

She nodded. "How'd you know?"

"Expected to hear you playing last night, and didn't." And it was normally true: a full-blood Tufa who'd been away from home all this time would've spent half the night playing. The silence once her door closed told her family everything.

"It ain't that I *can't* play," Bronwyn said quietly. "Everything works. This hole in my arm went right through, so it healed up pretty quick, like you said."

"It's the hole in your head giving you trouble?"

She smiled. Many times in her youth, her father had accused her of having extra holes in her head. "I wasn't *shot* in the head, Daddy, I had a skull fracture and concussion from the IED. It makes some things . . . fuzzy."

"Like what things?"

"Like . . . music."

They were both quiet for a long moment. "You tell your mama?" he asked finally, no accusation or judgment, just a question.

She shook her head. "You gonna tell her?"

"One of us is."

"Okay, okay. I will." She sipped her coffee and watched the porch chimes wave in the breeze without quite sounding. "Did I hear the phone ring before I got up?"

"It was that Major Maitland. He's a slippery fella, isn't he?"

"He may be president someday. What'd he want?"

"See how you were. See if them reporters was still around. I don't think he believed me when I told him they wasn't. I reckon he suspects they're hanging out in the trees like squirrels."

"That's what he's used to," she said. "He'll never understand this place."

"Not many from the outside would. He said people from Hollywood are calling. I got the idea lots of money was involved."

"What did you tell him?"

"That I'd tell you he called."

Chloe entered through the back door, stepped out of her

sandals, and went to the sink. As she washed a pair of fresh to-matoes she said, "Bliss Overbay'll be stopping by to see you."

"Good, I ain't seen her in weeks," Deacon deadpanned.

"Not *you*," Chloe scolded. "Girl like Bliss ain't got time for an old man like you."

"That's 'cause I'd flat wear her out," Deacon said with a grin.

Bronwyn recalled the bird, the bells, and the haint she'd put off last night. "Bliss is coming to talk to me?"

"Course. You saw her yesterday, so you knew she would."

"Didn't know it'd be right away. Thought she might give me some time to settle in."

"It's your home," Chloe said as she dried her fingers. "How settled do you need to be?"

Bronwyn sighed. "Reckon you're right." But she knew Bliss would not be making a simple social call. In the hidden, com-plex world of Tufa authority, Bliss Overbay wielded a mighty stick, and when she swung it, all the Tufa ducked. There was etiquette to a meeting like this, and Bronwyn would have to at least try to fulfill her part of things.

Chloe poured herself a cup of coffee. She kissed Deacon on the cheek as she passed him, then sat in the only other open chair. "You'll have to talk to that haint tonight, too."

"I *will*. Damn, Mom, I just got out of the hospital."

Her mother slapped her hand on the table so loud and hard, it was like a pistol shot; in fact, Bronwyn might've reflexively jumped aside if she hadn't been trapped by the pin frame. Her chest constricted and her eyes went wide.

Even Deacon looked surprised. "Honey?" he said to his wife.

Chloe's voice shook with suppressed anger. "Yes, I know, I've heard all about your sacrifices, your injuries, all about what a hero you are. And you know what? I *don't care*. As far as I'm concerned, you've spent the last two years playacting, and now that you're home where the real work is, you're trying to avoid it. You *will* see Bliss when she comes, and you *will* listen to your haint tonight. I don't want to hear any more about it."

Bronwyn could barely breathe. A new image, one she'd never recalled before, came unbidden through her fog of memory, shaken loose by her mother's slap. It was the same flash of orange light, but then it turned white, and she realized it was a flashlight. Beyond it was a swarthy face with a jet-black mustache and dark, panicky eyes. He said something she couldn't catch—her Arabic was terrible—and then reached for her.

She shivered, and realized she was sweating. When she looked up, Chloe and Deacon both stared at her. "One of them flashbacks?" her father asked softly.

She nodded. She could still smell both the gasoline from the wrecked truck and the burning flesh of the man trapped behind her. "One of the Iraqis was trying to get me out of the truck."

Deacon's voice changed very slightly, but it was enough to express his sincere, extreme concern. "You sure it was a real thing, and not just something you imagined?"

"No," she said bitterly. "I'm not sure. You hear about something enough, your brain starts to believe it. The whole time I was in the hospital, I heard about how the Iraqis pulled me out of the wreck and then . . . well . . . did stuff to me." She actually blushed, something she hadn't done in years, at talking about this in front of her parents. "But I don't know if it's true."

"There's ways to find out," Chloe said quietly. "If it matters."

"No," Bronwyn said. "It doesn't, really. I've got enough pain that I *can* remember." She shifted her weight, wishing she'd brought a pillow to put beneath her butt on the hard chair.

Aiden finally emerged from his bedroom. "Did I hear a gunshot?"

"Your mama was just making a point," Deacon said, his gaze on Chloe. He kissed her on the cheek and went outside. Chloe turned on the water and began washing the breakfast dishes. She kept her back to her children.

Aiden leaned close to Bronwyn and said, "I hear you've got a haint."

"You hear a lot," she said. For just a moment, her old big-sister annoyance with Aiden threatened to appear, but it faded. Would she be numb this way forever?

"Well, if you want, I can sit up with you and run it off when it shows up again."

She snorted. "You'd pee your pants if you saw a ghost. You know you would."

"Uh-uh. I'd look it right in the eye and say, 'Hey, leave my sister alone, she's a war hero.' Then I'd chase it with a hatchet."

"What if it didn't have any eyes? What if it just had big black sockets where its eyes *used* to be?"

He thought this over. In utter deadpan he said, "Then instead of a hatchet, I'd use a socket wrench."

They both burst into giggles. Without turning Chloe said, "Aiden Hyatt, get down to the bus stop now. Nobody's got time to drive you in to school if you miss it."

"Yes, ma'am," he said with a full-body shrug. He grabbed his book bag and dragged it across the floor behind him as he slouched out the door.

As Bronwyn watched her brother leave, something swaying

in the breeze caught her eye. Through the screen door she saw a bundle of feathers tied together with hexwound guitar string and hung from a wind chime's clapper, giving extra purchase to the wind and producing a constant, soft tinkling.

She frowned. She knew what this was . . . didn't she? The hawk feathers, mixed with those of a crow and tied to the clapper between three chimes that, in the right order, played . . . what song? What did it mean?

Her father must've built it; he loved putting chimes together in different musical combinations, and had racks of aluminum and wooden tubes in the shed. But she wouldn't ask him, because goddammit, she should *know*. She was a Tufa, a First Daughter, heir to the songs and rider on the night wind.

At last she said, "I think I'm going to lay down for a while. I'll see you at lunch."

In her room, she once again opened the mandolin case. The instrument gleamed in the sun coming through the window; its finish reflected the red, white, and blue from the curtains. She rested her fingertips lightly on the strings.

The calluses she'd earned had softened a little in the time she'd been away, but her skin still seemed to hold the memory. Her thumb curled as it would to pluck a string. But the experiences that connected these things, that allowed her to coax music from Magda, were still missing.

Because of her sudden media notoriety, the military doctor who'd tended her when she arrived stateside from Iraq had tried to be kind, but clearly lacked experience in real doctor–patient relations. "You may have some memory loss. Most of it will be connected directly with the accident, when your brain suffered its trauma. But it could crop up with other things. You may forget people you've known all your life, how to do certain tasks, and so forth. You can relearn the skills; the memories may or may not return."

Since she'd been semiconscious with a feeding tube down her throat, she'd only been able to nod. Really, though, what other response could there be?

She turned the mandolin in her hands. It was light, and felt fragile compared to the heavy, solid things she'd handled for the past two years. She had refused to take it with her to basic training, and from there to her deployment in Iraq, because she wanted nothing to remind her of Needsville. But now it was more tangible than the metal guns, equipment, and vehicles she'd gotten to know intimately.

"Shit," she sighed, and felt her eyes itch as tears tried to form. But like her memories, they never quite appeared.

7

Don Swayback sat down at his mother's kitchen table. He used to think of it as his table, too, but since he'd grown up, he had a hard time feeling connected to this old house, these old things, even this old woman now settling into her own seat across from him. Even the town, Rossell, had grown and expanded until it was unfamiliar and alien.

"It's good to see you, son," his mother said. Her name was Gloriana, although everyone called her Glory. "And it's not even Mother's Day. Shouldn't you be at work? You didn't get fired, did you?"

"You know, if you keep picking on me, I'll stop coming at all," he teased.

"Then I wouldn't have to do dishes more than once a month," she shot back. She was eighty-two, still self-sufficient except for the twice-weekly cleaning woman.

Don sipped his coffee and buttered a biscuit. "Mom, can I ask you something? Which side of the family has the Tufa in it, yours or Dad's?"

Glory's eyebrows rose in surprise. "Lord, son, why are you asking something like that?"

"I have to get an interview with Bronwyn Hyatt."

"Who?"

"You know, that girl from over in Needsville who was captured by the Iraqis? Got rescued on live TV?"

"Oh, I sure remember *that*. They played it enough on the news. Well, now, that's just something," Glory said with a shake of her head. "Hasn't she been talked to enough?"

"That's just it," Don said as he added homemade pear reserves atop the butter. "She's been talked *about*, but not *to*. No one's really had an in-depth interview with her about what it was like to be a Needsville Tufa so far from home."

"And that carpetbagger you work for wants *you* to do it?"

He nodded. "The Tufas don't cotton to outsiders, so I figure the best way would be to go through family. I know we're related to some Tufas somehow, but I don't know the particulars."

"Well, what makes you think I do? We don't associate with that Needsville trash, never have."

"Then where'd I get this?" Don said, and tugged on a lock of his black hair.

Glory sighed. "If you must know, son, it's through your late daddy's side of the family. The Swaybacks mixed with the Tufas when your great-granddaddy Forrest married a Tufa widow woman named Benji. I can't remember what that was short for. They met working on one of them Roosevelt WPA projects during the Depression. Something about 'documenting the rural lifestyle,' or some such nonsense." Her disdain for Roosevelt, Democrats in general, and the Tufa all combined to give her words a sour, bitter flavor.

"Do you know Benji's family name?"

Glory shook her head. "Your daddy's family never talked about Grandaddy Forrest very much. He'd passed on by the time I met your daddy." She suddenly snapped her fingers. "But you know what? I bet it's writ down in the old family Bible that your aunt Raby has. She's the last of your daddy's brothers and sisters, so I know she's got it, probably tucked away in the attic or something. You might drive out there to see."

Don nodded. He took a bite of biscuit, and was transported for a moment back to Sunday breakfasts when he was a child. He had felt a part of things then, with the Swaybacks and his mother's family the Dorchesters all around, cousins and in-laws liable to appear at any moment to join in post-church fellowship. But the instant passed almost with his act of swallowing, and once again he realized he had virtually nothing in common with the old woman seated across from him.

"I haven't seen Aunt Raby in a while," he said. "I might just do that."

When Bronwyn awoke from her nap, the house was empty.

Deacon was working in the fields, Aiden was in school, and Chloe was no doubt off running errands. In any other situation, such neglect would be unforgivable: she was supposed to be watched at all times for any relapses, physical or psychological. The VA doctors stressed that she could, essentially, freak out at any time. But the Tufa, especially purebloods like the Hyatts, would know if she wasn't safe. They could not see into the future exactly, but could sense if certain actions were likely to have unwanted consequences. It was not a perfect ability— Bronwyn had sensed nothing before her ambush in Iraq, for instance—but in the Needsville valley, in the heart of Tufa country, it was as infallible as it was possible to be.

She moved from her bedroom to the living room couch. The clock read eleven thirty. She felt sticky, and wished for the billionth time that she could take a proper shower. The open windows let in the cool breeze and the soft tinkle of the wind chimes. She considered turning on the TV, but didn't want to come across any news stories about herself. She still hated the fact that she was now a current event.

There was a firm knock on the door and a cheerful voice said, "Special delivery for the Bronwynator."

She turned to see a heavyset man in a postman's uniform, a large mail sack at his feet. "Hey, Ed," she called, and waved him in. "'Scuse me for not getting up."

Ed opened the door and dragged the sack in after him. "Now, never you worry about that, young lady. Your job right now is to mend those boo-boos, and that's all you should be concentrating on."

"Boo-boos?" Bronwyn repeated with a grin. "I'm twenty years old, I don't think I still have 'boo-boos.'"

Carvin' Ed Shill, the lone mailman for all the widely dispersed families in the valley, was only one-quarter Tufa, but it informed his whole being: he shone with the Tufa spirit even though his hair was sandy brown and freckles covered his face. "Sure you do," he said, and kissed her on her cheek. "You'll always be mean little, I mean *sweet* little Bronwyn to me, who didn't go a summer without her knees and elbows scraped all the time. You used to run up and show me your boo-boos then."

She gestured at her leg. "Well, this is my latest one."

"Lord A'mighty, it looks like a sausage caught halfway through a grinder."

Bronwyn laughed. "What's in the bag?"

"The best medicine in the world: get-well cards from your fans."

She stared at the bag, then at him. "From my *fans*? I don't have fans."

"Well, you got a lot of people mighty concerned about you. There's five more of these back at the post office, but I didn't want to overwhelm you."

"*Five* more? Holy shit, Ed, you're kidding me."

"No, ma'am." He took one card from the bag and looked over the envelope. "This is from little Emma from up in Kentucky. I assume she's little, she could be a big girl who just never mastered turning her *E*'s the right way. And it's sealed with a USA sticker."

Bronwyn numbly took the card. She couldn't bring herself to open it, and placed it beside her on the couch. "Thanks, Ed. It's weird thinking that so many people know about me, you know?"

"Are you telling me the Bronwynator has gotten stage fright? Say it ain't so, Bro! You used to crave attention like a sponge does dishwater."

"I did not."

"So writing 'Bronwyn was here' on every school bus in the county was your idea of being discreet?"

"*Dwayne* did that. I just kept watch for the cops. And besides, that was before I got a truck dropped on my head."

"Yeah," he said sadly, and touched her cheek. "I had an uncle in Viet Nam. They say he was a cut up, class clown guy before he went. Now he barely sleeps and won't sit with his back to a door."

"I hope I'm not that bad," she said with a wry smile. She'd been warned about posttraumatic stress at Walter Reed, and offered the kind of psychiatric help the army provides; she knew she'd be better off trepanning herself with a hammer and nail.

"Well, if you need anything, just let ol' Carvin' Ed know." He touched the brim of his cap in a salute. "Some days, especially during deer season, this job feels like the armed forces. Wouldn't think a mail carrier looks much like a buck deer, but I've got two caps with bullet holes in the brims. And they say *postmen* are trigger-happy."

"I'll swap tours with you. Baghdad's bound to need some mailmen."

He chuckled. "No way. Least with *my* job, there's days people *ain't* trying to kill me. Oh, and before I forget: I made you a little something, too."

From one of his voluminous pockets he pulled a small wooden box about the length of Bronwyn's hand and perhaps two inches high. Vaguely Celtic designs decorated the corners.

She took it. "Ed, that's so sweet. Really."

"It's not the *box,* bonehead. Open it."

Carefully Bronwyn lifted the lid and pulled the object from its cradle of cotton.

The figure was about three inches high, carved from a single piece of catalpa wood. It depicted a young woman playing a mandolin, standing on one foot as if dancing. From the figure's back extended a large pair of curved, two-lobed wings, similar in shape to a butterfly's.

The resemblance to Bronwyn was unmistakable. "Wow, Ed," she whispered. "It's beautiful."

"Only 'cause the subject is."

She ran her fingers lightly along the edge of the wings. They were carved so thin that even slight pressure caused them to bend. She felt a sympathetic tug in her own shoulders. "It's been a while since . . ."

"I figured. But you never lose it."

She looked up at him. "I hope you're right."

He grinned and playfully yanked one loose strand of her hair. "I know I am."

After Ed left, Bronwyn stared at the mailbag for a long time. A robin sang outside the window, encouraging her. At last she tentatively opened the card Ed handed her earlier.

Dear Private Hyatt, it began. The handwriting was clearly a child's, much younger than Aiden. *I hope you are getting well. We saw your rescue on TV and want you to know we are praying for you. You're my hero.* It was signed simply, *Emma,* with a backwards capital *E.*

A picture was included as well. It was a school photo of a pudgy little girl with lank brown hair put back in barrettes. An adult had written, *Emma, age 6* on the back.

Bronwyn stared at it, trying to imagine the girl's feelings as she wrote this. No doubt her whole class had done so as well; Major Maitland told her that schools all over the country were sending her get-well cards. But she could find no common ground. Whatever emotions left to her did not include this degree of empathy.

And yet a fragment of melody and a long-hazy lyric sprang to her mind:

When love gets you fast in her clutches,
And you sigh for your sweetheart away,
Old Time cannot move without crutches,
Alas, how he hobbles . . .

And that was all.

She put the picture and card back in the envelope. Then she went back to bed. She placed Ed's carving of the mandolin-playing fairy on her bedside table.

8

"Bronwyn," her visitor said. The figure stood in the bedroom door, backlit by the hall light.

Bronwyn blinked, looked at the window, and saw it was now dark. The clock on the bedside table read 1:45 A.M. "The hell?" she said sleepily, dragging her leg up the bed until she could rest against the headboard. She'd been asleep over twelve hours.

"Bronwyn," the voice said again.

I can't deal with the haint yet, Bronwyn thought fearfully. She felt her immobility more than ever, and winced with each crushing heartbeat; for an instant she thought she might really be having a coronary, her body too weak to survive this level of terror.

Then the voice registered. "Bliss?"

"You knew I'd be coming," Bliss Overbay said. "I'm going to turn on the light now."

Bronwyn scrunched her eyes shut, but still saw the sudden illumination through her lids. She blinked into it and waited for her vision to adjust.

"You look awful," Bliss said with a smile.

"You look exactly the same as you did when I left," Bronwyn replied. And it was true: Bliss was still slender, broad shouldered, and straight backed. She wore her long jet-black hair in a single braid that fell down her back almost to her waist. Her dark face had deep smile lines bracketing her wide mouth, which made guessing her age difficult for outsiders; she could've been anywhere between twenty and fifty. Her eyes seemed light blue or green, and often actually twinkled like they were illuminated from within. She wore faded blue jeans and a sleeveless jersey that displayed the snake tattoo around her upper arm. There was something disconcerting about the inkwork; it was the only thing in her appearance that hinted that she might be more than just another backwoods girl.

Bliss closed the door, knelt beside the bed, and examined Bronwyn's broken leg. As an emergency medical technician, she knew how to interpret the damage. "Wow. Broke the femur in three places?"

"Four. The last one was a hairline crack that didn't show up on the X-rays until they'd already put this thing on. And my fibula was practically pulverized."

"That is one messed-up leg," Bliss agreed. "How's your arm?"

"This?" She pushed up her T-shirt sleeve. The puckered hole on either side of her biceps was scabbed and red, but no longer required a bandage. "It's nothing. The bullet went right through. Except for being sore, it's good as new."

Bliss tenderly brushed a strand of hair from the younger woman's face. "And your head?"

"I get headaches sometimes. And the crack is still sore if I touch it, so I try not to touch it."

"I meant the inside of it."

Bronwyn paused, then shrugged. "I've been better."

Bliss nodded. Then she smiled and said, "We'll have these pins out of your leg in a week, you know."

"The doctors said six."

"And if *they* were looking after you, it might be six. But you're home now."

"I don't feel like it," Bronwyn said, and gazed out the window. Nothing moved in the night. Had the haint already come, been unable to rouse her, and departed? Chloe would be livid.

Bliss folded her arms on the edge of the bed and rested her chin on them. "So you're having some problems. Other than all the extra holes."

Bronwyn couldn't look at her. "Yeah. Two big ones. One is a haint that Mom says wants to talk to me. If she came tonight, she didn't knock loud enough. And the other . . ." Now those tears threatened again. "Bliss," she said very quietly, "I can't play."

"Because your arm's hurt?"

"No, because I can't remember *how*." And then the tears really did come, weeks of them silently bursting free and running down her cheeks. She felt her face contort with the sobs aching to follow, but she held them at bay. "It's like someone deleted the file from my brain."

Bliss leaned over and hugged her. "That's awful," she agreed. "But not permanent."

"What if it is?" Bronwyn whimpered into Bliss's hair. "What if I never remember?"

"Then you'll learn it all over again."

Bronwyn pulled away and wiped furiously at the tears. "I'm a little old to be starting over."

"What choice do you really have? You have to play. You have

to learn the song when your mother passes it to you. You only have brothers, there's no other option."

Something in her tone got through to Bronwyn. That sense of danger returned, stronger and more tangible. She remembered the bird pecking at the window. "Wait a minute, is that why you're here?"

"I'm here representing the other First Daughters. Something's come up that affects you, and us, and we need you with us."

The rhythmic pain in her chest returned. "What?" Bronwyn asked slowly.

Bliss paused before speaking, allowing her words to accumulate the weight they would need. "Peggy Goins saw one of the chairs on her motel porch rocking with no wind. Mandalay Harris had a picture of her mom with Chloe that fell off the mantel. I dreamed of muddy water. And your mama saw the sin eater come out of the woods and stop at your door before moving on."

Bronwyn knew all these things were traditional omens of death, just like the bird she saw. But the sin eater changed everything. Suddenly she knew why her father had fashioned the strange feathered chime clapper, a time-honored way to ward off or delay malefactions. "It's not me," she whispered. "My *mom's* gonna die."

"Don't know for certain. But someone's marked for it, and the picture falling pretty much says it'll be in this house."

Bronwyn knew Mandalay's mother was already dead, having expired from the complications of giving birth to her. So she read the signs the same way Bliss did. "Well . . . we have to stop it, then."

"There's no stopping it, you know that. You're either marked or you're not. You weren't. That's why you didn't die in Iraq.

Chloe might be." Now Bliss spoke with the quiet authority of a Tufa leader. "And maybe that's why you were spared. You *have* to learn her song. *Now.*"

"But I can't," she said simply. "I can't play. When I pick up Magda, there's nothing."

Bliss walked to the window and looked out into the blackness. "You have to learn to play so you can learn the song. There's no way around that. A First Daughter who loses her mother's song diminishes all of us. We're diminished enough already." She faced Bronwyn with all her Tufa authority. "If *we* don't know the melodies hummed in the night wind, then all that's left is the shiver of the grave."

"But how will I learn? Will you come and give me lessons?"

Bliss shook her head. "Not me. I play guitar, anyway. But someone will turn up."

Bronwyn nodded. The conversation had left her more numb than usual. "Okay, I'll give it a shot. But can I ask you something?"

"Chloe knows," Bliss said, anticipating the question.

Bronwyn nodded. It explained her mother's outburst that morning, at least.

Bliss looked out the window again and said, "And I'll take you into Knoxville next weekend to get those pins out. I can use the county ambulance. It's good PR for when we have to apply for funding next year."

"Thanks."

Bliss kissed Bronwyn on the top of her head, then saw the figure Ed had given her. She picked it up and looked it over, paying special attention to the delicate wings. "Pretty good resemblance," she observed.

"Maybe two years ago," Bronwyn said.

"You've been through a lot. But you're home, and we care for our own." She put down the carving and made a slow, elaborate hand gesture. "You know that."

Bronwyn responded with another similar gesture, but it was weak and weary, as she now was. "I know. But they tried that with Humpty Dumpty, too. Didn't work out."

Bliss smiled. The authority of a leader was replaced with a sisterly affection. "They just didn't know the right song."

9

Bliss's headlights raked across the bedroom window as she backed from the yard, turned, and drove away. Bronwyn wondered if the visit had even awakened Deacon, Chloe, or Aiden. There was etiquette involved when one First Daughter visited another on official business, but this seemed more clandestine: not secret exactly, but certainly discreet. If Chloe was marked, if Bronwyn really did need to take her place soon, then the less fuss, the better for the community at large.

Mom . . .

Bronwyn had a sudden, vivid image of her mother in a coffin, her face still and pale, her dark hair arranged around her shoulders. This merged with a flash of memory, of Steve Caffaro sprawled on the sand beside her, eyes open but sightless. Then came the blow that crushed her like a swatter coming down on a fly as yet another IED went off nearby.

"Private Hyatt . . . Private Hyatt . . ."

She opened her eyes. Had she been asleep? Someone

had turned off the light, and the room was black. She felt a shiver along the back of her neck as the situation's reality set in. The voice could be only one thing. Her haint, a genuine *ghost,* was calling for her from the darkness outside. Apparently it was just waiting its turn.

This wouldn't be the first haint she'd encountered. When she was nine, she'd spotted one walking slowly along the curve of County Highway B. It had been just after midnight, and she was returning home with a pillowcase full of bullfrogs. The haint resembled an old man, and hummed to himself as he shuffled along. His footsteps made no sound as he scuffed across the gravel toward her, and he vanished in the headlight beams of her father's truck as he arrived to pick her up. She'd gotten six swats from Deacon's belt that night, which took priority over the haint. So she'd never told anyone except Dwayne about it.

She'd seen another haint, a little girl this time, when she was thirteen and stumbling drunkenly along the tractor path between her father's land and the Hamilton farm. And she thought a third encounter was a haint, but it turned out to be simply wild child Curnen Overbay, Bliss's forest-roaming, possibly retarded sister.

But this was the first one that called her name, in a voice so soft, she wasn't sure at first it was even more than the wind. It was the first one specifically haunting *her*. And it was creepier than she ever imagined.

She rolled onto her side as much as her shattered leg allowed and peered past the American flag curtain. A shape materialized out of the darkness, lighter than the surrounding night. She swallowed hard as it resolved into a young woman in desert combat fatigues, with strands of dark hair dangling from under her helmet. Her left side was missing a basketball-sized chunk of flesh, leaving a jagged gap from the top of her hip to her rib cage. The edge was black with blood.

Bronwyn swallowed hard. "Not now," she whispered.

"Private Hyatt . . . ," the haint repeated.

She drew courage from the blue glass on the windowsill. Still soft, but more firmly, she said, "Soon. But *not now.*"

The haint tilted its head and silently, expectantly gazed at Bronwyn. It was hard to look directly at it; when Bronwyn focused on any specific part, like the face or the gaping injury, the details went fuzzy. It was like something glimpsed in the corner of your eye that vanishes when you turn toward it. Then it seemed to both back away and fade until the shadows reabsorbed it. In moments it was completely gone.

Bronwyn rolled onto her back and sighed. She was sweating, the chill kind that comes after a narrowly avoided disaster. There was a tingle in her throat that, for a moment, seemed about to develop into a sob. But like the haint, it too faded into nothingness.

Still, there would be no sleeping anytime soon. She turned on the lamp and laboriously used her crutch to drag the mailbag to her bedside. She took a handful of cards and letters and put them on her stomach.

The first one said, *We hope and pray for your swift recovery. God bless you for your service to our country.*

The second one said, *Without people like you, the ragheads would have struck us again. I think you deserve a medal for every one of those bastards you sent to hell. Stay strong, and keep the faith.*

The third said, *You're no more a "hero" than my fucking dog. You're a pawn being used by the right wing to pander to its illiter-*

ate, TV-sucking constituents. *Between you,* American Idol, *and global warming, we've proved without a doubt that the human race is worthless.* The letter was signed, *A global citizen.*

Bronwyn stared at this one, trying to decide how she felt about it. It should piss her off; these were the cowards who didn't *know* they were cowards, people who didn't understand the need to meet violence with violence. She'd joined her fellow soldiers in mocking them, and truly felt they were as big a danger as those wild-eyed grunts who craved the experience of killing another human being.

Something Bliss once told her came back vividly. They'd been seated on the edge of a cliff looking down over the valley, their bare feet dangling in the breeze. Bronwyn had been maybe ten. "There is no sanctity of life," Bliss told the younger girl. "There's always something that has to kill something else, either to eat it or to protect itself from it. And even with people, there's some that just need killing. I remember a fella named Ardis, who used to live down by Trebbel Creek. He was the meanest fella anyone ever knew."

"Meaner than Rockhouse Hicks?" Bronwyn had asked. Even among the children, the old man was notorious for his vindictive cruelty.

"Honey, he made Rockhouse look like a dang pussycat. But Ardis was Tufa, he had his song, and we put up with him as long as we could. But finally . . ."

"What'd he do?"

"Beat a fella's dog to death. Tied the dog's paws and beat it to death with a baseball bat. Started with the back legs and worked his way up so the dog would suffer the most."

"Why?"

"The owner accidentally cut him off on the highway. So Ardis followed him home, stole his dog, beat it to death, and left it back on his driveway."

Bronwyn was silent for a long time.

"You *should* feel bad hearing that," Bliss finally said. "Just because we're Tufa and can ride the night wind doesn't make us above the rules of right and wrong. Ardis thought it did, thought that we'd protect him."

"We didn't? I mean, you didn't? *They* didn't?"

"'We' is always right. No, we didn't. A man who'll kill an animal that way will eventually move on up to people if he's not stopped. The legal system says you have to wait until *after* the crime to remove them from society, but we have our own rules, and our own ways of dealing with things. He showed up at the barn dance to play, and no one stayed to listen. The next day he was found right there." She pointed down, where the cliff ended eighty feet below at the tops of the trees. From this height, the highway resembled a gray ribbon.

"Wow," Bronwyn said, imaging the impact as the body crashed through the tree limbs before striking ground she knew was rock hard. "So he killed himself?"

"Our songs are important," Bliss said. "We have to know them. We have to sing them. And someone has to listen. That's why we meet and play, that's why Rockhouse's people meet and play."

"But he *did* kill himself?" she persisted.

Bliss looked into the girl's eyes. "He *needed killing,* Bronwyn. Whether he did it to himself or someone else did it, the result was the same."

Now Bronwyn recalled that conversation in a whole new light. Had Bliss confessed to murder? Had she personally shoved Ardis the dog-killer off the cliff? And ultimately, was she right? Hadn't Bronwyn been trained to kill, quickly and efficiently, anyone her superior officers said "needed killing"? Bliss had at least made the determination herself; Bronwyn simply followed orders.

She put the letter aside and picked up another. It read simply, *Get well soon. The Davis Family: Bill, Suzy, Brittany, and Joshua.*

Her laptop was still packed away. She hadn't checked her e-mail in three days, since leaving the base for the flight home. Would it now be full of similar greetings? She'd learned in the hospital that Web sites devoted to her, or rather to the media's image of her, had sprung up like mushrooms after a summer rain. She'd deliberately avoided them; did these people not have *lives*?

She considered trying to get to the refrigerator for a beer to help her relax. She'd been sneaking beer out of that same fridge since she was twelve, and climbing out the window through which she'd spied the haint for almost as long. Lying in a drugged stupor in the hospital, she'd wished for this room with almost feral ferocity, but now that she was here, all the feelings that drove her away from it had returned. She felt more trapped than ever before.

She wanted a drink. She wanted to kiss a boy. She wanted that boy to put his hands all over her. She wanted to drive like a maniac, and pick fights with other boys' girlfriends, and with other boys. She wanted to spray-paint something rude on the water tower in nearby Mallard Creek.

Instead, she was on her ass in bed, her leg assimilated by the Borg and her head numb and fuzzy. The Bronwynator had left the building.

She yawned. *Now* she was tired, after all those deep thoughts. She pushed the envelopes and cards aside and turned off the lamp. The sense of foreign objects under her skin was so palpable, she could barely stand it, so she closed her eyes and began whisper-singing one of the oldest songs she knew, something that always gave her comfort. She was so weary, she did not realize that this was the first whole song she'd been able to recall since her injuries. She just knew it felt wonderful to sing it.

> *Oh, time makes men grow sad*
> *And rivers change their ways*
> *But the night wind and her riders*
> *Will ever stay the same. . . .*

The transition from song to dream passed without notice. Unlike her recent nightmares, in this reverie she reclined naked on soft grass, the night air warm and humid, the silver full moon overhead. Her skin was smooth and bore no injuries, no scars. In the dream she began to cry with happiness.

10

Deacon eased the tractor along the rows of knee-high corn. Dirt stirred by his passage sparkled in the morning sunlight.

He'd been up since before dawn, unable to really sleep. He'd heard the front door open, the creak of passage across the floor, and the distinctive squeak of Bronwyn's bedroom door. He had a good idea who had come to visit, and why. At least this time it hadn't been that damned Gitterman boy, but the knowledge did not help him relax.

He wiped his sweaty face with the back of his arm. The day was starting out muggy, so even though the temperature was pleasant he still dripped with perspiration. It wasn't hard to farm in the valley, and this field was small but blessedly flat. All he had to do was keep the dirt turned, hum the right tune, and everything came up easy. They'd have enough corn for the family, and a little to sell besides.

Over the tractor's rumble he heard a sharp whistle.

He looked around, saw the source, and froze. He reached under the seat for the .22 revolver he kept handy to chase off rabbits and starlings and tucked it into the waistband of his jeans.

He left the tractor idling as he hopped down, feeling the impact in his knees and lower back. He strode across the field to the barbed wire fence, where Dwayne Gitterman stood leaning on a post. His truck was parked in the middle of the road behind him. He looked like he'd been up all night, with red eyes and a beer-stained shirt. Dwayne grinned and said, "Hey there, Mr. Hyatt. How's the corn coming? Keeping the horseweed under control?"

"What do you want, Dwayne?"

Dwayne put one foot on the lowest strand of wire and lifted himself off the ground, using the pole for balance. "I was driving by, and when I saw you, I thought I might come by tonight and see Bronwyn."

"Hm. When I saw *you,* I thought I might shoot you and bury you where nobody would find you."

"Now that's fucking harsh, Mr. Hyatt. I never did nothing bad to you or your daughter."

"And you never done nothing good for anyone else in your life. Get outta here, Dwayne. If you come to the house, I won't have to shoot you. Bronwyn'll have your balls for paperweights before you get to the porch. And not a soul will miss you."

"Well, I might still do it. I'm only a frog's-hair less pure-blooded than you, you know, so I expect y'all to be civil." He hopped down off the fence. "You might come outside sometime when I'm squirrel hunting and catch a stray bullet, you never know. Be a real tragedy. My conscience would never get over it."

"I might mention you threatenin' me to old Trooper Bob

Pafford. He's still got an eye out for you, and he'd love the chance to pull you over."

"That asshole don't scare me," Dwayne said. "And he could never catch me."

Deacon met Dwayne's eyes. He was silent for a long moment, then said softly, "Do you want me to sing about you at the barn dance, Dwayne? Want me to come up with your dirge? Because if that's what it takes to get Bronwyn shed of you, I'll do it."

Dwayne's cocky grin slipped a little. "You be overreacting a little, Mr. Hyatt," he drawled.

"No, you be taking up too much of my time. Go back to your hole and bother somebody else. You come anywhere around here again, it'll be *my* trigger finger that slips before I can stop myself. And your dirge might get a thimbleful of tears out of the whole valley."

Aunt Raby's attic smelled like she did: a musty, abandoned accumulation of decades sticking around for reasons unknown even to her. The boxes stacked along the walls and at the eaves were unmarked, and bore the logos of defunct produce companies and other products that no longer existed. Don banged his head on the beam running down the center of the peaked roof and muttered, "Shit!"

"What was that?" Aunt Raby's trembling voice called. She waited at the bottom of the rickety ladder, propped on her upstairs walker.

"Nothing, Aunt Raby." He shone the flashlight around until he saw the box she'd mentioned, then crawled on his hands and knees to it. Dust puffed when he opened the flaps.

Inside the box were the contents of an old writing desk: innumerable pens, small white envelopes, and blank reply cards with faded images of birds and flowers. But beneath them, at the bottom of the box, he found the Swayback family Bible.

It was a large book, nearly two feet square and over six inches thick, with a heavy purple bookmark ribbon attached to the spine. The page edges were gilded, except near the top corner where it was worn away by decades of turning. He tucked the book under his arm and backed his way down the ladder.

When he'd brushed the dust from his jeans and washed his hands, he put the big book on Aunt Raby's kitchen table and opened the cover. The first half-dozen pages were listings of family births, deaths, and marriages. It was somehow touching, he thought, that no consideration was given to possible divorce and remarriages. He scanned the listings, which began in 1803, until he found Forrest Swayback.

The date was June 11, 1912. On that long-ago day, Forrest Leon Swayback had been joined in holy matrimony with Bengenaria Oswald. Their three children, including Don's own father, were listed under that. Don followed the line to the date of his own birth, in July of 1972.

Aunt Raby put one gnarled hand on his back. "Did you find what you're looking for, honey?"

"I did, Aunt Raby. Did you ever know Grandma Benji?"

"I sure did. She was one of them Needsville Tufas, you know."

"I know."

"She could sing like the voice of heaven, that's a pure fact. Only she wouldn't sing a hymn to save her life. She'd sing country and western songs, even nigra songs, and of course those weird ol' Tufa songs when she thought no one was listening. But she'd never praise the Lord, she sure wouldn't."

"Did you like her?"

"She was never nothing but kind to me. Sometimes it's a shame to think about someone that sweet burning in hell, but the Bible says it true, and she never accepted the Lord Jesus Christ that I know of. She and Grandpa Forrest got married by a judge over in Mississippi, even, because she wouldn't have a church wedding."

Don nodded, copied down the dates of her birth, death, and marriage, then took the bag of garden tomatoes Aunt Raby insisted on giving him. As he drove home, he thought about the phrase *weird ol' Tufa songs*. He'd never heard a song that was specifically Tufa; he wondered idly what they sang about that was so weird.

Brownyn stood propped on her crutches at the end of the hall. She stared through the living room into the dining area; it was really a single big room divided by the edge of the rug separating the hardwood kitchen floor from the couches, chairs, and TV. So she had an unobstructed view of the strangest thing she'd seen in a while.

Her wheelchair was on the table upside down, its big wheels removed and propped against the kitchen counter. Deacon's toolbox sat open on a chair. But Deacon wasn't the one working. Instead a dark-haired boy, tall and lanky and instantly familiar, adjusted the ball bearing mechanism as he hummed to himself.

Her heart began to pound, and another, more basic response swelled within her. *Dwayne.* Suddenly she could barely stand, and it had nothing to do with her injured leg. She fell against the wall and dropped one crutch, which clattered against the floor.

The boy, startled, dropped the wrench in his hand and spun

around. They stared at each other, mouths open, words frozen in their throats.

Finally Bronwyn managed to speak. "Don't just stand there looking like a damn carp, Terry-Joe, get my crutch before I bust my ass here."

Terry-Joe Gitterman rushed over and scooped the crutch from the floor. He tried to push it under her arm, but that only caused her to stumble into him, and he caught her around the waist as she fell. He grunted at her weight, which made her scowl and say, "It ain't all me, you know, it's this damn office building on my leg."

For a moment they stayed like that, gazes locked, each secretly ashamed of the way they enjoyed the other's body pressed so close. Then Terry-Joe blushed and said, "Sorry." He stepped away as she got her crutches in place.

As she steadied herself, she blushed as well, although for different reasons. Terry-Joe was Dwayne's little brother, and he'd be sixteen or seventeen now. He looked distressingly like Dwayne from the back, but the family resemblance ended there. Dwayne's face was always set in a smirk that said he knew exactly what you were thinking, especially if you were female. In Bronwyn's case, it had been true damn near most of the time. His eyes had a twinkle that at first seemed to be mischief and laughter, but time revealed it to be the enjoyment of cruelty. He had matched her sexually, and in rambunctiousness, but ultimately his touch had disgusted her and his presence filled her with dread. She didn't like who she was with him, and no matter how often she told him to go away, he kept coming back, like basement mold. He'd been one big reason she'd joined the army in the first place.

Now she laughed and said, "No, Terry-Joe, I'm sorry, I . . . you surprised me. I didn't expect you to be here."

"Bliss Overbay asked me to see if I could clean out the bearings on that chair so it'd move better."

"Yeah. Well, look, don't let me keep you from working, I'll just hobble on out to the porch and soak up some sunlight." She really didn't want to go out, but if she stayed, she'd just make both of them nervous.

He rushed to push one of the chairs aside to make a clearer path for her. It caught on a rug crease and he fell over it. He jumped up so quickly, she burst out laughing, then choked it down when she saw the instant of hurt feelings on his face. He was *so* unlike Dwayne, who would've thrown the chair across the room in a rage for daring to make him look foolish.

"It's okay, Terry-Joe, I can make it," she said. He jumped to hold the screen door for her, but since it opened out, he had to stand with his back against the inner door, arm extended. She had to turn sideways as well, which meant they again pressed against each other as she passed. She sensed the heat of his body through her clothes, and the same distinctive tingle announced itself. She also thought she felt his erection through their jeans. Both looked anywhere but at the other.

Then she was outside, in the bright sunlight, looking down at the yard she'd grown up on. She dropped heavily into a rocking chair, and dragged another one over to support her leg. The pain of moving was still severe, but there was that added sensation, the itchy sense of the presence of strange metal things in her body. Did that mean she was, in fact, healing? Was Bliss's timetable accurate?

"You're looking perkier," Deacon said as he came around the

end of the house. He was dusty from the cornfield, and his shirt had big sweat rings soaked into it.

"Thanks," she said. "I do feel better."

"That's not what I mean. Your high beams are on."

She looked down at the front of her T-shirt, then blushed anew. "Dad," she said, trying to sound scolding.

He tousled her hair. "Ah, your mom does the same thing whenever that Australian guy comes on the radio. Beats me how a foreign guy named Urban can claim to be a *country* singer, but hey, I don't make the rules. . . ." He went inside.

She closed her eyes and leaned her head back into the sun. Well, the hell with it. It *had* been nice to feel like a live human being again, even if it was for an instant, even if it was due to a jailbait boy three years her junior. He was cute, and sweet, and apparently good with his hands, if he was working on her wheelchair. Why *not* get a little horny from that?

Then she recalled the handsome young minister and sighed with renewed shame. She never had much sense of propriety to begin with, but had she lost it *all* now?

"Hey, Dad!" she called. "Could you bring me a cup of coffee?"

"Get it yours— Oh," he answered. "Yeah, right, forgot. Sure thing."

A moment later the door opened, only instead of Deacon, Terry-Joe appeared holding a cup on a saucer with both hands. It still didn't keep the two pieces of porcelain from clattering. "Uh . . . here," he said as he extended the cup to her. "Finished your chair, too. Should roll a lot smoother now."

She placed it on the small table beside her. "Thanks. You've changed a lot in the past two years, Terry-Joe."

"You, too. You didn't have an oil rig on your leg last time I saw you."

She smiled. "That's a fact. So shouldn't you be in school?"

"I graduated in the spring. Doing odd jobs until the fall, when I go to college at UT."

"And Dwayne?" She tried to make the question innocuous, but there was no hiding the catch in her breath when she said his name.

"He's still around. Out on parole, not that he's acting like that matters. Want me to tell him anything?"

"No," she said quickly. She felt far too weak, in every sense, to deal with Dwayne Gitterman. "I'll catch up with him one of these days."

Terry-Joe put his hands in his jeans pockets and seemed about to say something. Finally Bronwyn prompted, "What is it?"

He leaned close. "Bliss also wants me to, ah . . . teach you."

"Teach me?" she repeated, eyes wide.

"Mandolin," he added quickly. "Help you relearn how to play. She said you were having trouble with that."

"She did."

He nodded.

"I didn't know you played."

He shrugged. "I don't talk about it much."

"I never saw you at the barn dance."

"Back then I didn't want to go because Dwayne was around."

She nodded. "That makes sense. Well, mine's under my bed. Go get her and let's hear you."

He retrieved Magda, sat on the porch steps, and spent a moment getting the feel of the instrument. Then, with no introduction or warning, he launched into a blistering instrumental version of "June Apple." He stared into the middle distance, not watching his fingering. He played with the certainty of instinct married to skill, and Bronwyn's mouth dropped open in response.

In the kitchen, Deacon heard the music and smiled. Chloe came in the back door, and he swept her into his arms and kissed her passionately.

She responded, her arms twining around his neck. When his hands began to roam knowingly, she quietly warned, "There's kids just outside."

"Then we best be quick and quiet," he said as he nibbled her neck.

She giggled. "You're *never* quiet."

On the porch, Terry-Joe finished with a flourish and looked up to see Bronwyn's reaction. She clapped, genuinely delighted. "Wow, Terry-Joe, you've been hiding that light under a bushel, all right." Then she made a gesture, fingers curled in a specific way, she hoped he would recognize. But his expression didn't change.

He stood, dusted off his pants, and extended Magda to her. "Want to try?"

She shook her head. "Not now."

"Bliss wants me to—"

"And I will, Terry-Joe, just . . . not now." She looked away. "I'm supposed to get this monster off my leg this weekend. Come by next Monday and I'll seriously try, okay?"

He nodded. "Okay. 'Scuse me while I put this away." He went back inside.

She watched robins dancing across the still-damp lawn as they sought worms. She'd known Terry-Joe wasn't a full-blooded Tufa; he was close, but that difference could be crucial. Why would Bliss send someone like him to teach her? She was a First Daughter, after all. But Bliss would have her reasons, and most likely they would become clear later on. All she could do was wait, and endure, two things the Tufa mastered long ago.

Terry-Joe returned, followed by Chloe. "See you Monday, then," he said as he went down the steps, awkwardly stumbling at the bottom. He rushed to his dirt bike propped under the tree and zipped off down the driveway.

Chloe shook her head. "That boy has a crush on you, you know."

Bronwyn nodded, frowning at her mother. Chloe's hair was disheveled, and her shirt was now on inside out. "He has since he was fourteen and caught me skinny-dipping with his brother."

Chloe took several quick, deep breaths, as if calming down after some exertion. "Have you heard anything from Dwayne?"

"No, and I don't want to. I've seen enough combat to do me for life."

"Good," Chloe said as she sat down on the steps. "That boy was bad news on toast. I wouldn't have swerved to miss him if I'd seen him lying in the road."

"He wasn't that bad, Mom."

She looked up at her daughter with the clear, steady eyes Bronwyn always feared. "He's wired backwards, Bronwyn. He smiles when someone's hurt."

"Well, he won't be around anymore." Then she took a deep breath and added, "And some people worry the same about you."

Chloe nodded. "I know. There's been some signs. But there's two things to remember: One, a sign can mean more than one thing, and sometimes we read them wrong. And two, nothing's set in stone. The night wind don't blow the same way twice."

Bronwyn nodded at the charm hanging inert in the still morning air. "And better safe than sorry."

Chloe smiled and undid the tie holding her black hair. "I've seen you and Kell graduate high school. I intend to see Aiden. Like to see grandkids before I'm done."

Bronwyn wasn't fooled by the optimism. "But you'll teach me the song."

She nodded. The passage of the family song from mother to eldest daughter was a major thing to the Tufa, and in this case, since both Chloe and Bronwyn were hereditary First Daughters, it was monumental. The loss of this song would devastate their community. "As soon as Terry-Joe has you able to play."

"I'll work real hard, Mom," she said softly.

11

Susie Swayback stood in the bedroom doorway, hands on her hips, and said, "Donald Carter Swayback, what the hell are you doing?"

Don looked up from the floor, where he knelt as he pulled things from the closet. "Looking for my old guitar. Have you seen it?"

"Lord, do we still even have that thing?" Susie put her purse on the bed and sat down to remove her shoes. Susie had been adopted from China but raised across the line in Georgia, so she had a thicker Southern twang than even Don. It often disconcerted people when they traveled. "And why do you want to find it? Planning to sell it online?"

"No," he said petulantly. "Thought it might be nice to start playing again. Just fooling around with it, you know. Is that okay with you?"

"You didn't lose your job, did you?" Susie said accusingly.

"No!"

"Well, good," she said as she took off her scrub pants. Susie was an X-ray technician at the county hospital, and for the past three months she'd been pulling third and first shifts to cover vacations, which meant she went to bed almost as soon as she got home in the evening. Don was beginning to feel like they were college roommates with mismatched class schedules instead of husband and wife.

"Ah-ha!" Don said. From the very back of the closet he pulled out the battered black cardboard case. He placed it flat on the foot of the bed.

"Don't get dust on my comforter," Susie warned. "And put that other stuff away." She went into the bathroom; a moment later he heard the shower start.

Don opened the case. Inside was his cheap old Sunburst acoustic guitar, now some thirty years old. The remains of a sticker, probably for Nirvana or Pearl Jam, marred the surface. He lifted it, rested it across his lap, and lightly strummed. The sound shimmered, mingling with the shower noise. He adjusted the G string slightly, but otherwise it sounded in tune.

He strummed again. The room abruptly seemed to grow clearer, as if a hazy curtain had been yanked away. He looked around, seeing his home as if for the first time. The cheesy landscape painting they'd bought on their honeymoon hung over the bed; straps of Susie's bras protruded from the top dresser drawer. His brown loafers, one upright and the other showing the worn sole, lay on the carpet beside the door. The effect quickly faded, though, and then Susie came out of the bathroom, tying her robe.

Inside the case was a spiral notebook. He opened it and saw lyrics and chords in his own handwriting. He remembered that he used to write lots of songs, documenting his life through music; how long had it been since he'd done that? And why did he stop?

"I declare, that Coletta is going to get herself in trouble before long," Susie said as she sat on the bed and began brushing her black hair. "She was an hour late, and I swear she smelled just like pot. She can only slip past so many pee tests before they catch her, I tell you what."

Don looked steadily at his wife. He admired her shiny black hair, pale skin, and delightful slanted eyes. Her legs, where they emerged from under the robe, were smooth and soft. By the time his gaze returned to her face, she was also staring at him. "What," she asked, "are you looking at?"

He smiled. "The most beautiful redneck Asian woman I've ever seen."

She continued to stare; there was an unmistakable rumble in his voice. "I've been on my feet for sixteen hours," she said warningly.

He crawled across the bed and growled teasingly, "Then you won't mind being on your back for a while."

He kissed her shoulder, and she giggled. "What's got into you, Don?" she demanded, but did not resist as he pushed her back onto the pillows.

Later, she turned to him and said, "Now I need another shower. But if this is your idea of a midlife crisis, I have to admit I like it."

"I'm not middle aged," he disputed with a tired grin.

"And my eyes are round like Ping-Pong balls," she said in a cliché Asian accent, swapping the *l*'s and *r*'s. She ran her fingertips across his chest; the remains of his youthful muscles were still there beneath the layer of sedentary fat he'd accumulated. "Seriously, what brought this on? Did you imagine I was that cute little clerk down at the Q-Mart?"

He shrugged. "I don't know, I just . . . I was out at Aunt Raby's today getting the old Swayback family Bible. I hope I can find some family connection between me and Bronwyn Hyatt's family that might let me get that interview with her."

"You're part Tufa?"

"Yeah, my right leg below the knee and the three fingers on my left hand. One of my ears is suspect, too."

"Seriously? I guess it explains the hair and the teeth, but you never mentioned it before."

"Never really thought about it before. But my great-grandmother was Tufa, and if I can track down her family in Needsville, it might give me an in with the Hyatts." He paused, looking down at her hand now drawing lazy circles on his bare stomach. "The thing is, Aunt Raby mentioned that Grandma Benji used to sing weird Tufa songs. I checked online, and at the library: nobody knows anything about any Tufa songs. I mean, any songs that are specifically Tufa."

"And all this made you think, 'Hm, I want a quickie when my exhausted wife gets home'?"

"No, all this made me think about my guitar and the songs I used to write, which made me feel kind of . . . I don't know, young, I guess. And *that* made me want a quickie with my exhausted wife, who I might add was up to the challenge." He playfully yanked a stray strand of her hair.

She giggled, then stretched luxuriously. "Boy, I'll sleep now. You know, one of the ambulance drivers who drops people off at the hospital is a Tufa. Bliss Overbay. I could ask her if she knows any Tufa songs."

Don shook his head. "Nah, doesn't matter. Just thought it was odd."

Susie looked into his eyes. "I like you like this. All interested in something. It's been a while since I've seen you this way."

"Been a while since I've *felt* this way."

"Think it'll stick?"

He shrugged.

She kissed his ear and took the lobe in her teeth. "Anything I can do to *help* it stick?"

He turned to her. "You're doing a fine job already," he said as he kissed her.

It took forever for night to fall.

The sunlight faded and at last the moon rose, casting enough light that Bronwyn could see the yard outside her window where the trees didn't cast shadows. In that clear spot of silver, the haint would again appear. Eventually.

She rubbed around the point where the largest pin went through the skin of her thigh. Scratching was totally forbidden, but the itch had grown exponentially. She would be immensely glad to be shed of this monstrosity, and would hold Bliss to her Tufa timetable. She dreaded what she'd see when the Ilizarov mechanisms were removed, though; her legs, once the envy of all the other Tufa girls, would be permanently scarred. She pretended it didn't bother her, but it did. She *liked* being the Bronwynator, the hell-raising hot chick all the other girls hated and all the boys wanted to take out on a quiet gravel road. That would be hard to maintain once she looked like she'd been through a blender, and she never, ever wanted a mere pity fuck.

She looked at the banners across her ceiling. Tomorrow she

would take them down while Aiden was at school. She didn't want to hurt his feelings, but there was no longer any meaning in the symbol for her. She would leave the army when her enlistment was up. Stop-loss wouldn't apply to her; she was more valuable as a PR tool if she vanished back into the hills anyway. If she emerged into the public eye again, she might say something Major Maitland wouldn't like. Besides, she knew her immediate future was here.

That should've brought a sense of relief, but instead the tight panic in her chest increased. The challenge she now faced was even more daunting. Her mother appeared so young, alive, and filled with music that it seemed impossible the night wind would take her. Her absence would send reverberations all through Cloud County, and probably to every Tufa who'd left as well. A First Daughter didn't go without leaving a mark.

She heard cows lowing somewhere in the distance and glanced at her clock. Three minutes after twelve. The sound of cows after midnight was supposed to be another herald of death. Then again, it could just be insomniac cows. Not all superstitions had that supposed grain of truth to them.

The wind suddenly billowed the flag curtain into the room. Then it snapped back against the screen, as if the air pressure outside had suddenly dropped. At that moment a soft voice said once again, *"Private Hyatt . . ."*

Bronwyn swallowed hard and realized she was sweating. A haint could do nothing, she knew, except appear and speak to those meant to hear; nevertheless, knowing a dead person wanted to chat sent chills up her spine. She often wondered if the Tufa afterlife was the same as the regular one; Tufa passed through time differently, but once it stopped, they were like any other dead thing. When their song was over they decomposed, in both the literal and ironic sense.

So when someone crossed back to this world to deliver a message, everyone assumed it must be pretty important. Yet to be the recipient of that message left Bronwyn with a tingly, tangible fear completely different from the one she'd known during her ordeal in Iraq. Those people had wanted to do her physical harm; this haint might be after something else entirely.

But she'd never know until she engaged it. So she turned to the window and said, "I'm here."

The haint emerged from the shadows beneath the red oak trees. As before, it stood so that the missing tissue in its side was plain, the wound looking for all the world like it had been made with a giant cookie cutter. Blood soaked the edges, but otherwise it was surprisingly neat. It took off its helmet, revealing the same dark hair all true Tufas sported. It had been a lovely young girl in life, but was now free of both flesh and gender.

Bronwyn forced herself not to look away. The haint's eyes sparkled with moonlight as if they glowed. Its expression was wide eyed and blank.

"Okay," Bronwyn said at last. "Come in here and let's get this over with."

The haint did not move. Slowly it pointed at the window. The blue glass still rested on the sill.

Bronwyn took a crutch and, after three swings, finally knocked the rocklike chunk of glass to the floor. It landed with a thud that reverberated throughout the house.

By the time she settled back against her pillows, the haint stood at the foot of her bed.

"Yah!" Bronwyn cried. She waited to catch her breath, then said, "Okay. What's up?"

"I'm Sally," it said in a voice that was just a hair slower, and considerably more sepulchral, than a normal speaking voice. *"Sergeant Sally Olds. I died on the road to Basra in 1991."*

Bronwyn's mouth went dry. Everything had happened on that road. "I drove that way myself."

"I know. I saw you. I watched."

Bronwyn shifted on the pillows; the pins in her leg ached more than ever. When she looked up, the haint had vanished.

A slightly darker shade stood in front of her dresser. Bronwyn said, "Oh, come on out here, will you? If I can't even scootch around without freaking you out, this isn't going to work."

"It's very hard to stay this way," Sally said. *"And I'm here for something important."*

"Yeah, I know. My mom's gonna die, and I have to learn her song."

"No," Sally said. *"I'm here just for you."*

Bronwyn's breath caught in her throat. "For me," she said flatly.

"You are surrounded by walls, Bronwyn. They were there before you were hurt, and even though your body is weak now, these walls are stronger than ever. They must come down if you are to be what you must."

Rage flared in her heart; she hated being lectured. "And what's that? Somebody's wife? Mom to a brood of barefoot heathens just like me? I put those walls there for a reason, to keep me from marrying the first guy who made me come and being stuck in this valley for the rest of . . . of *time!*" She had no idea where this sudden insight came from, but she grasped its truth even as she blurted out the words.

"Yes, just like you've always known, none of that is for you. Your path is . . ."

The haint made a hand gesture that left Bronwyn speechless. For a moment the only sound was the night wind through the open window.

"I will help you," Sally continued. "I know what happened. As I tell it to you, you will recall it. And relive it. That can't be helped."

"The hell it can't," Bronwyn snapped.

"There is no time for your pain, Bronwyn. It has to be drawn out, looked at, and dealt with. What will happen, will happen, and you must be ready for it."

"Yeah, but—"

"Be ready for me tomorrow night," Sally said, and turned toward the window. It gave Bronwyn an unobstructed view of the wound. Pieces of ragged organs dangled like the ribbons on a war hero's chest. Before the haint took three steps, it vanished.

Bronwyn stared off into the night. Crickets and tree frogs gradually grew louder. The breeze stirred the banners and curtains.

She turned on the bedside lamp. There would be no sleeping for a while, and now she had to pee. Bedpans quickly lost their charm, and although getting up and going to the bathroom was a production even with her mother's help, this time she was determined to do it herself.

The worst moment was when the weight of her leg hung free before it tipped downward. She felt it in her lower back and, oddly, her triceps as she braced herself, lowering her leg as slowly as she could until her heel touched the floor.

As she caught her breath, she saw an envelope half-hidden by her nightstand. Leaning as far as she could, she managed to retrieve it. The effort made her break out in a fresh sweat.

She turned the envelope over. It had fallen from the mail sack when Deacon moved it against the wall. The writing was a child's, and the address in Jasper, Alabama. She opened it and pulled out the card.

Dear Private Hyatt, it said. *Thank you for protecting our country. Someday I hope to join the army, too. Maybe by then they'll let girls fight.*

Bronwyn smiled at that. The girl would learn quickly enough how often girls fight, especially in the army.

> *But one thing makes me sad. I'm a Christian, and I'm sure you are, too. The Bible tells us not to kill people, and yet you had to. I feel very sad knowing you had to do that. All people are brothers, and we shouldn't go around killing each other. But I know God forgives you, and I know Jesus loves you.*
>
> *Your friend,*
> *Adelia*

A small photo of a gap-toothed little black girl had been enclosed. Bronwyn gazed into those wide, dark eyes. She saw nothing she recognized.

She put the picture beside her on the bed. Someone was sad, not because she was nearly killed, but because she had to kill other people. Bliss's words came back to her once more: *Even with people, there's some that need killing.*

She realized with renewed vividness that she truly was different from other people, even most other Tufas. The haint knew it. And maybe that's why Bliss entrusted her with that pragmatic truth so long ago.

She no longer had to pee. She lifted her leg back onto the

mattress, wincing at the slight, almost obscene movement of metal bolts penetrating her skin. This would *have* to end soon. She took three Vicodin, one more than her doctor recommended, and closed her eyes, waiting for the effects to kick in. But she found herself still awake as the sky outside lightened at dawn, her curtains waving in the last of the night wind.

12

Craig Chess waved to George Landers across the Shoney's. Craig had already claimed a booth, and the older man sauntered over with the easy grace of someone content with his place in the world. This particular Shoney's was located at an exit equidistant between Craig's home in Smithborough and George's in Unicorn, and they'd met here several times so Craig could pick George's brain.

An elderly lady stopped him and said something that made him smile. He patted her hand before continuing on. Craig felt a tingle of envy, because it was exactly that sort of moment he craved. He wanted the respect he saw in the old woman's eyes. But he also knew George had spent years building it, and he, Craig, had yet to preach his first sermon in his own church.

When George reached the booth, Craig stood and offered his hand. "Reverend Landers."

"Reverend Chess," the newcomer replied. Then he

laughed. "Craig, it's both a pleasure to consider you an equal, and a little disconcerting. I have golf shoes older than you."

"I'm not your 'equal,' George. You're still my elder."

"Ouch. 'Elder.' I should be wearing bifocals, then, and using a walker."

Craig knew George ran three miles every morning, even on Sunday. "You know what I mean."

They sat, ordered coffee, and when the waitress was gone, Landers asked, "So how goes the new church? Ready for opening morning? Is it next weekend?"

"No, it's this Sunday. If anyone shows up, I'll be surprised."

"Reaching the Tufa has defeated many a young zealot, I reckon," Landers agreed. "I knew a man who'd once been a top vinyl siding salesman before hearing the call. His first post was in Needsville itself, if you can imagine that. Not only did no one show up, he couldn't keep his piano in tune. For some reason that aggravated him more than anything else. He asked for a post in China soon after."

"That's a big reason I wanted to meet with you," Craig said. "I've been spending time in town, just hanging out and introducing myself, offering any help I can. Everyone's friendly enough, but I can't imagine any of them in a pew on Sunday morning." He sipped his coffee. "What do you know about them that I don't?"

"They're quiet, keep to themselves," George deadpanned.

"I already know *that*. But why don't they come to church?"

"Why doesn't anyone? We're not relevant to them."

"Are the Tufas even Christian?"

Landers shrugged. "Son, greater men than you or I have puzzled over that. The real Tufas, the ones with family ties back to pre-Revolutionary times, won't talk. The ones that do talk, don't know anything. So it's a tough little nut."

Craig recalled Deacon Hyatt's comments. "They must believe in something."

"Sure, they do: music. I've never met one yet that didn't sing or play some kind of instrument. And play the heck out of it, too. If they ever wanted to, about half of 'em could probably move to Nashville and be on everyone's iPods within six months."

"Why don't they?"

"Some do. Ever heard of Rockhouse Hicks?"

"Sure, he sits outside the post office every day. I've met rabid skunks who were friendlier."

"That's him. Well, back in the late sixties, he almost made it as a big bluegrass star. Put out a record, traveled with Bill Monroe, was right on the edge. Then he got caught in a sex scandal, and that was that."

Craig didn't hide his surprise. "A sex scandal? That's a little hard to picture."

"He's just a man," Landers said. "Prey to the same temptations as us all. But my point is, that tends to happen to any of the real Tufas who leave their little valley. Look at your latest celebrity, Bronwyn Hyatt."

"Being hurt in a war is a little different from having trouble keeping your pants zipped."

"Maybe. But both happened away from Needsville."

The waitress refreshed their coffee. "So they play music, and they fare badly when they leave home. That still doesn't help me get them to church."

"No. But in six months when you get moved to another position, you'll at least understand a little about why this didn't work."

"That's pretty fatalistic for a minister."

"Oh, don't get me wrong, if God wants them in church, they'll go to church. I believe that, and apparently so does the annual conference, because they keep sending new ministers until they find one who can reach these people."

"Do *you* believe God wants them in church?"

Landers looked around, then leaned over the table and spoke softly. "Here's what I think, and if you repeat it, I'll deny it. I believe God wants everyone in church, but I'm not entirely sure our God and their God are the same thing."

"There's a school of thought that would call that blasphemy."

"And they'd be right, but there it is. We also have noses that run and feet that smell. Sometimes the universe just doesn't make sense."

Don Swayback pulled his car to the side of the road beneath an oak tree. The sporadic shade made the sunlight dance on his dusty windshield. He picked up the road atlas and compared it to the Internet maps he'd printed out at home. Both agreed; so where the hell was the turnoff?

Ahead he saw the intersection of Highway 23 and Curly Mane Road. A tractor reached it and slowly pulled onto the highway, headed away from Don. Far behind him, though still visible in the mirror, was the turnoff for Jenkins Trail. And in between should have been the road that dead-ended at the Hyatt farm, called simply Hyatt Way. But he'd been up and down this stretch of blacktop a dozen times without finding it.

He thumped the steering wheel in annoyance. He'd always heard the Tufa could disappear when they wanted to, although he assumed that meant they vanished right before your eyes, which of course was impossible. It was typical of the stories that grew up around small, isolated places, and that white folks tended to spread about any group with darker skin. But he supposed that being impossible to *find* was the same as disappearing.

He jumped when an unmistakable electronic shriek sounded right behind his car. In the rearview mirror he saw the state trooper's cruiser; in the side mirror, he watched the trooper emerge and swagger toward him. The officer took his time, planting each large foot flat and square so every step sounded like approaching retribution.

When the trooper reached the driver's open window, Don looked up and saw his own reflection in the mirrored shades. "Sir, are you having car trouble?" the trooper asked, in a tone that seemed more suited to a Guantánamo guard.

"No, I'm looking for—"

The square face, with its huge flat-brimmed hat, leaned down. The name tag on his chest caught the light, and Don saw the word PAFFORD. "I asked you a yes-or-no question, not for your life story. If you're having car trouble, I'll call you a tow truck and make sure you get to a garage. If not, I expect to find you gone when I come back by here. Understand me?"

Don blinked in surprise. "I was just going to ask for some help with directions. I'm trying to find the turnoff for—"

Pafford smiled. Don suspected it was for the benefit of the trooper's dashboard video camera, because his voice was a snarl of contempt. "Get smart with me, son, and I'll shove a Taser so far up your ass, your nose will light up like Rudolph's. I ran your license plate; I know you're one of them reporters making a big deal out of Bronwyn Hyatt. Around here she ain't no hero, she's just white trash from the hills who ended up in the wrong place at the wrong time. You makin' over her just means every other half-nigger Tufa will think they can smart off to the law and get away with it."

Don stared. He'd encountered all sorts of cops in his job, but never one so brazen in his prejudices. "Officer," he said carefully, "I don't believe I'm breaking any laws sitting here. I'm certainly not bothering anyone."

"You're bothering *me*. And if you look up and down this highway, you'll see that's the worst thing you *could* be doing, because ain't nobody gonna come help you out. Now *git* before I lose my good nature, and you lose an awful lot of time and money to the Great State of Tennessee."

Don's hands shook as he turned the key and pulled slowly out onto the highway. The trooper stood watching, hip cocked, one hand on his gun. Don wanted to turn around and go back the way he came, but instead drove straight, forty miles out of his way, to make sure he didn't have to pass the trooper again.

By the time he hit the junction to Highway B near the interstate, his anger had truly peaked. He thought of calling Sam at the *Horn* and getting a lawyer involved, but he had no proof of anything. After all, the trooper let him off with a warning, and the dashboard camera would show nothing out of line.

"Fuck," he snarled. He was as angry as he'd ever been, just like he used to get as a young man. But this was no frat-house bully, he reminded himself. This was a cop, who could beat him senseless—or kill him—and get away with it.

He stopped at the intersection. There was no other traffic, and he took a moment to calm down. But it was hard to do; it felt like something long buried was now free and unwilling to go back in its box.

"You're not chasing me off," Don said to the air. "I'll find that goddamned road. Just wait and see if I don't. And if I see your blue lights again, I'll make my own recording of what goes down, and we'll see what happens then."

But first, he decided, he needed some lunch. His anger had left him ravenous. He turned onto the access road that ran parallel to the interstate until he reached the exit with a Shoney's restaurant. He parked and gathered his atlas and printouts; maybe he was just disoriented, and the turn was actually obvious. He'd make another run before giving up, and if he ran into that trooper again, he'd be sure to have his cell phone on to record the conversation.

As he entered the restaurant and waited for his eyes to adjust, someone called, "Don!"

He turned. George Landers waved from the cash register. Don went over and shook hands. "You're a long way from Unicorn," Landers observed. "Is one of our softball teams in a tournament I don't know about?"

"No, I'm on double-secret assignment," Don said with mock drama. "I could tell you, but then I'd have to write your obituary."

Landers turned to the young man beside him. "Don, this is Craig Chess, the new minister at the Triple Springs Methodist Church in Cloud County."

Don's eyebrows rose. "There's a Methodist Church in Cloud County?"

"Why does everyone react like that?" Craig said with a smile. "And no, technically it's not. The county line is on the highway right past the church driveway, so we're actually in Smithborough."

"Ah," Don said. "So it's wishful thinking by the diocese."

"District," Landers said. "We're not Catholic."

"I stand corrected. At any rate, Reverend Chess, it's nice to meet you." The two men shook hands.

"So what's with all the maps?" Landers asked. "Are you looking for old Colonel Drake's Confederate treasure?"

"I'm supposed to interview Bronwyn Hyatt, the war hero. I went out to visit them, but I couldn't find the turnoff."

Landers turned to the younger minister. "You've been out there, haven't you, Craig?"

"Yes. It wasn't hard. The turnoff is on Highway 23 just past Jenkins Trail."

"I know, that's where I've been looking."

"That's odd," Craig said. "The road they live on is a dead end, so there's no other way to get there."

Don nodded. "Yeah. The Tufa curse strikes again, I suppose."

"The what?"

"Oh, it's just something people say about the Tufa: that if they don't want to be found, you won't find them. Old wives' tale."

"There's a lot of those about the Tufa," Landers said. "Craig and I have just been discussing some of them. Well, good luck."

Craig said, "Don, pleasure meeting you."

"Likewise," Don said.

Outside, Landers shook Craig's hand and went to his car. Craig glanced back at the restaurant, and saw the reporter take a seat in a window booth. Like a lot of local people, the reporter bore the visible traces of Tufa ancestry, but seemed not to be one; certainly he lacked the flat, noncommittal stare the Needsville Tufas presented.

As Craig unlocked his own car, a loud rumble made him

look up. An ancient pickup driven by a skinny middle-aged man parked in the handicapped spot near the door. A blue state placard permitting this hung from the rearview mirror. The truck bed was filled with children, the boys all skeletally thin like the driver, the girls round like Christmas ornaments. All had black hair, dead eyes, and suspicious expressions focused on Craig.

"Hi," he said with a smile. "Beautiful day, isn't it?"

The father stepped out of the cab and said, "We teach 'em not to talk to strangers, mister. Can't never tell these days."

"That's a sad truth," Craig said, and offered his hand. "I'm Craig Chess, the new minister at the Triple Springs Methodist Church."

The man's hand was strong and wiry. Craig noticed the pinkie was missing. "Nice to meet you, Father," he drawled.

"We're trying to get a children's program started at the church; we'd love to see you bring your family. It's just across the county line in Smithborough."

"Oh, I reckon we're too busy for that sort of stuff," the man said. "We live way up in the hills, anyway."

Craig knew not to push the issue. He was a minister, not a missionary. All he could do was let them know his church was open to them. "Well, think about it, and if you can find the time, we'd be pleased to have you."

The man's wife, as large as he was thin, herded the children inside. As Craig pulled out of the parking lot, he turned on impulse away from the interstate, toward Needsville. To date, the Hyatts were the only Tufas who had been pleasant to him, and he had to admit the memory of Bronwyn Hyatt kept reappearing in his imagination, especially when he was in bed at night.

The best way to exorcise such fantasies, he'd learned, was to confront them directly. Besides, they *had* invited him back.

He found the turnoff with no trouble. But at the last minute, he chickened out.

Sam Howell laughed the way a man does when he finds out his bitchy wife has run off with his best friend. The newspaper editor slapped the arm of his patio chair and said with undisguised delight, "So you ran up on Big Bobby Pafford, huh?"

"You know him?" Don asked. He'd gone straight to Howell's house after leaving Shoney's, needing to share the experience with someone. They sat on the back patio with cold beers, Howell shirtless and barefoot.

"Sure I do. So do you. You know those stickers they have on gas pumps saying if you run off without paying, you'll lose your license? That's his picture."

"He's not the friendliest guy."

"No, for him protecting and serving means kicking ass and taking names."

"How do you know so much about him?"

"We've crossed paths before. They say all bullies are cowards, but not him: he just likes making people afraid of him. He went in the marines right out of high school, I believe, but we weren't at war with anybody, so there was nobody for him to kill. Poor bastard: he was born in the wrong time. Being a state trooper is the best he can do now."

"He's a piece of work. Wonder what his discipline file looks like?"

Howell suddenly turned serious. He sat forward so that his

back skin pulled free of the chair's plastic with an audible pop. "*No,* Don. No bullshit. You leave Bobby Pafford alone and out of this. You had one run-in and got away without a ticket or a cracked skull. Count yourself lucky. He's the kind of man who wouldn't take kindly to being investigated, and since he's a cop, you'd have nowhere to turn."

Howell's voice actually trembled a little, as if describing a fear he knew firsthand. Don shrugged. He was no crusading reporter. "Okay, Sam. No problem."

"Good," Sam said with real relief. "So you never did find the Hyatt place?"

"No, and I'm damn sure I was looking in the right place. I double-checked the map and the atlas. It's almost like . . ."

"What?"

"You know what. You've heard the same shit I have, that the Tufa can disappear if they wanted to. That you could look forever but if they didn't want to be found, they wouldn't be."

"Them big-time New York reporters sure found them. They've been all over the TV."

"I know. But either I can't follow directions worth a damn, or they covered up the end of that road sometime in the last few days and made it look like it'd always been that way." *Or,* he thought, *the stories of the Tufa have more truth in them than I used to believe.*

Howell leaned back and laced his fingers behind his head. He shifted into his Jason Robards mode, the fatherly editor who knows what's best for his staff. "You've still got the assignment, Don."

"I know, Sam."

"No, I mean it. Your job is riding on this. I let it slide when you skipped those high school football games and wrote the stories from tapes off the radio, or when you 'pretended' to accidentally delete those spelling bee shots that you never took in the first place. This is your last chance, and I'm not feeling too generous about it right now. I admit running into Bobby Pafford can make a man a little shaky, but it's not enough. You clear on this?"

Don nodded. He felt like a kid in the principal's office. "Yeah."

"I want it for next week's issue. All original, with your own photos, not cobbled together off the Internet. In fact, I want to hear the tape of it."

"You don't trust me?"

"Don, I like you. That's why you've still got a job. But no, I don't trust you. You've lied to me enough times already."

Don stood and walked back to his car, feeling a numb tingling on his face and neck. In the rearview mirror, he saw that his skin was still red with shame.

13

Marshall Goins looked up from painting the Catamount Corner's porch rail. A white Altima pulled into the parking space right in front of him, and by the time he put down the brush and stood, Craig Chess was already bounding up the steps. "Good morning, Mr. Goins," he said cheerily, extending his hand.

Marshall displayed his palms. "Sorry, Reverend, wouldn't want to get paint all over you."

"Isn't it awfully early on a Saturday to be working so hard?"

"When you run your own business, every day's a workday. And with my wife in charge, I'm lucky to get off for Christmas or the Fourth of July."

Craig saw an opening. "You celebrate Christmas, then?"

He laughed. "Hell, don't everybody?"

"Not Jews or Buddhists."

"But I bet they still get the day off, don't they? Well, that is, unless they're married to Peggy."

Craig laughed. Once again a Tufa had blocked any further religious conversation. "Beautiful morning, though, isn't it?"

"Is that."

"Is the café open so a fellow can get a cup of coffee?"

"I believe the wife's in there. We've got a full house for the continental breakfast, so I'm not sure anything's left."

"Ah, just some coffee and a visit is all I need."

Marshall sadly shook his head as Craig went inside. He liked the young minister, and there was something poignant about the boy's doomed sincerity. He just hoped Craig didn't take it personally when his church went belly-up.

Craig went through the lobby and into the little café. It was empty, and the table of goodies was pretty well picked clean. The carafe still held some coffee, though, so he put some into a Styrofoam cup, along with a package of sugar. He grabbed a plastic spoon, returned to the lobby, and leaned on the front counter. "Good morning, Mrs. Goins."

Peggy looked up and smiled. "Why, Reverend, you can call me Peggy, you know. Everyone does."

"Good morning, then, Peggy-you-know."

She giggled. Craig was exactly the kind of man she would've found irresistible some thirty years earlier, on the trailing edge of the sexual revolution. She still fondly recalled venturing forth into the world and finding her Tufa forthrightness no longer sent men screaming for the hills. Now, though, her perspective, if not her libido, was considerably different. "I never knew a minister could be such a flirt."

"Can I expect you and Marshall at church tomorrow? I

promise a ten-minute sermon, no shouting about eternal damnation, and absolutely no speaking in tongues."

"Oh, we can't take the morning off, Reverend. We have guests that need tending. Some of them are even Yankees, and Lord knows what they might get into if we left them on their own."

Craig expected her response; he looked on this as just another early skirmish in a long and concentrated campaign. "Well, if things work out so you can make it, I'd love to see you there. How much do I owe you for the coffee?"

"Not a thing, Reverend. And stop by anytime." She smiled and momentarily resembled the girl she'd once been. Then her eyes opened wide. "Oh, goodness, would you look at that."

"What?"

She tapped the plastic spoon in his coffee. It split, revealing two spoons stuck together. "I always heard that if you accidentally put two spoons in a coffee cup, it's a sign you're about to get married."

He chuckled. "That'd be a miracle for sure, Peggy. Right now I haven't even got a girlfriend."

"Well, you might want to keep your eyes open. I'm pretty good at reading signs, they tell me."

"I'll sure do that."

Outside, Craig asked Marshall, "Mind if I leave my car here? I was going to stroll around town a little bit, enjoy the breeze."

"Reckon so," Marshall said as he painted the railing's underside.

Craig walked toward the post office. Sure enough, Rockhouse Hicks was in his usual place, all alone at one end of the long, narrow porch. Craig sat down in the rocking chair beside the old man and said cheerily, "Good morning."

"It's morning," Hicks said without turning. He wore threadbare jeans, old loafers, and a flannel shirt whose collar points had worn away.

"You pretty much run this place, don't you?"

"The porch?"

"The town."

Now Hicks turned very slightly toward him. "Me? I'm just one more retired old fart with nothing to do all day."

"Yeah, but I've seen how people treat you. They look up to you."

Hicks frowned, then resumed his neutral expression. "I think somebody's been talking out of turn, Reverend."

"No, sir, I just pay attention. I see how people defer to you. And I was always taught to respect my elders."

"You want me to get people to come to that church of yours, don't you?"

"No, sir. I'd just like to invite *you* to come."

Hicks almost laughed out loud. "I don't think that's too likely, Reverend. Not too likely at all."

"Why?"

A new voice said, "This Yankee bothering you, Uncle Rockhouse?" The word came out *Unca*.

Craig looked up. A tall, broad-shouldered young man stood on the sidewalk leading up to the porch. His face was almost femininely handsome, with thick pouty lips and sleepy eyes. He wore a faded cowboy hat with the side brims rolled up, and black hair fell to his shoulders.

"Naw," Hicks said. "This-here's the new preacher over to Smithborough."

Craig smiled, stood, and extended his hand. "Craig Chess, of the Triple Springs Methodist Church."

The younger man was a full head taller than Craig. "Get the fuck away from me," he snapped contemptuously. "You need anything, Unca Rockhouse, you call me."

"Sure thing, Stoney," Hicks said.

The tall young man went into the post office. He sauntered, just as Dwayne Gitterman had done in the convenience store, but with even more arrogance.

"Reckon I'll leave you to your rocking, Mr. Hicks," Craig said tightly. His temper seldom flared, but it did so now, and he knew he needed to leave. He crossed the highway toward the Fast Grab. He did not check for traffic, but in Needsville, that was not terribly risky.

Inside, he found Lassa again behind the counter. "Morning, Reverend," she said brightly.

Her cheer defused most of his annoyance. "Good morning, Lassa."

"You're in town early."

"I wanted to catch a few people and extend personal invitations for them to come to services tomorrow. Including," he added with what he hoped was a charming smile, "you and your family."

Lassa giggled. "I'm afraid we can't make it, Reverend. But it's sweet of you to ask."

He leaned on the counter and asked seriously, "Lassa, why won't any of you Tufas come to church? Any church?"

She looked down, studiously rearranging a display of portable lighters beside the cash register. "I don't know about anyone but me, I'm afraid. I have to work tomorrow morning, six A.M. to two in the afternoon."

"I just spoke to Mr. Hicks over at the post office. If he came, would you?"

Lassa looked up, eyes wide. "Did he say he would?"

For an instant Craig seriously considered lying. "No. But if I convinced him, would that convince you?"

"What's that old man to me?" Lassa said flippantly. "I hate to see him come in the door. He pays for things out of a tube sock full of pennies."

Craig contemplated pushing the point, but again remembered this was a preliminary scuffle, not a final battle. He patted her hand and said, "Well, just know you're always welcome." As he turned to leave, he spotted the young man referred to as Stoney kneeling beside Rockhouse, deep in conversation. When he opened the Fast Grab's door, both men turned to look at him. He was too far away to see their expressions, but he felt a chill that had nothing to do with the mountain breeze.

Bronwyn returned from Knoxville that night with her leg in a removable fiberglass cast.

As promised, Bliss drove her there in the Cloud County Emergency Services ambulance. Bronwyn asked that no one else accompany them; she never again wanted to wake up in post-op and find a ring of concerned Hyatts hovering over her the way she had at the VA hospital.

The office visit had been scheduled for the weekend in case there was a mob scene with the media, but not a single reporter seemed to know about it. After examining Bronwyn, the astounded doctor scheduled immediate surgery to remove the pins and screws; normally this was done with local anesthetics, but her injuries were so complex, they decided to put her under a general. The surgeon, called in from his son's soccer practice, was also amazed at the rate of recovery, and for one brief moment thought he might have to rebreak one place to get the metal out. But eventually they left the two pins that would be permanently needed and closed the incisions.

While she waited for Bronwyn to wake up from the anesthetic, the surgeon appeared, still in his scrubs, and took Bliss aside into a conference room. He seemed agitated, and frequently scratched under his beard. "Ms. Overbay, may I ask you something? You seem to know your stuff, and I know you're from the same small town as my patient. Is there anything unusual in Ms. Hyatt's medical history that might not be mentioned in her files?"

"Unusual?"

"Yes. Something in her family history, perhaps. Frankly, if I didn't have X-rays showing what her leg looked like six weeks ago, I'd be convinced this was a whole different patient. She's healed a good three months ahead of any normal prognosis."

"That's good, isn't it?"

"It depends on the reason. If she's just a freakishly fast healer, then yes, it's good. If not, then it's the sign of some deeper condition."

"Such as?"

"Hell, I don't know. It's just weird. I looked over the army's medical records on her, and I can't imagine that the woman I just worked on was really in as bad a shape as they said she was."

"You saw her on the news."

"Yes, but the news is no different from the drunk in the corner bar: he might have a good story, but that doesn't mean you can trust it." He paused, considering his next words carefully. "I'm worried that the army might have treated her injuries as more serious than they were, in order to get more PR use from them. That would be a gross mistreatment of the patient, needless to say, but sadly it's not outside the realm of possibility. Has Ms. Hyatt given you any indication that might be the case?"

Bliss almost laughed. "Doctor, I promise, Bronwyn's injuries were real. What you see now is the result of rest, good home care, and following doctor's orders. I've watched it happen. If it's faster than normal, then it just is."

The doctor nodded, although he didn't appear convinced. "I'll make lots of notes about this, should Ms. Hyatt ever need them to pursue any legal action against the army. Or the Iraqis, for that matter."

"Thank you. I'll make sure she knows."

After Bronwyn woke up, drank some water, and was able to answer basic questions, the doctor returned to explain the results of the surgery. "There's a lot of rehab still to go. Realistically you're looking at months, maybe years before you can walk fully unaided again. But all in all, it's close enough to a miracle to have me looking over my shoulder for angels."

She looked down at her withered, pale leg. The sutures were fresh, the incisions stained orange by antiseptic and already starting to scab over. Patches of long, soft hair grew between the surgical sites. Her other leg, smooth and muscular, only made this one look even more deformed. She felt something in her chest like a sob struggling to escape.

Bliss stroked Bronwyn's hair and asked the doctor, "How

soon until we can head back? I know it's Saturday, but I'd like to miss as much evening traffic as possible."

His eyes widened. "Back? Tonight? I really think we should keep her at least overnight, just for observation." Then he turned to Bronwyn. "Sorry, I don't mean to talk about you like you're not here. But you've been through a lot, not just today's surgery, and I'd feel better if we waited."

"I've been observed enough," Bronwyn said, her tongue still heavy with the dregs of sedation. "I want to be the audience, not the show. I want to go home."

"She'll be in an ambulance with an EMT," Bliss said. "And clearly, whatever she's doing at home is working."

The doctor chewed one end of his mustache for a moment. "It's against my better judgment. But you can't argue with the results you've been getting." He threw his hands up in a shrug. "Drive safely, ladies. And call me if you need anything."

The trip home was uneventful; Bronwyn slept most of the way. Bliss hummed all the songs of comfort she knew. When she heard Bronwyn moan once, either in pain or a nightmare, she began to sing a tune originally written as a hymn. For the Tufa, though, its symbolism carried a far different meaning:

> *When I can read my title clear*
> *To mansions in the skies,*
> *I'll bid farewell to every fear*
> *And wipe my weeping eyes.*
>
> *I feel like, I feel like*
> *I'm on my journey home.*

I feel like, I feel like
I'm on my journey home. . . .

It was almost ten o'clock when they passed through Needs-ville, and twenty minutes later Bliss backed the ambulance up the hill to the Hyatts' porch. Deacon carried his semiconscious daughter from the stretcher inside to the couch. Bliss undid the cast, exposing the sutures to the air. Bronwyn awoke to find Aiden, hair tousled from sleep, kneeling beside her and staring at her leg.

Aiden said, "Wow."

"Yes, that's where the pins went in," Bliss said. "And came out. Your sister's been through a lot today."

"Wow," he whispered again, and tentatively extended one hand.

"Touch them," Bronwyn croaked, "and you'll draw back a nub. I mean it."

"Leave your sister alone," Deacon said firmly. "Go get her a glass of tea."

"Yessir," Aiden mumbled and shuffled, head down, into the kitchen.

Bliss turned to Deacon and Chloe. "The doctors were pretty surprised. She's way ahead of schedule. I told them it was all this clean mountain air."

"Good an explanation as any," Deacon agreed.

"Thanks for taking care of her," Chloe said to Bliss. "I've been worried all day, and tonight the wind's been high in the trees."

Bliss nodded. "I noticed that. Best you stay close to home for now."

Brownyn closed her eyes and listened for the night wind. It lurked outside among the upper branches, waving them against the stars. It was hard to tell over the pain medication if the wind was dancing, or instead flitting from place to place like something stalking its prey below.

"Not my mom," Bronwyn whispered.

"What, honey?" Chloe asked. But Bronwyn was asleep again.

14

"Good morning," Craig Chess said to his congregation.

All seven people, in a sanctuary that could seat three hundred, replied in unison, "Good morning."

He leaned casually on the pulpit. "I don't think there's going to be a mad last-minute rush, so why doesn't everyone come down front?"

Don Swayback looked at Susie. They rose from the last pew and came down the side aisle, passing through beams of sunlight tinted by the stained glass windows. On the opposite side, a well-dressed family of five left their seat on the next-to-last pew and moved in an orderly line to the front. The two groups took seats at opposite ends of the first pew.

Craig almost laughed. "Thanks. I don't have to shout this way, at least. I'd like to thank you for coming to my inaugural service, and I hope you'll tell your friends and family about it as well." He opened his hymnal. "I think it's appropriate to begin both this service and my full-time pastoral career with 'What a Day That Will Be,' page one hundred forty-two."

He looked back over his shoulder. Mrs. Gaffney, the elderly pianist he'd recruited, began to play.

Craig's voice, a well-modulated baritone, was the loudest. His congregation sang softly, none of them risking any public display of enthusiasm. He knew George Landers had sent them from his own church to make sure Craig didn't face an empty building on his first day. Later, when two hundred-dollar bills showed up in the collection tray, he'd known they originated with George as well. Still, seven people now faced him expectantly, if not exactly enthusiastically, and he owed them a sincere effort.

"I'd like to read from Psalm 111, verses one through ten." He concluded with, " 'The fear of the Lord is the beginning of wisdom: a good understanding have all they that do his commandments: his praise endureth forever.' " He closed his Bible and added, "Which, as I'm sure you know from looking at the bulletin, leads into today's sermon, 'The Beginning of Wisdom.' "

It wasn't a great sermon; he knew it wouldn't be. But he also knew it was the right sermon for this day. He told them about his own life, his crisis of faith, and his subsequent certainty that he'd been called to the ministry. He tried to be self-deprecating without being irreverent, and was rewarded by one muffled snicker from Susie Swayback. He was establishing, as much to himself as to them, his viability as a spiritual leader, and as he progressed he grew more certain, more comfortable, more right.

The children fidgeted during his talk, but he held the adults' attention. When the service ended thirty-five minutes after it began, he moved to the door for the exit meet and greet. He

THE HUM AND THE SHIVER 151

gave each of the three children a silver dollar, telling them they "fell from heaven just that morning."

After the family left, he shook Don Swayback's hand. "We met at the Shoney's the other day, didn't we?"

"That's right. This is my wife, Susie."

"A pleasure to meet you. So, Don, were you ever able to find the road to the Hyatt place?"

"No, I haven't been back yet. But I intend to."

"If you want, give me a call and maybe I can ride out there with you. I've been meaning to go back out there myself, so surely between the two of us we can find it."

"We'll see what my schedule is like," Don said. "Thanks for the offer."

As they walked to their car, Susie said quietly, "You still haven't done that interview?"

"Not yet," he said testily as he held her door.

She swung her legs into the car and smoothed down her skirt. "I can't keep working these double shifts, you know. You have to keep your job."

When Don had closed his own door and buckled his seat belt, he said, "I know that, Susie. I really couldn't find the road, it wasn't an excuse."

"Is it because of that state trooper everyone's terrified of?"

"Do you *want* to have to bail me out of jail?"

She looked evenly at him. "If you're in jail for standing up for yourself and what's right, yes."

He felt a mixture of shame and pride. "Well, it's a big county. I probably won't ever see him again." Then he turned on the ignition and slapped the old mix tape into the player before Susie could say anything else. They pulled out to the strains of "A Country Boy Can Survive."

Craig watched the two vehicles depart. He heard Mrs. Gaffney closing up the piano behind him. He knew he should've been disappointed, but somehow he felt elated. He could *do* this. That last nagging bit of doubt in the back of his mind was now gone. This *was* his calling, and even if he only momentarily reached one out of the four adults, then it had been worth it.

He looked up at the clear blue sky and said a heartfelt, "Thank you."

"So," Terry-Joe asked seriously, "what *do* you remember?"

The morning sun twinkled through the trees as a breeze rippled the branches. A mourning dove plaintively announced itself. "Terry-Joe, I'm still a little fuzzy from yesterday," Bronwyn said. "I did have surgery, you know. And we agreed to start tomorrow."

They sat on the Hyatts' porch. Terry-Joe's own mandolin rested across his knees. Brownyn's leg was propped up and exposed to the air, per the doctor's instructions; with the antiseptic stains and fresh scabs around the puffy, bruised incisions, it looked especially grotesque. She used the Sunday paper's *Parade* magazine to shoo flies drawn to the shiny Neosporin.

Terry-Joe made no mention of it. Instead he said, "I'm just trying to find out where you're head's at, so I know where to begin."

"Okay." Bronwyn pointed at the instrument. "That's a mandolin. How's that for a start?"

He smiled. "Sure it's not a tater bug?"

"Not with a flat back."

He held it by the neck. "Remember how to hold it?"

She took the instrument and placed it under her right arm. He offered a small white pick. After turning the flat plastic in her fingers a few times she said, "It's lighter than I'm used to."

Then she frowned. There was no conscious memory associated with that, but the pick *did* feel wrong in her fingers.

He traded her a green one. "Try this."

She touched the pick to the strings, but before she strummed, she said, "The action doesn't look right."

He scooted closer so he could see what she meant. "Show me."

"Give me a nickel."

He fished one from his pocket.

"It's too high. Look." She slid the nickel under the twelfth fret. It lay flat against the neck, not touching the strings.

He looked at her and smiled. "I think it's coming back to you."

She realized he'd set the action high to see if she'd notice. It would make the instrument louder, but the fingering would be much harder. "That's sneaky," she said, but couldn't repress a smile. "Have you got a screwdriver to adjust it?"

He twirled one in his fingers. "Always."

After the action was reset, she plucked the two bottom strings and winced at the sound. "That's not a G," she said.

"No, that's a bug screamin' right before it hits the windshield. You want me to tune it, or you want to try?"

Despite the morning breeze, she was already sweating from the intensity. This had been second nature to her before she left home. The Bronwynator could retune a mandolin, make out with a boy, and sneak tokes off a joint without short-changing any of the tasks at hand. Now, though, she couldn't quite recall how to tune the instrument, despite her best efforts. *God,* she thought, *I hope I remember how to do those other things.*

Before she had to admit it, though, Terry-Joe reached around so that his left hand covered hers on the neck. This brought her close against him. "Here's how you do it when you ain't got a tuning pipe or a guitar handy," he said, and guided her fingers to the pegs. "Keep plucking the fourth string for me."

She did. As he slowly adjusted the peg, the discordant sound of the two parallel strings merged into one clear note. "That's it," he said softly.

She turned to him, and suddenly, like in the movies, their faces were millimeters apart, close enough to feel the other's breath on their lips. They gazed into each other's eyes, and all she could hear was her own blood pulsing.

After a moment he blinked, smiled, and said, "Now you do the next one. Remember how?"

It took real effort for her to turn away. "I think . . . you hold down the fourth and get the third to sound just like that, right? That gives you the D."

"Yeah," he said. Her black hair brushed his cheek. "Tune the whole thing. That'll be lesson enough for one day."

He went to the edge of the porch and looked out over the yard, his back to her so she wouldn't feel nervous under his gaze. Bronwyn did as he instructed, adjusting the deliberately discordant strings into the correct tones. As she worked, her memory gave up little flashes of experience so that she gradually recalled the proper tuning.

Movement drew Terry-Joe's attention to the tree line at the edge of the yard. A greenish brown bird six feet tall, with long spindly legs and an erect neck, emerged tentatively into the open. It looked around, then darted its long neck down to test the grass. Two more emus peered out from the bushes, waiting for their scout to signal the okay.

Bronwyn saw it, too. She put the mandolin aside and raised herself with her arms to get a better look. "What the hell—?"

Terry-Joe waved his arms and shouted, "Hey! Get on outta here! Now!"

The lead emu shivered, its feathers rippling, then turned and dashed back into the woods. All three vanished.

Bronwyn said, "Was that an *ostrich*?"

"Naw, one of Sim Denham's emus."

"Does he know they're loose?"

"Know it? He *let* 'em loose. He had to file bankruptcy because of those stupid things, and when he couldn't find a buyer, he just opened the pen and off they went. There's probably a dozen of 'em in the valley, and if they survive the winter, they'll start breeding."

"When did that happen?"

"Back around the first of March, I suppose."

Just before the mission that made her a celebrity, she calculated. "Wow. That's weird, even for here."

"Yeah. Most likely they'll freeze to death, though." He turned to face her. "So, back to work. How are you doing?"

She ran the pick across the strings. The sound shimmered in the morning air.

"Nice," he said.

"Thanks."

"So what sort of music did you listen to over in Iraq?"

"Whatever everyone else was listening to. Hip-hop or country, pretty much. Not a lot of middle ground."

"Anything good?"

She shook her head. "It all sounds the same after a while. And it's all . . ." She sought the right word. *"Mean."*

He nodded. "I know. Gave up on the radio myself. Been listening to stuff from England lately, pipers and such. Ever heard smallpipes? Like a bagpipe, 'scept not as nails-on-a-chalkboard sounding." He looked at his watch. "Okay, your homework: Get Aiden, if he ever wakes up, to knock Magda well and truly out of tune, then you retune her. Right now I have to get down to Jack Tenney's to help him unload some seeds, but we'll check your work tomorrow." He met her eyes in a way that said more than any words. "It's been a pleasure working with you, Ms. Hyatt."

"Thank you, Mr. Gitterman," she said, knowing exactly what the look meant and more, how much courage it took for him to risk it. She'd been his brother's girlfriend, after all. It made her feel good in a totally new way. He walked down the hill to his dirt bike, the mandolin case in his hand. His wide, straight shoulders and narrow waist lent an echo of Dwayne's swagger to his stride.

Terry-Joe's bike passed another vehicle that pulled into the driveway and stopped. Craig Chess parked in the sun, willing to brave the hot interior rather than deal with the sticky residue dripping from the pecan tree. He waved to Bronwyn as he approached. "Good morning. Hope you don't mind me stopping by."

Bronwyn managed to keep her voice steady as Craig strode toward her. Terry-Joe was a good-looking boy, but Craig was a *man,* and the awkward feeling in her belly returned. "Not to tell a man his job, but shouldn't you be in your pulpit?"

"Already done. The turnout was pretty light. Makes the service go quickly." He sat on the porch steps at her feet. When he looked up at her, the sunlight edged her in a halo. It was a bit disconcerting. "You look like you feel better."

"I do. Getting the Eiffel Tower off my leg helped."

"I bet." He nodded at the mandolin. "Do you play?"

"I'm learning," she said truthfully.

"I read somewhere that music's good therapy for head trauma. And, in my experience, for making life a little better in general."

"Do *you* play?"

"I tinker. Piano, organ, some guitar. Never tried a mandolin, though."

Chloe emerged from the house, barefoot and wearing a comfortable summer dress. Her black hair hung loose. Craig immediately stood. "Mrs. Hyatt," he said.

"Reverend Chess, what a surprise." She looked around. "Where's Terry-Joe? Jack Tenney just called for him."

"He's on his way there," Bronwyn said.

"I hope I'm not intruding," Craig said. "I wanted to check on Bronwyn and see if she needed anything from town." *And,* he thought to himself, *to see what the devil Don Swayback meant about not finding the road. And to make up for being a coward on Thursday.* "I'm going into Johnson City later this week, so if you all need anything picked up there, I'd be glad to."

Chloe smiled, and for an instant Craig felt a little dizzy. The resemblance between mother and daughter was extraordinary, but the differences were even more pronounced. There was a hard edge to Brownyn, but Chloe was all soft curves and gentle feelings, an earth mother in the truest sense. And, he realized uncomfortably, as sexy in her mature way as Bronwyn was in her youthful one.

Chloe's smile grew into a grin, as if she'd followed his thoughts. "I'll pour you kids some iced tea," she said, and went back inside.

Craig turned to Bronwyn. "So . . . what sort of music do you listen to?"

She didn't want to give him the same answer she'd given Terry-Joe; a non-Tufa might not get it. She tapped her temple and said, "Things are still a little scrambled up here. I'll have to take a rain check on answering that. What about you?"

"Ironically, my favorite musician is *John* Hiatt."

"No relation to us, I reckon."

"Well, it is spelled differently."

"Not exactly religious, though, is he?"

"You think religious people can only listen to religious music?"

"I thought *professionally* religious people had to, yeah."

"Maybe at one time, and maybe some still. But I don't hold with isolating yourself from the world. I may not watch MTV or play on the computer every night, but I try to leave myself open to new things. If I disagree with something, I like to be able to explain why. To myself, if no one else."

"So do you agree with the war?" she asked, then mentally slapped herself. Why was she trying to pick a fight?

He didn't seem offended. "Me? No. The whole 'thou shalt not kill' rule is pretty clear." Suddenly he remembered whom he was talking to. "I hope you don't take that personally."

She laughed. "No. I've seen plenty of Christian killers, and Muslim killers, and the occasional Jewish killer. As near as I can tell, believing in their various gods just eggs them on."

"What denomination are you?" he asked as casually as he could.

"My family's Tufa, Reverend. We believe what we've always believed."

Smiling, he pressed on. "And what's that?"

"That it's not polite to discuss religion with company."

He leaned a little closer. "And how long until I'm not company?"

"I'm afraid you'll always be company to most of the Tufa, Reverend, even if you married me."

Instantly she blushed bright red and looked away. Where the hell had *that* come from?

Craig stood, brushed off his jeans, and said, "Well, I didn't mean to be rude. It was nice to see you again, Bronwyn."

Chloe came out with two glasses of tea, and looked puzzled when she saw Craig on his feet. "Not leaving so soon are you, Reverend?"

"I don't want to tire Bronwyn out. Thanks for the tea, Mrs. Hyatt. I'll take a rain check, if you don't mind?"

"Of course. You're welcome any time."

Chloe watched Craig get into his car and drive away. "He is a handsome man, isn't he?"

Bronwyn said nothing, instead staring at a viceroy butterfly as it danced across the yard. She'd seen the flash of hurt in Craig's eyes, and had let him go without a word. Was the Bronwynator, who'd once propositioned her sexy-bald high school principal, suddenly ashamed she found a man attractive? Had she deliberately driven him off?

Chloe sat down, sipped the tea she'd intended for Craig, and said, "You think you're up to doing it?"

Bronwyn's eyes opened wide. "What, with the *preacher*?"

"No, learning to play again. What did you think I meant?"

"Never mind. And it's not like I have a choice, is it?"

Chloe looked down. "I reckon not. You have to take it on."

"Because you're ready to die." It came out as an accusation.

Chloe sighed. "No, Bronwyn, I'm not ready to die. I'm not like you, I never sought it out to see what it felt like. And it beats me where you get it from; your daddy's the most sensible man I ever met, and your brothers are both level-headed, even

Aiden. I never thought I was a wild one, but it had to come from somewhere, and you and me, we're Tufa women, so we're pretty connected."

"Don't feel guilty for me, Mom," Bronwyn said with no sympathy. "I did what I wanted, every day of my life. The time to turn me from that road was when I was little and still scared of you. It's too late for both of us now."

"No, ma'am," Chloe said seriously. "It's never too late, not for a Tufa. We got all of time to play in, if we want it. You don't like who you are, change it."

"Do you like who you are?"

"I've got a good man who loves me, two fine sons, and a war hero for a daughter. I know my songs, I know my stories. Yeah, I like who I am."

"You never wanted to be more than that? More than some Tufa jukebox?"

"You seem to think that ain't enough. It is for me. Lots of people never know their purpose, never know their songs or their stories. Rich ain't just about money."

"So you're rich."

"You may understand that sometime. You might even feel the same way. I sure hope you do, Bronwyn, because it's the sweetest feeling in the world. I ain't in no hurry to give it up, but if the night wind wants me, I'll go with no regrets. When them Iraqis had you, could you have said the same thing?"

Bronwyn started to get angry. "No, Mom, I couldn't because I was too fucking busy fighting to stay alive. I didn't just sigh and accept the next song on the playlist, like you're doing. You want to leave Aiden without a mother? You think that'll make *him* rich?"

"I think you need to calm down," Chloe said. Her voice was

even, but Bronwyn heard the edge to it. "You left. You made your choice. You really don't have the high ground on this."

Bronwyn wanted desperately to leap up, stomp inside, and slam the door. She wanted to hop into her truck, tear off down the road with the radio blasting while she smoked a joint to calm down. But she could only sit and look at her mother, at the unaccustomed anger simmering in her face, and endure it.

"Maybe there is no high ground," Bronwyn said after a moment. "Maybe the night winds don't carry us anymore. Maybe they just drag us along."

15

The road between the Hyatt farm and Needsville was empty except for one tractor pulling a rusted old combine. The driver was kind enough to pull aside and let Craig pass. He waved at the farmer, turned up the music on the radio, and headed into Needsville on his way back home.

He was fuming, although he wasn't exactly sure why. Sure, the "even if you married me" bit could've just been a joke, but Craig was pretty sure Bronwyn knew he was attracted to her. If so, why would she be so snotty about it? Had that cruel state trooper been right? Was this the *real* Bronwynator, only now reemerging from the haze of her wartime experiences?

He saw the Needsville post office ahead on the right. Even though the building was closed, Rockhouse Hicks sat on the porch, his eyes resolutely straight ahead.

Impulsively Craig whipped his car into a parking place, stopping so hard, the belt yanked tight against his shoulder. The old man did not acknowledge Craig until he settled into the empty rocker beside him and said, "Morning, Mr. Hicks."

Hicks grunted a reply. His chair squeaked rhythmically as it went back and forth.

"What's been happening in town today?"

"Sun came up, you sat down," he said with no inflection. "That's about it."

"Pretty much all that ever happens, isn't it?"

"During the week the postman raises the American flag."

Craig sat back and rocked in unison with the old man for a few moments. "Missed you in church this morning."

"Didn't know you were shooting at me," Hicks said.

Craig chuckled. "That's a good one." After more silence, he continued, "The town sure looks different than it did when Bronwyn Hyatt's parade came through."

Hicks leaned over and spit off the edge of the porch. "Hyatts," he said. "I know you been keeping company with 'em. Nothing but white trash, all of 'em."

Craig hid his annoyance. "Yeah, I've been to visit a few times, but that's kinda harsh, isn't it?"

"That Chloe Hyatt? Back when she was Chloe Smith, you could find her out in the fields with a different boy every night. Sometimes even with boys whose blood was a little too close to her own, if you take what I mean. That sound harsh to you?"

"Well, yeah, actually. Sounds like gossip."

"Ain't no *gossip*. That's pure-D *fact*. Come up on her a few times myself when I'd be out hunting or fishing. Scared up her and whatever boy she was with. All I seen was assholes and elbows." He snorted at the memory, a sound so full of bile that Craig understood anew why everyone left the old man alone. "And that daughter of hers is the same way. Before she run off to join the army, she made sure every boy in the county knew what a girl's mouth could do for them."

"I'm sure you have a few youthful indiscretions in your own past, Mr. Hicks," Craig said, but he found it hard to keep his tone even. How did Hicks know he'd visited the Hyatts unless one of them told him?

"Not like that Bronwyn Hyatt. She was a hellion for sure. Had an abortion when she was sixteen, did you know that? Wouldn't never say who the daddy was. I figure it was that oldest Gitterman boy, Dwayne, but hell, could've been anyone old enough to stand at attention, the way she carried on. Might as well have strapped a mattress to her back."

"If you'll excuse me, Mr. Hicks," Craig said as he started to rise.

"Sit down!" Hicks barked. "You don't walk off when I'm talking to you!"

Craig stared; the old man's sudden burst of fury was overwhelming, like a volcano that had previously been merely placidly steaming. His face blazed bright red beneath his cap, and his eyes shone as if lit internally. *Demonic* was the word that first came to mind.

Craig slowly sat back down. He forced himself to step outside his immediate resentment. Whatever else, he could at least spend a few minutes listening; perhaps Hicks had been unpleasant for so long, he knew no other way to be. Christ wouldn't stomp off in a huff.

Hicks glared at him, showing more animation than Craig had ever seen. "Let me tell you about your 'war hero,' Reverend. That little slut spent four months in juvenile jail for stealing a car when she was fourteen. She was arrested twice for selling dope, but shook that little ass of hers and got out of it. Does that sound like some goddamn hero to you? It don't to me, that's for certain. Yeah, sure, she got all shot up and got rescued on live TV, but that ain't nothing. Sure as shit ain't *heroic*."

Then as quickly as it rose, the storm of rage passed. His color returned to normal, and he resumed his methodical rocking. After a long moment Craig said, "Anything else?"

"Naw," Hicks said, looking straight ahead. He seemed content, satisfied that he'd somehow done his job.

"Well . . . I'll be going then." He stopped halfway through standing to see if the old man would bellow at him again, but there was nothing. He left the porch as quickly as he could without running.

Back in his car, the air conditioner blasting in his face, he had time to evaluate. Maybe Hicks was sliding into dementia. Yet his anger had not been irrational, just out of proportion. Perhaps it was simply the ire that can fester in isolated small towns, especially when one person is singled out for notoriety. Craig had witnessed that before, just never out in public and with such an abrupt, 180-degree shift.

Or maybe, he thought with sudden insight, this was all designed by a much greater hand to show him that Bronwyn Hyatt would never be a suitable partner for a preacher. Perhaps the pain he endured now would spare him a greater pain later.

As he pulled out of the lot, he noticed that the door at the building's back corner, marked with a tiny sign as NEEDSVILLE CITY HALL, now stood open. In the three months Craig had visited Needsville regularly, he'd never seen that, so he immediately pulled the car back into its space and got out. He avoided eye contact with Hicks until the old man was out of sight.

He knocked on the doorframe, then stuck his head inside the tiny office. "Hello?"

Marshall Goins looked up from behind an old wooden desk. A green filing cabinet stood against the wall, along with a photo of Bill Monroe where, in most city halls, the current governor's portrait would hang. "Well, howdy, Reverend," he said with a big grin. He stood and offered his hand. "Just getting the water bills ready to go out. What brings you around?"

"I've never seen the city hall open before," Craig said honestly.

Marshall laughed. "That's true enough. Not a lot of civic business in a town of less than three hundred. But we do have to send out the bills, and every so often, somebody'll need something notarized."

"Are you the mayor?"

"'Fraid so. Hard to get shed of the job when no one runs against you."

"Could be a sign of confidence."

"Or laziness," Marshall said with a laugh.

Craig looked around. "So this is the seat of power for Needsville."

"I don't know about 'power.' You got the two Tufa tribes each with their own place, and—" Suddenly he scowled and shook his head. "Listen to me, sounding like I know something. You know, Reverend, you got a way of making a fella so relaxed, he forgets his good sense."

Craig knew he'd just lucked up on something and had to proceed carefully. "I think it's just because everyone here is so friendly. Sure can't be because you're used to preachers."

"That's true," Marshall said. "Hope you can make it work, though. You're a lot more easygoing than some have been."

"Marshall, why don't you go to church? Why don't *any* of the Tufa go to church? We *are* in the Bible Belt, after all." He deliberately kept the same jovial, carefree tone, but inside he was alive with anticipation.

"The Tufa." Marshall snorted. "Do you know what the Tufa are, Reverend? We're people they ain't got any other name for. We ain't white, we ain't black, we ain't red, we sure ain't Mexican or Chinese. I don't even know what the word means. And maybe it means nothing at all. If I was to leave Needsville, nobody'd look at me twice. They sure wouldn't need a special name for me."

Craig smiled. "Is that the truth, Mr. Goins?"

Marshall laughed. "I reckon so. Who'd lie to a preacher?"

"Somebody with a guilty conscience."

"My conscience is as white as the first winter snow," he said, looking heavenward and batting his eyes.

They both laughed. Craig decided to take a risk, based on his sense of Marshall's innate decency. "Hey, can I ask you something and have you promise to keep it between us?"

"Of course, Reverend."

"I've been hearing some gossip about Bronwyn Hyatt. I know she was pretty wild before she joined the army, but what I've been told goes way beyond that. Wondered how much of it was true."

Marshall paused and thought. "Well, Bronwyn *was* a hellion. They called her the Bronwynator, you know. She'd take a drink, a draw, or a dare from anybody. And she ran with a rough crowd. But I tell you, I've known Deacon and Chloe all my life, and they wouldn't raise a child with a bad song in her soul. Besides, she's too important to us."

"Because she's a hero?"

He looked startled, shook his head, and laughed again. "Boy, you can sure put a fellow off his line, Reverend. You don't be worrying about Miss Brownyn Hyatt. That leg of hers may be a little stiff, but a year from now, I bet you won't even know she was hurt unless you're close enough she shows you the scars. All that other talk—" He held up a bottle of Wite-Out. "Time has a way of covering up mistakes, just like this stuff does. She mighta sowed some wild oats, maybe even done some things that crossed the line of the law. But a fella's got to have faith in his fellow man, or woman, doesn't he?"

"I've always thought so."

"Of course you have, that's your job."

"Yes, but it's also what I believe. It's what made me want to *take* the job."

Marshall gestured at the stacks of bills and envelopes. "Well, my wife made me take *this* job, so I best get to it. The wrath of God ain't a patch on the wrath of an angry woman."

Craig left more perplexed than ever, but convinced he'd been on the verge of learning something significant about the Tufa. And he *had* learned quite a bit about Bronwyn Hyatt. Now he had to decide how he felt about it.

16

Susie Swayback opened her front door and muttered, with more than her usual annoyance, *"Baptists."*

Don looked up from tuning his guitar. "And tigers and bears, oh my?"

"No, that stupid Ethelene Hightower." She kicked off her shoes beside the door. Ethelene was a member of a tiny Baptist congregation that refused to let its members work on Sundays. Therefore, whenever Ethelene rotated to weekend duty, she would pass on any Sunday calls to one of the other X-ray techs. Susie had been paged on their way home from church to do a chest series on a drunken young man who'd driven his ATV into a tree as he chased a coyote. "I have to go all the way in to work just so her husband won't beat her up."

"He beats her up?"

"He does if she tries to work on a Sunday. She had a black eye for a week the last time she tried to. That's why we all pitch in for this." She sighed with disgust as she plopped beside him on the couch. *"Baptists."*

He leaned over and kissed her. "Good thing we're Methodists, then." He resumed noodling a blues lick as he adjusted the tuning pegs, but took the time to write down a lyric that came to him. He hummed as he wrote:

> *He beats her to show her the way*
> *Because she can't find it on her own*
> *He's sure she'll always stay*
> *This bed of pain is her home*

Satisfied, he began strumming chord progressions, seeking a melody.

"Honey, please," Suzie said, annoyed. "It's been a bad day already, and finding Blind Lemon Jefferson on my couch just makes it worse."

Without changing expression, he strummed the opening bars of "Rocky Top."

"Oh, stop it." She leaned her head back on the cushion and closed her eyes. "I don't feel like cooking tonight, do you want to go out somewhere? Maybe the buffet over in Sturgeonville?"

He put the guitar aside and said casually, "*I* was thinking we might drive out to the barn dance in Cloud County."

She opened one skeptical eye. "What barn dance?"

"The one they have every Sunday night. Thought it might be fun, maybe dance a little, sit in with the players and such."

She opened both eyes. "You mean you want to play in public? You haven't done that since college, have you?"

He shrugged. "No. But it might be fun to get back into it."

"Are you still good enough?"

"If I'm not, I'll just keep rhythm."

"Do you know any of those people?"

"Won't know until I get there."

"Who told you about it?"

He started to answer, but then realized he had no idea. Someone must've mentioned it, because it was firmly fixed in his head, so much so that he could even see the route clearly even though he'd never been there. He shook his head. "I don't know. Must've been a notice in the paper or something. Anyway, what do you think?"

She closed her eyes again. "I think I've been vomited on by a drunk redneck once already today and do *not* feel like dancing with a bunch of Cloud County hillbillies who would probably say 'konitchy-*wa*' and shout at me because they think I don't speak Engrish. You go if you want to."

He knew better than to take that last statement at face value. And truthfully, even though she was exhausted, Susie inspired a sudden amorous urge in him that momentarily overrode all thoughts of music. He leaned close, brushed her hair aside, and kissed the curve of her ear. "On second thought, I think I'd like to stay in. We can order pizza or something."

She opened one eye and looked at him. "Don, I'm *really* tired."

He ran his fingers lightly along her jawline. "Give me five minutes, and if I haven't gotten your attention, I'll quit."

"I'll give you two minutes."

"Three."

"Two and a half."

"Done." And with that he crawled off the couch, knelt on the floor at her feet, and slid her scrub pants slowly off, all the while humming low and deep.

She giggled, her eyes closed once more.

———

Chloe, Deacon, and Aiden stood at the front door. "Are you sure you'll be okay by yourself?" Deacon asked. "One of us can stay if you want."

Bronwyn, from her pillow-packed spot on the couch, held up a small black device. "I can call you if there's any problem."

"That's the TV remote," Chloe pointed out.

Bronwyn sighed, put down the remote, and picked up her phone. "Okay, *now* I can call you if there's any problem."

"Maybe I should stay with her," Aiden said.

Bronwyn looked at them. They were silhouetted against the last of the day's sunlight, each carrying a musical instrument in a well-worn case. Deacon had his fiddle tucked under his arm, Aiden's guitar case barely cleared the floor as it waved in his hand, and Chloe held her autoharp close to her chest. Bronwyn felt entirely left out. "Will you—*all* of you—get on out of here? I don't want any pity company. Tell everyone at the barn dance I'll see 'em soon, okay?"

"Come on, everybody into the truck," Deacon said. He was the last one out the door, and glanced back at his daughter. "Normally I'd tell you not to have a wild party while we were gone."

She smiled. "Normally I'd say I wouldn't, then I would."

The screen door slammed. Bronwyn sat on the couch and stared at the dark TV screen until she heard the truck's engine fade into the distance. The silence unique to the mountains settled in around her, broken only when the refrigerator's compressor kicked on.

She turned on the TV and began flipping channels, careful to avoid any news. She stopped when she got to some horrid science fiction movie about a half man, half mosquito. For ten minutes she laughed at the inanity. Then, as darkness settled in outside, she fell asleep.

In her dreams she saw, as if flying above it, the supply convoy rumbling down the highway to Basra. The sun blazed through the dust and sand. She banked to the left, changing direction as easily as a bird, and watched the scurrying insurgents, black against the bright sand, take position for their ambush. Their gun barrels waved like insects' antennae.

She was not alone. She felt the presence of her haint Sally Olds beside her on the wind. Bronwyn did not turn to look.

Then she snapped awake as a car horn blared the first bars of "Dixie" from right outside the door.

She started to jump up, then remembered her leg. She wrapped the plastic cast around it and fastened the Velcro straps. She got to her feet just as someone pounded heavily on the door. A tall figure stood outlined in the glare from headlights. She flicked on the porch light, knowing who it would reveal.

Dwayne Gitterman stood there, his hands insolently on the top of the doorframe. The pose displayed his muscular body to great effect, and his smile beneath his cowboy hat was the same knowing leer it always was. His eyes were red from dope and drink, but everything else was as attractive as she remembered it. Behind him his truck was parked in the front yard, its headlights cutting through the night. Insects danced in the horizontal shafts.

"Hey, baby," he said. "Home alone?"

"I ain't your baby," she said through the screen. "Go away, Dwayne."

"Aw, you don't mean that." He picked up a twelve-pack box of Budweiser and waved it back and forth. "You ain't gonna send me out to drink this all alone, are you?"

Bronwyn was caught between two equally unexpected reactions. One was purely physical: Dwayne would always be someone whose mere presence got her blood racing and juices flowing. She remembered one night when he'd bent her roughly over the dropped tailgate of that very same truck, hiked up her denim skirt and gone at her with a ferocity that put bruises across the tops of her thighs. She'd never thought she could feel that kind of desire again, and having it strike so unexpectedly disoriented her a bit.

The other response was pure loathing. This was Dwayne, the boyfriend who'd spent six solid months trying to get her into a threesome, who'd abandoned her topless on a gravel road after an argument, who'd forgotten to take the condom off after drunkenly coupling with another girl just before he picked her up, and who generally treated her like a convenient piece of meat most of their time together. Now he showed up unannounced, no doubt after hiding and watching everyone else leave for the dance, certain that his lazy smile and country-boy charm would have Bronwyn's panties on the floor in no time.

"Dwayne, so help me I'll get the shotgun and blow new holes in you if you don't get out of here," she warned.

"You couldn't hurt me, Bronwyn," he said smoothly. "There's too much history between us."

"Yeah, just like between Iran and Iraq."

He held up a plastic bag. "I've got something to take the edge off that pissy mood."

She sighed. "Dwayne, *please.* I had surgery yesterday, I'm really not in the mood. Call me later this week and we'll see."

"We'll see? That's not a no."

"Boy, nothing gets past you, does it?"

"Nothing as hot as the Bronwynator, baby."

Something flared deep in her chest at the use of that nickname, and she slapped the wall beside the door so hard, the impact rippled in her aching leg bones. She could almost feel his throat crushing between her hands, and was grateful for the screen separating them. She hissed, "Get the fuck out of here, Dwayne. Now! Don't say another goddamn word."

"Okay, I'm going, jeez." He stumbled down the porch steps to his truck. "Goddamn, must be on the rag or something," he muttered as he fumbled into the cab. The engine roared to life, and she felt the thump of the truck's bass playing some hip-hop tune. Things rattled on shelves throughout the house. He turned sharply, cut deep ruts in the yard, and roared off down the driveway.

She stayed looking into the darkness for a long moment, letting her emotions sort themselves out. At some point she realized tears had run down her face, but she hadn't noticed until she tasted the salt on her lips. She switched off the porch light, turned, and nearly screamed.

Sally the haint stood between her and the TV. In the bright light, the gaping wound in her side was even clearer. The broken ends of the ribs showed white through the red meat of her flesh, and the tattered dregs of multicolored organs dangled in space.

"Y'all did the right thing," she said. Then she vanished.

Bronwyn stared at the space Sally had just occupied; she was close to hyperventilating. She managed to hop to the couch, where she pressed herself back into a corner, a pillow clutched to her chest. She stared at the TV, where a tall actress hawked cell phones.

A line popped into her head:

Shall the sycamore branch bend for you?

She sat up straight. That wasn't a song she remembered; that was something new. She found a pencil and scrawled the lyric along the edge of the *TV Guide* cover.

She was asleep when Deacon, Chloe, and a very tired Aiden returned home at 2 A.M. Aiden mumbled, "G'night," and slumped off to bed. Chloe draped a blanket over Bronwyn and tucked it in around her shoulders.

"Want me to carry her to her room?" Deacon asked softly.

Chloe shook her head. "Let her sleep here. I need to wash her sheets tomorrow anyway."

He nodded. "I'm going to check the weather for in the morning. I'll be along in a bit."

Chloe kissed Deacon and went off to the bedroom. He settled on the other end of the couch and muted the TV, putting on the closed-captioning so he wouldn't wake Bronwyn. He watched the Weather Channel until he, too, nodded off.

Bronwyn awoke around three and lay very still so as not to disturb her father. Her leg ached from being in one position for so long, and she desperately needed to pee, but she didn't want to move.

In the changing light from the TV, she studied Deacon's face. He was a handsome man; he was, in fact, her *standard* of handsome. His jaw was firm, his eyes steady without being cruel, and his mouth settled into a nice neutral line when he wasn't actively smiling. He wore his hair longer than most men his age, which also made him look younger. In her sleep-fuzzed mind, she realized that if he wasn't her father, she'd definitely find him attractive and probably let him know. The thought woke her all the way, and she blinked hard to dislodge the idea.

And yet he was, always, her father. From her earliest memories he'd been the strong, steady influence that she both craved and rebelled against. He was fair but unafraid to be tough, and whenever he'd taken the belt to her backside, she knew she deserved it. She'd never forget the time he'd whipped her for nearly setting the house on fire with a bottle rocket; she found him later sitting under a tree, looking sadly at her baby picture in his wallet. No amount of blows to her ass could ever make her feel as bad as that tableau.

She carefully changed position so she could rest her head in his lap. When she was a little girl they used to watch car races and football this way, Deacon stroking her hair and explaining the intricacies of the sport to her. She wanted to be a football player and a race car driver then, so he'd be proud of her. He never told her she couldn't.

His breathing was steady and deep, and he smelled of hay from the barn dance and the old-fashioned aftershave he always wore. The fabric of his jeans, warm from his body, pressed into her cheek. She closed her eyes and tried to remember how safe and happy she felt here, with her daddy in front of the TV. But the emotion hovered just out of reach.

Then she felt his hand lift and gently run down the length of her hair. She closed her eyes and sighed. "Worried about your mama?" he asked sleepily.

"Worried about everything."

"That's a big plateful. Maybe you shouldn't get everything from the buffet all at once."

"Aren't you worried?"

He shifted a little as he stretched and yawned. "You know, I suppose I am. But honey, the song goes on. The music carries on the night wind. If your mom goes, I'll still hear her again when my time comes."

She was silent for a long moment. Then she said, "I've seen people die, Daddy. I may have even killed some. It's not pretty like you taught us. There was no song, no night wind."

"That was them. This is us."

"And what if I never learn the song? What if—?"

He lightly pinched her cheek and said, with mock sternness, "What if I turn you over my knee and smack you? I know that no-account Gitterman boy was out here tonight. He tore up the front yard with that big truck of his. You ain't never too big for me to spank, you know."

She smiled. She didn't have to tell him that she'd sent Dwayne packing. "Yes, sir, I know."

He twirled one strand of her hair around his finger. "We're the Tufa, honey. Our songs go on, just like they did in the Green Country, just like they have since we got here. You'll learn your mama's song." After a moment he added, "And you need to get well enough to come to the dance. You need to stretch your wings."

"I know it, Daddy," she agreed.

17

Dwayne popped open a fresh beer and took a long swallow. He closed his eyes to savor it, then heard the rippling buzz that meant he'd drifted onto the warning ridges at the shoulder of the highway. He overcompensated and swerved into the other lane. Luckily there was no traffic, and he managed to get back on his side of the road. The yellow and white lines in his headlights grew hazy and split into multiples the farther they were from his truck.

He had an erection that *ached*. All he could think about were the times he'd had Bronwyn Hyatt. In the two years she'd been gone, no other girl had come close to turning him on the way the Bronwynator did. He *needed* to fuck her again, to muscle and slam that wiry, strong little body until he found release as deep within her as he could manage. He needed to hear her scream and moan, to feel her retaliatory blows as he hurt her.

Seeing her had been awful. He shouldn't have gotten

stoned first, he realized as he inhaled the smoke from the joint. That was his mistake. It always dulled the edge of his charm. He should've watched patiently until her family departed, then maybe taken a few tokes for luck. He definitely shouldn't have smoked a joint and a half, as well as shotgunned three beers, as he waited for the Hyatts to leave.

Yes, if he'd been straight, she would've dropped to her knees and sucked him off before even saying hello. He was certain of that. He recalled the many times he'd looked down at the top of her head, her wide bare shoulders visible below her tangled black hair as she willingly serviced him, and the ache only intensified. God, he *had* to fuck her again, and soon. His balls would explode if he didn't.

He almost missed the curve where the road turned toward Needsville. Low branches slapped his windshield as he came close to the ditch.

He took another drink and tried to form a plan. If he could get Bronwyn alone, he could have her; there was no way she could physically overpower him, and he wasn't above tying her down if she gave him any trouble. In fact, he remembered times when she'd enjoyed that. But the opportunity to do that was twenty minutes ago, when he'd stood outside her door. Just a simple yank to open the screen, then a few slaps to show her how much he needed it. He'd make it up to her later, after his urges had been sated. Her cast might be a problem, since it meant she couldn't wrap those thighs around him. He could always turn her facedown, he supposed, and take her that way. He was sure Chloe Hyatt kept some Crisco in the kitchen that would do in a pinch to ease things along.

But she's a First Daughter, the seldom-heard voice of his conscience managed to say. *Just like her mom.*

He was so lost in the sudden fantasy of a threesome with Bronwyn and her mother that he didn't notice the blue lights pull out of the roadside darkness and onto the blacktop behind him. By the time he spotted them, the state trooper was almost on his bumper.

"Fuck!" he yelled, tossed the roach into the open beer, and threw the can out the window. He slammed the gas pedal to the floor.

Bob Pafford didn't need to run the license plate of the truck in his headlights, especially when he saw the beer can fly out the window and bounce into the dark. He knew it at once, and he smiled grimly at the thought of who was inside. Would he be lucky enough to catch Bronwyn Hyatt as well as Dwayne Gitterman? Or would it just be the redneck thug alone? Perhaps some other girl was with him, one willing to do anything to keep from getting a police record. . . .

He thanked whatever urge sent him off the interstate and onto the Cloud County secondary roads. Normally there would be so little traffic on a Sunday night that he might not see another car at all, let alone one he could pull over and ticket. But on this night, the Cop God had smiled on him.

Suddenly Gitterman's truck leaped away like a spooked frog. Pafford floored it, and the big Crown Victoria's rumble rose to a solid, intimidating whine. The hash marks between the lanes blurred into a single line.

At the last second, Dwayne saw the road that led past the fire station. His truck skidded wide as he tried to turn, and both tires on the passenger side left the pavement. He cut ruts into the grass bank and felt the rear bumper slam into the side of the ditch before the tires got traction and shot the truck up, its front end now off the ground. It slammed down onto the blacktop, and Dwayne winced as he bounced up into the cab's roof. But he was back on the road, and he both floored it and switched off his lights.

The cloud of dust where Dwayne's truck skidded off the road was momentarily lit red by the truck's brake lights. Then it vanished. The Interceptor shot through the dust and for a moment Pafford saw no sign of the truck. Then he spotted the reflection from a distant license plate.

It took Pafford a moment to realize what had happened; the drunken fool was running blind on a moonless night. This could only end one way.

That made Pafford smile.

Dwayne leaned so far forward, his forehead touched the windshield. He knew the road ran straight for about three miles before it began to weave with the rising terrain. He had to put as much distance as possible between him and the asshole cop before the curves started, because there was no way he could navigate them without headlights.

"Come on, cocksucker," he whispered. "Come *on*. . . ." Thoughts of fucking Bronwyn had been replaced by the chest-wrenching memories of the time he'd spent in jail. He'd rather end up wrapped around a tree than endure that again.

Pafford gritted his teeth in rage. The truck was slowly pulling away, the license plate now a dim glow at the far end of his headlights. "You're not getting away from me, Gitterman," he said aloud. "It's not happening."

Then the truck was gone. Ahead he saw only empty road.

His roar of rage made his own ears ring.

As if in response, the license plate reappeared. Now it rushed toward him, and he realized the vehicle ahead was traveling much more slowly than his car. He stood on the brakes, his shoulders straining back against the seat, hands fighting to hold the wheel steady. He stopped barely a car's length behind the other vehicle.

The old tan Chevrolet station wagon put on its right turn signal and pulled off the road. It sat there with its emergency flashers blinking in the night.

Pafford gasped for air. He smelled the skid-scorched tires and the fresh sweat from his own body. He waited until the blood no longer thundered in his ears before he took his foot off the brake pedal. The cruiser crept forward, and he eased it to a stop, almost touching the station wagon's bumper. He got out, adjusted his hat and belt, then strode with practiced arrogance to the driver's window. His legs felt wobbly; he hoped it didn't show. He shone the flashlight inside the vehicle.

Rockhouse Hicks squinted into the light. "Problem there, Officer Pafford? I got out of your way quick as I could, but you come up on me awful fast. Surely I wasn't speeding, this ol' heap barely cracks fifty going downhill."

Pafford clenched his teeth again. He knew Hicks carried some weight among the Cloud County Tufa population, but there was something indefinable about this old man that always gave him the creeps and, although he'd never admit it, scared him. "Mr. Hicks," he said, "I was in pursuit of a pickup truck running with its lights out. Did you see it?"

Hicks cleared his throat and spit phlegm past Pafford into the night. "Dwayne Gitterman's truck?"

"That's the one."

Hicks's expression didn't change, but somehow he conveyed mockery with his eyes. "No, 'fraid not. Only other car I've seen is yours."

Pafford's free hand automatically went for his gun, as it always did when faced with an uppity motorist. But he caught himself. Calmly he asked, "Are you absolutely sure about that, Mr. Hicks? There's no place along here he could turn off. He had to pass you."

"Maybe he flew over me, then," Hicks said. "You mind getting that light out of my eyes? Makes 'em water."

Pafford switched off the light. For a moment afterwards, Hicks's eyes seemed to glow red with some inner illumination, and their surfaces looked compound, like those of an insect. Then it faded, and the old man said, "Unless you're going to give me a ticket for not knowing where Dwayne Gitterman is, I reckon I'll be heading on home. Good night, Officer."

Hicks started the engine, put on the left turn signal, and pulled out onto the empty highway. His taillights slowly faded into the distance.

At the first curve, Dwayne had pulled his truck into a tractor path and hidden it behind a stand of trees. He killed the engine, so the only light came from the starry, moonless sky. He guzzled another beer and watched the road for any sign of the trooper. He heard no approaching engine, only the insects in the trees and the pops of his own cooling motor.

Then he jumped and shrieked when someone knocked on the window.

He scooted across the seat to the passenger door, holding the beer can out in front of him like a weapon. He saw a shadow beside the truck taller than the cab. His first thought was *It's fucking Bigfoot!* and he started to reach for the pistol he kept under the seat. Then a voice muffled by the glass said, "Don't be such a pussy, man."

He switched on the dome light. It revealed the handsome, blank face of Stoney Hicks outside the door. "What the hell are you doing out here?" Dwayne said, his voice high.

Stoney laughed. He was physically very similar to Dwayne, except writ large: taller, broader, and if possible, even smoother with the ladies. He'd left a trail of broken hearts and lovelorn suicides among the non-Tufa population all around Needsville starting when he hit puberty. His voice always sounded sleepy and bored. "Watching you piss your pants, I reckon. What's wrong with you?"

Dwayne scooted across the seat and out the driver's door. "That asshole Bob Pafford was after me. I barely got away."

"Guess it's your lucky night, then," Stoney said.

Headlights appeared through the trees as a vehicle approached on the highway. "Shit," Dwayne said, and started to jump back in the truck.

Stoney grabbed his arm. "Just relax. That's Uncle Rockhouse. He probably wants to talk to you, seeing as how he saved your ass and all."

The station wagon pulled in behind Dwayne's truck and

stopped. The headlight beams stayed on as Hicks emerged. He hitched his pants, spit into the dark, and walked over to Dwayne. "Ain't you a piece of work. Running from the law with no lights on a moonless night. How drunk are you?"

Dwayne swallowed hard, looking from uncle to nephew. Stoney Hicks intimidated him as few men his own age did, and Rockhouse *terrified* him. The stories whispered about the old man would not have been out of place in a *Saw* movie. "I dunno . . . I've had a few."

"You been out to see your old girlfriend?"

Dwayne's mouth went dry. "Yeah."

"Yes, sir," Stoney corrected, and painfully squeezed Dwayne's right biceps for emphasis.

Dwayne repeated, "Yes, sir."

"Good. You be sure you keep after her, now. Don't want her running off with somebody from outside the county." He stepped close. "Ain't that right?"

"Yes, sir."

"Good. Hate to think what might've happened to you if I hadn't been here tonight. Come on, Stoney."

Stoney released Dwayne's arm, muttered, "Pussy," and smacked him lightly on the back of the head.

Dwayne watched the two Hicks men depart. He stood there for a long time trying to sort through the evening's events, and it was quite a while before the two strangest things registered on him.

What the hell had Stoney Hicks been doing out here? And why did Rockhouse care about him and Bronwyn?

Stoney watched Dwayne's taillights recede, then turned to his uncle. "That boy's dumb as a damn snail shell. He's been smoking dope so long, he ain't got but three brain cells left, and they don't all work at the same time."

"That's okay," Rockhouse said, and spit into the night. "All he's got to do is get Bronwyn Hyatt back under his thumb."

"Why don't you let me do it?" Stoney said. "Hell, ain't a girl out there I can't get on her back." He wasn't bragging; in his entire life, he'd never had a girl refuse him. Most Tufa girls knew not to go anywhere near him, but there were plenty of others around.

Rockhouse glared at him. "Yeah, you can *git* 'em, but you leave 'em useless, so eat up with love for you that they wither up and die."

He shrugged. "Ain't my fault."

"That ain't what I mean. I want everyone to see the little Hyatt whore bring herself down, not have her be took down by one of us. I ain't making no martyrs." He spit again, then shook his head. "She shoulda died in that damn desert. She left here, she took herself and her song away from us, she shoulda fucking gotten her brains blown out. Instead she comes back a hero."

Stoney said nothing. Now he understood why Rockhouse hated the Hyatt girl so much. Like Rockhouse himself, she'd gone away and found disaster, but unlike his uncle, she'd come back a hero. Even if she'd been part of their clan and not Mandalay's, the old man would've hated her.

"She's home now," Stoney said at last. "She'll be back to her old habits soon enough."

"Damn well better be," the old man muttered, and slapped his keys into Stoney's hand. Then there was a rustle of large age-battered wings, and Stoney stood alone in the dark. He hummed as he walked to his uncle's station wagon.

18

The sun touched Bronwyn's face through the window. She blinked and frowned as she awoke; there was no way the sunrise could come through her bedroom window at that angle. She rose on her elbows and squinted into the glare before she realized she was still on the couch, and the light was reflected from a car's windshield. At the same moment, she comprehended whose car it was.

The excitement was almost too much for her as she struggled to get the Velcro straps in place around her leg. When that was done, despite the protests of her sleep-stoked bladder, she grabbed her crutches and hobbled toward the front door. "Kell!" she almost screamed.

She blinked into the dawn as she emerged onto the porch. Chloe and Deacon sat with her older brother, all of them looking at her. It was the first time she'd seen Kell in two years, and he looked broader, older and more mature. His black hair hung in unruly strands to his shoulders, and his chin was fashionably stubbled.

When he stood, she swore he was a good two inches taller. She hopped toward him and he met her halfway with a big wrap-around embrace.

"So this is the big war hero," he said.

"Nah, there's some lots bigger than me," she said into his chest. She grabbed a handful of his T-shirt and anchored herself for the fiercest hug she could manage, pressing herself into him. For the first time, she felt like she was truly home, and that everything would be all right.

She pulled back and looked up into Kell's face. The maturity in his eyes was different, much more like Deacon's than it had ever been before. She tucked his hair behind one ear. "You need a haircut, mister."

"And you need dancing lessons," he said with a grin, then picked her up and twirled her around. She laughed, the first time she'd done so without an edge of bitterness since she'd been home.

He put her down, kissed her on the forehead with a loud smack, and said, "I was beginning to think you weren't ever going to wake up. Let me see the leg."

She extended the plastic-sheathed limb for him.

"Ouch," he said. "Weren't you also shot in the arm?"

"That was nothing," she said with a dismissive wave. The gesture toppled her off balance, and Kell caught her. Both laughed and hugged again.

"You better sit down so you won't have so far to fall," Deacon said dryly, and pushed a chair out for her.

"Wait, I'll be right back, I really have to pee."

"Holler for your brother while you're in there," Chloe said.

Bronwyn used the bathroom quickly, yelled for Aiden to get out of bed, and returned to the porch. As she settled into a chair she said to Kell, "I thought you were coming home Saturday."

"I pulled an all-nighter Friday night to get ready for my last final," Kell said. "I was too tired to drive Saturday night, and then Sunday morning I got a call from the warehouse that one of the other stockers drove his ATV into a tree. So I worked an extra shift, then got up early this morning and headed home."

"You could've called."

"He did," Chloe said.

Bronwyn scowled. "Well, no one told *me*."

"Has she been like this all week?" Kell asked.

Deacon nodded.

The door opened and Aiden emerged, rubbing his eyes against the light. "Nobody woke me up," he slurred. "I'll miss the bus."

"You can stay home today," Chloe said.

"Yeah, you can help me unload my car," Kell added.

At the sound of his big brother's voice, Aiden squealed and jumped into his lap with such force that, had the chair not slammed back into the wooden porch rail, he would've knocked them both over. Everyone laughed.

"Nice to be missed," Kell croaked as Aiden hugged him.

"Aiden, let your brother breathe," Deacon said.

"Let's all play something!" Aiden cried. "C'mon, we're all here, let's do 'John Barleycorn.' "

Kell looked at Bronwyn. "What do you think? You up to it?"

Sweat beaded along her spine at the thought, but she managed to sound casual when she replied, "Sure, why not?"

Kell got his banjo from the car, and Aiden fetched Magda for Bronwyn. The others gathered their instruments, and for a moment the morning air filled with various tunings and adjustments. Then Deacon said to Aiden, "You're the one who wanted to play, hotshot, so you sing it. And count us off."

Aiden grinned happily. He lightly slapped the guitar as he counted four, and then the Hyatt family played together for the first time in over two years.

Aiden sang,

> There were three kings came from the west,
> Their victory to try;
> And they have taken a solemn oath,
> John Barleycorn should die.

The others joined in:

> Fol the dol the did-i-ay,
> Fol the dol the did-i-ay-ge-wo.

Bronwyn held to her mandolin like a life preserver. She played tentatively, sneaking peeks at Aiden's chording to see if she was both remembering correctly and putting her fingers in the right places. She sang softly as well, her voice tight and thin. But she *was* singing, she *was* playing, and she felt the stirring of her long-neglected wings in the music.

And then it happened. First her injured leg began to tingle, that maddening itch sensation that signals healing but makes you wish you were still injured. She flexed her toes and felt the muscles work more strongly than they had in weeks. Her calf, weakened from disuse, ached a little in protest but didn't give out. And despite the rigid support of the temporary cast, her bare heel began inexorably tapping against the wooden porch.

At first she didn't even notice it. After all, according to legend,

Tufas were born with their feet tapping. But then Deacon lowered his fiddle, looked at her with his slightest smile, and winked. He resumed playing before the others noticed, and she had to bite her lip to keep from giggling.

Terry-Joe Gitterman slowed his bike as he approached the Hyatts' home. Something in the air felt different. He stopped just out of sight, hidden by the overhanging trees. He let the engine die, then listened.

Music drifted down from the house. He recognized "John Barleycorn," and Aiden's adolescent voice. Then he picked out the instruments. Guitar, also Aiden. Chloe's autoharp, Deacon's fiddle. A banjo, which meant Kell Hyatt had returned from college at last. And . . .

He felt a lump rise in his throat. A mandolin.

He should feel a sense of accomplishment, he knew. After all, Bliss Overbay, second in line of the First Daughters, had given him an important task, and now he knew he'd accomplished it. Bronwyn was once again playing Magda. Yet he felt the sting of tears behind his eyes aching for release. He didn't understand until this moment how much he was looking forward to spending time with Bronwyn again, how he wanted to slip his arms around her slender body and guide her strong fingers to the right place.

But there was nothing for it now, he knew. She was playing with her family, and he would definitely be the odd man out. He turned the bike, kicked it into life, and sped away, grateful for the sharp wind in his eyes.

———

That afternoon, Don Swayback found the turnoff with no trouble.

He stopped in the middle of the highway and stared at the blatant turn he was certain had not been there before. He saw the intersection of Curly Mane Road, and the turnoff for Jenkins Trail. He saw the spot where he'd had the run-in with the state trooper. But this road, the one now plain before him, simply hadn't been there that day. There was no way he could've missed it. If only he'd thought to take photos for comparison.

He checked his watch. It was two forty-five. He shot several pictures of the turnoff in case it vanished again. Then he considered his options. He could go back to his office and show Sam the photos, proving he'd at least tried to do the interview. Or he could suck it up and actually try to do it for real.

He thought of Susie's disappointment if he came home with more excuses or, worse, no job at all. He sighed, turned off the highway, and headed toward the Hyatt residence.

The road dead-ended at their driveway, and the gate was open. He parked along the fence; after all, he hadn't been invited. Then he took a deep breath, checked his hair in the sun visor mirror, and got out.

As he climbed the hill toward the house, he saw a woman working in the flower bed off to one side. She hummed to herself, and had her back to him. He stopped a respectful distance away and said, "Excuse me?"

She turned, shielded her eyes with one gloved hand, and said, "Can I help you?"

He recognized her from his research, and his mouth was suddenly dry. His whole career might ride on what he said next. "Ma'am, my name is Don Swayback and I'm with *The*

Weekly Horn newspaper over in Unicorn. I'm guessing you're Mrs. Hyatt?"

She stood, removed her gloves, and walked to him. She wore cutoff shorts and a sleeveless top. Her skin was tanned dark brown, and her jet-black hair was pulled back in a ponytail. "I'm Chloe Hyatt," she agreed. "Swayback . . . I knew an Oswald who married a Swayback fellow."

"Bengenaria? Everyone called her Benji?"

"That's her."

"That's my great-grandmother." He frowned, taking in Chloe's comparative youth. Despite having three children, the woman looked younger than he did. "You *knew* her?"

"Knew *of* her."

"That's not what you said."

She smiled. It was beautiful, dazzling even, and Don suddenly felt decidedly uncomfortable. "Mr. Swayback, are you calling me a liar?"

He smiled as well. "No, ma'am, I'm sorry it came out like that. I'm here because I'd like to make arrangements to sit down with your daughter and do an interview with her. I know she's been badgered by the press, and I can appreciate that she still needs to recover from things. But I think the local readers have been ill-served by the national media, and I'd like to speak with your daughter about things other than the war or politics."

Chloe smiled faintly. "'Ill-served'?"

Don laughed. "Well, you know. . . ."

Movement caught his eye. A tall young man with hair to his shoulders emerged from the house and leaned on the porch rail as he watched them. Don tried not to let it rattle him.

Chloe made a strange motion with her left hand, almost like

she was trying to speak in sign language. He might not have noticed, except at that exact instant he felt a sharp pain above his left eye that made him wince. It faded immediately.

"So what would you want to talk to my girl about, if it's not the war or politics?" she asked.

"What it's like to be home, what she missed, what she didn't miss, and what she plans for the future. Her favorite memories of Cloud County that helped her get through her troubles, that sort of thing. We're not trying to beat the news channels at their own game. People read our paper for football scores and coupons."

"Howdy," a male voice called behind Don. He turned and saw an older man, dressed for farming, stride across the lawn. The young man now watched from inside the screen door. "Don't believe I've had the pleasure," the newcomer said neutrally.

"This is Don Swayback," Chloe said. "He's a reporter. But Benji Oswald was his great-grandmother, so he's one of us as well." She said that with a wink, although Don noticed the man looked a bit puzzled. "Mr. Swayback, this is my husband, Deacon."

"Well, pleasure to meet you, then," Deacon said as they shook hands. "But our newsworthy family member is dead to the world right now, I'm afraid. She was up early, and after lunch she went out like a light. Just like she used to do when she was a baby."

Don felt a sudden, embarrassing rush of relief. No interview today, and it wasn't his fault. "If you'd do me the honor of passing on my comments, I'd be really grateful. You can reach me here." He handed Chloe his card.

"You a musician, Mr. Swayback?" Deacon said.

Don blinked. "Er . . . funny you should ask, sir. I just dug my guitar out of the closet after about six years."

"There's a regular ongoing shindig some of us have every night around here. It's a private thing, so we don't advertise it or nothing, but I think you might enjoy it. Starts around sundown, goes until our fingers fall off. Bring your guitar and come sit in." With a chuckle he added, "Nobody there expects anybody to be too good, and you might run into my daughter there."

"I might do that," Don said. "Where is it?"

"Just follow Spruce Line Road. You'll know the turnoff."

The pain above his eye momentarily returned. He *would* know the turnoff, just as he would've if he'd gone through with his plans last night instead of spending the evening with Susie. The emotional certainty overrode any intellectual skepticism. "Thanks for the invite."

"We look out for our own," Chloe said enigmatically.

As they watched the reporter drive away, Chloe undid her ponytail and shook her hair loose. "What'd you invite him to the barn dance for?" she asked.

Deacon shrugged. "Had a feeling about him. You spotted it, too. He's got some of us in him, and it's more'n just skin deep."

"If it's from Benji Oswald, though, he's more Rockhouse's people than one of ours."

"Benji left. She knew what her blood was. I'd say that leaves him free to choose." Suddenly he stepped forward and yelled, *"Get outta here!"*

He kicked at the plants. A brown and yellow snake turned and moved off across the yard toward the weeds at the tree line.

"That could've been close," Deacon said.

Chloe chuckled. "That little bitty thing?"

"It was a copperhead."

"And if it bit me, I'd have a sore for a while. There's a patch of snakemaster growing right down the hill, it'd clear it right up."

"Maybe," Deacon said, continuing to watch the snake until it vanished. "You remember when we first saw Brownyn in the hospital down in Virginia? We knew she'd be okay, so even though it was hurtful to see, we didn't get that ache that you get when you worry someone might die."

Chloe said nothing, but put her hand on his back.

He continued to gaze after the snake. "I told her that if something happened to you, it was because the night wind called you and I was okay with that. But that was a lie, plain and simple."

"I know," she said.

He turned to face her. "You look so healthy, Chloe. So alive. If I start dwelling on what you might look like in a coffin—"

"Don't," she said. "Seriously. I worry about you, too, trying to keep it together without me. But it's all signs so far, and we may be reading them wrong. Even if we're not, I'm not going to stop living before I have to, you know?"

Before he could reply, Kell came down the hill saying, "Who was that?"

"Local newspaper guy," Deacon said. "Wanted to talk to your sister.

"What'd you tell him?"

"That she was asleep." He spit casually to one side, then added, "Say, why don't you take your sister to the barn dance tonight?"

Kell blinked. "Because I'm tired? I'm running on four hours' sleep, you know."

Deacon waved his hand dismissively. "Ah, you can sleep when the night wind blows you away. It'll do her good. And you're the only one who could get her to do it without a fight."

"All right," he said wearily, and headed back toward the house. Deacon winked at Chloe; she shook her head and pinched his behind through his overalls.

When Kell went back inside, he found Aiden still watching TV, switching through channels with methodical boredom. "Man, there's nothing on during the day. I might as well have gone to school."

Kell sat down beside him. "What are you going to do when school lets out next week?"

"Die of fucking boredom," Aiden said, then caught himself. "I mean . . ."

Kell laughed. "I know the word. Just make sure you don't say it around Mom."

Suddenly their sister's picture appeared, and Aiden stopped switching. Beneath the photo of Bronwyn in uniform were the words, HERO NO MORE?

The news channel announcer said, "It's been a week since Private Bronwyn Hyatt returned to her tiny hometown in Tennessee following her spectacular rescue. In that time, more sources have confirmed that her rescue was little more than a staged publicity event, even as the military continues to defend its actions."

The image switched to a man identified as MAJOR DANIEL MAITLAND, U.S. ARMY. "Private Hyatt was severely injured in combat, was taken to an enemy hospital, and kept under armed guard. U.S. Marines risked their lives to bring her out of that situation. I'm sorry that some people feel the need to insert politics into this, but those facts are indisputable."

The next talking head was Cole Kincaid, Democratic representative from Tennessee. "It appears that this young woman was in the process of being turned over to the Red Cross for transport back to the U.S. Command when the marines attacked. The doctor making the arrangements was killed, some say execution-style, by American troops. I'm determined to get to the bottom of this, no matter how high it goes."

"Wow," Aiden said. "Sounds like they don't believe she's a hero."

"To them she's not a real person," Kell said. "She's just a face they can exploit."

"What does 'exploit' mean? Is it like 'explode'?"

Kell smiled. "No, it means they'll use her to make themselves look better."

The newscaster returned. "There has been no public statement from Private Hyatt since she returned home a week ago to great fanfare." Footage of the parade appeared. "The army has said she will be honorably discharged, and wishes to return to private life. But the question remains: Was this young woman a hero, a victim, or simply in the right place at the wrong time?"

Kell took the remote from Aiden and turned off the TV. "That's enough of that."

Aiden rolled his eyes and sighed. "Now what do we do, then? If I tell Mom I'm bored, she'll just give me chores."

"Can't have that," Kell agreed. He pretended to think hard. "Let's get our squirrel guns and go pop some beer cans."

19

Don Swayback was alone in the *Weekly Horn* office. Before he left for the day, Sam had congratulated him on speaking with the Hyatts, then reminded him that it wasn't the same as doing the interview, which he still expected this week. Then he told Don to finish up the obituaries before heading out. That wasn't hard, just tedious, and the sepulchral tones of the area's undertakers always got on his nerves. When would these ghouls get e-mail?

He was about to dial the next one on his list when the front door opened, sending a shaft of hot afternoon sun into the room. A figure stood silhouetted in it, and Don said, "Come on in, you're letting out what little air-conditioning we've got."

The figure stepped forward and the door closed behind him. He was a heavyset young man with unruly blond hair and a prominent fat roll under his chin. He wore baggy shorts and a T-shirt that showed Uncle Sam urinating, Calvin-like, on the United

Nations symbol. He clutched a thin MacBook Air to his chest.

When his eyes finally adjusted and he saw Don, he said, "Hi. Are you the editor?"

"No," Don said as he stood. "I'm the staff. The editor's gone for the day. Can I help you?"

The man looked behind him out the door as if he thought he might be followed. Then he scurried over to Don's desk and sat in the chair opposite it. He looked Don over with uncomfortable scrutiny, paying special attention to his black hair. "Are you," he asked finally, "one of *them*?"

Don said nothing for a moment. "Define 'them,' and maybe I can tell you."

"The Tufa People."

"Oh. Yeah, I've got a little in me. But everyone around here does, pretty much. Why?"

The young man extended his right hand. "I'm Fred Blasco, the blogger. *Fred, White, and Blue,* you know? Twenty thousand unique hits a day? Linked to *Drudge* at least once a week? Anyway, I'm here because I wanted to corroborate some of my online findings by doing some fieldwork. I drove all the way from Atlanta to see Needsville, the home of the Tufa People."

Don looked around for any reason to avoid this conversation. The empty office gave him nothing. "This is Unicorn, not Needsville. If you need directions, I'll be happy to—"

"No, I got those from Yahoo," Blasco said. "What I want to know is if you, the local media, know who's living in your own backyard. Or should I say, *what* is living there."

Blasco's excitement had made him sweat, and the odor began to permeate the space. Don grew nervous. "Look, I don't know what you mean, and I'm really kind of—"

"Okay, look, just give me a minute to catch you up. I've been following the Bronwyn Hyatt story ever since her rescue. The bluebellies—liberals, Democrats, blue states, get it?—are out there jumping through hoops to make her look like less than a hero. And as far as I can tell, she hasn't said word one in her own defense. I wanted to know more about her, so I found out she was one of these Tufa People, and I started looking into that. Do you *know* about them?"

"Just what everyone around here knows."

"Do you know they were already here when the first white people arrived in this area?"

"Yes."

"Do you know that there are reliable accounts of some of them living two and three hundred years?"

Don blinked. "I never heard *that,* and I've lived here all my life. And, since I also do the obituaries, I can assure you plenty of the Tufa die much younger than that. I think someone might be yanking your chain. Where did you get your information?"

"Never mind. And here's more for you. Did you know that some people say they can fly?"

Don laughed before he knew he'd done it. *"Fly?"*

"Mock if you want, but I've talked to a lot of people over the Internet. They say that when the Tufa People meet for their secret ceremonies, they grow wings and can fly. They say it happens because the Tufa People are actually the remnants of the *Tuatha,* the original fairy folk who left England and Ireland centuries before any settlers came to the New World."

Don just stared. "I just want to be sure I'm following this, Fred. You say the Tufa . . . the people living over in Needsville, Tennessee, as we speak . . . are actually a lost tribe of Irish fairies?"

"I know how it sounds, believe me. That's why I had to come up here and see for myself. But look, let me show you something."

He opened the laptop on the edge of Don's desk and spent a moment typing. "My mom got me this Air for my birthday, it's so cool," he murmured, as if Don were his best friend.

"We don't have wireless," Don pointed out.

"That's okay, this is a file. Now look." He turned the laptop so Don could see the screen.

It displayed a satellite shot of rural countryside. The trees were clear, and at one edge a paved road cut across the corner. But along the far left side were two white silhouettes. Don had to admit they did look like the traditional image of fairies: humanoid forms with large butterfly-like wings, apparently moving fast enough to cause a blur.

"See?" Blasco said excitedly. "This is a Google image filtered through enhancement freeware. Those are *fairies,* man. In flight over Cloud County, Tennessee. For *real.*"

Don looked at the nondescript countryside. "That could be anywhere."

"I trust my source."

"And those could be just a couple of bugs close to the lens."

Blasco looked at him. "Of a *satellite?*"

Don's wariness now mixed with amusement. Whatever the origins of the Tufa might be, he was certain they were flesh-and-blood people. "Fred, look. I'm serious here. I have lived in this area all my life, and this is the first I've ever heard of this. My own great-grandmother was a full-blooded Tufa, and she never sprouted wings and fluttered off. Wherever you're getting this, my advice would be to check your sources a little more closely before you make yourself look foolish."

Blasco's expression tightened. "So you're one of them."

"Because I don't agree with you, I'm part of the conspiracy?"

His eyes narrowed with suspicion. "*I* never said there was a conspiracy."

"No, I guess you didn't." He stood, hoping the blogger would take the hint. "I don't think I can be any more help to you, Fred. Sorry. Best of luck with your story."

Blasco closed the laptop and stood. His face was splotchy with emotion, and a fresh sweat ring circled his collar. "This is the biggest story in the *world,* friend. And I gave you a chance to be part of it. When it breaks, you remember that."

Don stared after Blasco for several moments after the door shut behind him. It was the silliest thing he'd ever heard in his life, the kind of thing only someone who stayed at home all day blogging could take seriously. And yet . . .

He sat back down, opened a search engine, and typed in the word *fairy*.

Blasco drove his rental car out of Unicorn and headed toward Cloud County, guided by Yahoo Maps printouts. He drove for four hours without finding any of the turns or roads that led into Needsville, and finally ran out of gas within sight of the interstate. The road he was on, though, went under the highway without any ramps. So, already exhausted from the heat, he started walking across a small field and into a stand of trees, toward the towering sign that indicated a gas station at the next exit ramp.

20

Bronwyn opened her eyes and saw Kell standing over her bed. She jumped, startled.

He smiled and said, "Boo."

She sat up and yawned. "Why are you watching me sleep?"

"I'm not watching you sleep, I'm waking you up. Get dressed."

Then she saw the darkness outside. "Holy shit, how the fuck long was I out?"

"You kiss our mama with that mouth? C'mon, wash up and put on some pants."

"Why?"

"We're going for a drive."

She looked at the bedside clock. "It's eight o'clock at night."

"And they said you had brain damage."

"Seriously, what's the deal?"

"Seriously, get your ass in gear and I'll tell you." He pulled a strand of her hair and winked. "Trust me."

She swung her legs over the side of the bed. Her broken leg was ridiculously smaller than its mate due to the muscle atrophy, but it looked surprisingly pink and healthy around the incisions. She wiggled her toes; the tingling was almost gone. "Hand me my crutches, will you?"

"Do you want your cast?"

"Hell no. I'm taking a goddamn shower like an adult."

He nodded at the stitched places. "Are you supposed to get those wet?"

"Probably not."

"Want Mom to help?"

Bronwyn used the crutches to stand and tucked them under her arms. "No, I don't. I'm twenty years old, I should be able to wash myself." She looked down and added quietly, "But do me a favor, stand outside the door and listen for a loud thud, will you?"

He laughed. "Sure."

An hour later they were in Kell's car, riding smoothly over roads guaranteed to rattle the bones of the non-Tufa. Bronwyn suspected she knew their destination, but hoped she was wrong.

She watched the light from the dashboard play across her brother's features. Kell had never been a skirt-chaser, being too focused on whatever task was before him, whether farming, studying, or working one of his many part-time jobs. But he'd grown into a handsome young man who no doubt drew the eye of many well-bred ladies on the UT campus. He knew full well the dangers of a Tufa man becoming too intimate with a non-Tufa girl, though; he'd seen Stoney Hicks's life marked by the suicides of desperate girlfriends he'd dropped with no more thought than if they'd been empty soft drink cans.

"So where are we going?" she asked finally.

"Don't be a moron. You know where we're going."

She felt a sudden chill, not of fear exactly, but certainly apprehension. "I'd rather not, Kell," she said, trying to sound casual. "I mean, I've only been home a week, and I just got the pins out of my leg on Saturday."

"I know," he agreed. "But you need to do this, and you're gonna."

She put her hands on the dashboard, fighting the panic. "I will, I promise, just not tonight, okay?"

He turned to look at her. "Why not?"

"Why not? Today was the first time I've played anything in two years."

He made a sour face. "I know, I heard you."

"Ha ha, smart-ass."

"Seriously, though, you weren't bad. Your song was there. So if a toe-dip like today worked, just think what a full dunking will do."

"Drown me," she said, but her real fear trumped her irony. "Kell, please, don't do this. Don't make *me* do this. I've got a bad leg, a haint on my ass, and all the worries about Mom. Let me figure out at least one of those first, okay?"

"I'm not making you. I'm *taking* you, but not making you. What you do when we get there is your business."

She stared into the night. The road became a path she could almost drive with her eyes closed, as any real Tufa could. Ahead a glow rose above the treetops. Her mouth was dry and her chest hurt from not breathing.

They rounded the last curve, and suddenly parked vehicles

lined either side of the road. Past them rose an enormous old barn, with SEE ROCK CITY painted in huge letters on its roof. Light spilled out through spaces between the wall slats, and shadowy figures moved inside. Down the hill below it, young teens danced around a bonfire.

Kell drove right up to the barn's side door. A large man in overalls and a weathered Tampa Bay Buccaneers cap sat on an old crate beside the door. He held a cigar box with duct tape reinforcement along its seams. Beside him, a ten-year-old boy sprawled on the ground playing a battered Gameboy.

The man's leathery face lit up when Bronwyn opened the car door. "Good gosh a'mighty, it's the Bronwynator!" he exclaimed. To the boy at his side he said, "Go in there and pass the word."

"Uncle Node, please," Bronwyn said as she eased her leg out. Kell got her crutches from the trunk and brought them to her. "I'm just here to listen and see people. We'll just slip in the back, that way we won't bother anybody."

"Bother, hell, this is an occasion." The boy had not moved, so he slapped him gently on the back of the head. "What'd I tell you?" The boy jumped up and scurried off.

"I'll go and park the car," Kell said. "Wait for me."

Noah Vanover, known to everyone as Uncle Node, stood and took Bronwyn by the shoulders. "You sure been missed here, Bronwyn. It does my old heart good to see you."

He released her and made a sign with his hands. She smiled and gave the appropriate sign back. Then she leaned up and kissed his cheek. It smelled of freshly turned earth after a rain. "I've missed you, too, Uncle Node. And this place."

Kell returned. "Anything special happening tonight, Uncle Node?"

"Just your baby sister coming back to us."

"I may not be all the way back yet," she warned.

"Well, if you ain't, you soon will be," Vanover said with certainty.

She followed Kell into the barn. As soon as the door opened, the music that had been barely audible outside hit her chest with a thump like a shell exploding nearby. For just a moment she smelled the desert's dry air, and burning blood, and cordite. Then she was back in the present, and the impact spread through her far differently than any mere ordnance concussion.

Kell sensed her change and patted her hand where it held the crutch handle. "Drowning?" he said over the music.

She shook her head. "Keep the life preserver handy, though, in case I hit a drop-off."

As always, the barn's interior seemed bigger than it appeared outside. It was lit mainly by thousands of tiny white Christmas lights. Hay bales covered with heavy blankets provided rough bleacher-style seating. The band riser was made out of old shipping pallets covered with particle board, and a row of ancient stage lights hung from the rafters directly above it.

Two hundred people danced on the hard-packed dirt floor, played music onstage, or just watched and socialized. Couples twirled in old-style formality, and some individuals also danced flatfooted on battered pieces of wood. The noise was rhythmic, twangy, and dug into Bronwyn's soul like a welcome parasite seeking blood from a host. And the itch it created was just as maddening.

Bronwyn surveyed the mass of dark hair, tanned skin, and wide, white smiles. Cliché said that all the mountain families were inbred, and to an outsider this sight would just confirm that; it looked like one enormous family, all close enough to share the same basic characteristics. But these were only the exterior signs; the real connection came at a deeper level, in the response to music that each of them experienced and shared. It was something so innate and deeply rooted that it was like drawing breath, and in a sense did link them as a single clan.

Heads turned toward her almost at once. She'd learned to dread that moment: lately, it was always followed by ridiculous praise, thunderous applause, and unearned standing ovations. But this time, except for some smiles of recognition and friendly nods, no one really reacted. It was as if she'd been away for days, not years. Or that she'd never left at all.

Kell led the way, making sure Bronwyn had plenty of room to maneuver her crutches. When the current song ended, old Mrs. Chandler stepped up to the microphone and said, "Ladies and gentlemen, we've got ourselves some real royalty here to-night, Cloud County's own hero, Bronwyn Hyatt. Why don't you come on up and play a little with us, Bronwyn?"

Before Bronwyn could answer, Kell said, "Now, Miz Chandler, she's just here to listen and visit tonight. Plenty of time for her to sit in later."

"That's fine, that's fine," Mrs. Chandler said agreeably. "We're just all mighty proud to see you back, Bronwyn. Mighty proud indeed."

"I'm sure glad to be here," Bronwyn called out, and waved. Then she turned to thank Kell for giving her a graceful way out, and let out a little yelp of surprise. Kell had vanished into the crowd, and now Terry-Joe Gitterman stood grinning before her.

"Hey there," he said. "Surprised to see you here."

"Wow, I mean . . . yeah," she said. He looked strikingly hand-some with his hair combed, in a dark blue polo shirt and faded jeans. There was surprisingly little resemblance to his brother.

Dwayne loved to get dressed up and show off, but he always seemed peacockish, preening and performing for his perceived audience. Terry-Joe had simply dressed up for the dance. "What are you doing here?"

He shrugged. "Just had one of those feelings this might be a special night."

Someone said, "Oops! 'Scuse me," and bumped her against Terry-Joe. He caught her easily, their gazes met, and suddenly she was in one of those moments when everything seemed to be frozen except for the two of them. She wanted to speak, to break the moment, but instead he seemed to be leaning nearer, his lips slightly parted. . . .

She blinked. He hadn't moved closer at all; had she imagined it? It wasn't impossible that he might *want* to kiss her; he clearly had a crush on her. But the fantasy had been hers, not his. She took a breath, forced herself back to the present, and said, "Thanks. Going splat wouldn't be very dignified."

"My pleasure," he said.

The opening notes of "I'll Twine 'Mid the Ringlets," played on Mrs. Chandler's autoharp, rang out. A fiddle and banjo joined in. The singer, an eight-year-old girl named Emaline, stepped to the microphone, which even fully lowered required her to tilt her head back and sing up into it. It did not affect her performance.

> *I'll twine 'mid the ringlet*
> *Of my raven black hair,*
> *The lilies so pale*
> *And the roses so fair. . . .*

Terry-Joe nodded toward the dance floor. "Come on."

"What, *dance*?"

"Sure. Trust me."

Bronwyn let Terry-Joe take the crutches away and prop them against the wall. Hopping on her good leg, she moved with him to the dance floor. The other couples gave them room and plenty of encouraging smiles. His hand went around her waist and pulled her close, forcing her to again look into his eyes.

He's seventeen, and he's never been out of the valley, she told herself. *He's a child, and not just legally.*

He leaned close. She felt his breath on her cheek. "My wings can hold us," he said like the wind sighing through the trees.

Emaline continued to sing:

> *I'll sing and I'll dance,*
> *My laugh shall be gay;*
> *I'll cease this wild weeping,*
> *Drive sorrow away....*

It reminded Bronwyn how glorious being a Tufa could be. The music formed around them like a physical entity dancing on sparkling wings. And then they, too, danced on wings that left trails of sparkles in the air as they swooped and twirled in time to the tune, merging with the music to become magical, timeless beings. Bronwyn's leg, unburdened by her physical self, no longer ached with the weight of injury and age.

And Terry-Joe was magical, too. He bore her into the music with the gracefulness of a true rider of the night wind. He may not have been a pureblood Tufa, but he was awfully close. His body felt hot and solid beneath her hands, and his fingers along her skin, even through her clothes, left little tingling trails. He brought her body to life like sunlight opening a morning glory blossom, banishing all traces of the numbness.

I chose not to love him,
Though he called me his flower
That blossomed for him
All the brighter each hour;
But I woke from my dreaming,
Took my life from his sway;
My visions of love
At last faded away.

When the song finished and they again touched solid ground, Bronwyn threw her arms around Terry-Joe and let him spin her through the air. The crowd applauded the music and dancing, and Mrs. Chandler returned to the microphone. "That sure was purty, wasn't it? Thank you, little Miss Emaline, and special thanks to Bronwyn Hyatt and Terry-Joe Gitterman. Now we'll be hearing from our own Paige Paine, back from the music college in Nashville."

As the next song began, Kell appeared holding two bottles of beer. He looked from Bronwyn to Terry-Joe, his face impassive. "Can't turn my back on you for a minute," he said as he handed his sister one of the drinks. "I thought I'd get the first dance."

"You snooze, you lose," she said, and took a long drink from the bottle. The beer was ice cold and felt amazing going down.

Kell turned to Terry-Joe. "That's some fancy footwork," he said, an edge of suspicion in his voice. "Didn't know you Gittermans could dance like that."

Terry-Joe shrugged modestly. "Your sister brings it out in me."

"She has been known to get men to do some crazy things," Kell agreed. He took a drink and added, "Men like your brother."

"Kell," Bronwyn quickly warned. From the time they were

children, Kell and Dwayne Gitterman had disliked each other; in fact, one reason Bronwyn had first dated him was to tweak her overprotective big brother. It had been one of her poorer decisions.

"No, that's okay, Bronwyn," Terry-Joe said. He met Kell's challenging gaze and said simply, "My brother ain't me. And family only goes so far. You have a problem with him, he's not hard to find. If your problem's with me, I'm right here."

Kell started to say something, then stopped. He nodded. "I reckon you're right. Everyone's their own. Sorry about that."

Bronwyn turned at the touch of a feminine hand on her arm. Bliss Overbay stood beside her. Her black hair hung in two braids beside her face and her tank top displayed the snake tattoo on her arm and shoulder. "Quite a dance," she said.

Bronwyn nodded at Terry-Joe. "Thank him; he held me up."

Bliss nodded approvingly. "He's true, all right." Then she turned to both men. "I need some private girl-talk with Bronwyn. If you'll excuse us?"

Both Terry-Joe and Kell made the hand gesture that signified respect for a First Daughter. Bronwyn took her crutches from Kell and hobbled after Bliss, past the hay-bale bleachers and out a side door into the night.

They moved away from the barn into the darkness at the edge of the forest. The teenagers' bonfire, where they pounded drums and danced around the flames, provided enough light for them to see each other. Bliss turned to her and said, "Was it a good idea leaving those two alone? I could smell the testosterone burning."

"They'll work things out," Bronwyn said. "Kell doesn't hate Terry-Joe, just Dwayne."

"That's not an exclusive club."

"No, not even among the Hyatts."

Bliss looked at her closely. "Are you sure you're over him? He had a mighty tight grip on you once."

As she said the word, she realized its truth: "Absolutely."

Bliss didn't seem convinced. "Have you seen him since you got back?"

"He came by the house last night after everyone left. He was drunk, probably stoned, and just wanted to fuck. I didn't even let him in. He's the past I'm not real proud of."

Bliss cocked one eyebrow. "Don't tell me the Bronwynator is *ashamed*?"

She was in no mood for teasing. "Did you bring me out here to lecture me on boys? When's the last time *you* had a date, huh?"

"Ouch," Bliss said.

Bronwyn sighed. A girl at the bonfire took off her T-shirt and began dancing in her bra. That kind of freedom seemed a million miles away. "I'm sorry, Bliss. I'm just tired of everyone knowing what's going on in my life. Being the center of the whole world's attention will do that to you."

Bliss continued to look at her with the penetrating, steady gaze. "Are you done?"

"Yes."

"Good. Because you know things are happening. How goes the music?"

"It's there, finally. Terry-Joe gave me a lesson Sunday morning, and then when Kell came home, everything kind of broke loose. I'm still rusty, but I'm not helpless."

"Also good." She stepped closer and spoke more softly. "The First Daughters are meeting at the next full moon, this Thursday. You have been specifically invited, to talk about the future."

Bronwyn nodded; this wasn't unexpected, but it was part of the whole reality of her mother's impending death that she didn't want to acknowledge. "I'll be there."

Bliss smiled. "And for your information, I had a date with a session guitarist two weeks ago, just before you got home."

"Really? Will there be a second date?"

"Maybe. I think I intrigue him, but he doesn't understand me. Kind of like you and that Reverend Chess, I imagine."

Bronwyn was glad the firelight hid her blush. "Him? He just keeps showing up. I don't encourage him."

"I think you should be careful."

She laughed. "Bliss, I can barely walk, I don't think I'm up to anything more strenuous."

"I'm not worried about what's between your legs, Bronwyn. I'm worried about what's in here." She tapped Bronwyn's chest over her heart.

"That? It's solid rock," Bronwyn assured her.

"That's not good, you know. Hearts melt; rocks shatter."

21

Don parked at the end of the line of cars. His chest felt tight with excitement the way it had on his first date with Susie back in college. The barn ahead glowed from within, as if some wondrous miracle was occurring among the hay bales and tractors.

As he got his guitar from the trunk, he impulsively picked up a couple of rocks from the gravel road. He stuck them in his pocket without really knowing why.

He heard the trilling, winding melody of a reel from inside the building. Fiddles, acoustic guitars, harmonicas, and mandolin melded in the tune. He smiled and hummed along, knowing the song even though he didn't consciously recognize it.

A bunch of kids sat around a campfire down the hill from the barn. A beautiful girl danced in low-slung jeans and a red bra as drummers provided a low, steady rhythm. One of the boys strummed a guitar and sang something Don recognized:

Don't feed the bear unless you know
You're faster than he is when it's time to go. . . .

Don stopped in the middle of the road. How *did* he know this stuff? Ever since digging his guitar out of the closet, he'd been surrounded by music, all of it beautiful, all of it somehow known. He had no trouble picking up the melodies, and even lyrics he was certain he'd never heard before felt like old rhymes learned in childhood. His trade, his skill was with words, cold and analytical descriptions of events denuded of any excess passion or meaning; so where did *this* passion come from?

A sudden burst of doubt made him look back at his car, then at the barn. He recalled Fred the blogger's insinuations about the Tufa, and his own Internet surfing for confirmation. He'd uncovered no link at all between the Tufa and fairies, which didn't surprise him. Still, he had learned that the true fairy folk, the Tuatha De Danaan, were considered anything but Tinker Bell–ish sprites. They were dangerous, and humans encountered them at their peril. And there were two perpetually warring tribes, the Seelie and the Unseelie. Some people said the same about the Tufa.

He shook it off. He wasn't here just to have fun, he reminded himself. He needed to find Bronwyn Hyatt and arrange an interview. He'd come this far; he might as well see it through.

An older man sat outside the side door, apparently collecting admission. He smiled as Don approached. "Howdy, neighbor. Beautiful evening, isn't it?"

"It is," Don agreed.

The man held out a cigar box. "Pay the toll, then rock and roll."

Don reached for his wallet, then happened to glance into the box. It contained no money, only stones of various sizes. Don put the rocks from his pocket in with them.

The man scrutinized him. "You're kin to Bengenaria Oswald, ain't you, son?"

Don blinked in surprise. "Yeah. She was my great-grandmother. She was from Needsville."

"Fine woman," he said sadly. "Sang like the wind. Shame she had to leave."

Like Chloe Hyatt, the man didn't look old enough to have known Great-grandma Benji. Don smiled nervously. "Never knew her myself. Nice to hear such good things."

Suddenly a ragged voice cried, "Hey! Hey, *you!*"

Don turned. A figure lumbered out of the dark woods, across the open space around the barn. Don reflexively raised his guitar case as a shield. Then he recognized the man.

"Holy shit, am I glad to see you," Fred Blasco gasped. He was covered in dirt and scratches, and his face gleamed with unaccustomed sweat. He still clutched the laptop to his chest, and used his free hand to lean on Don's shoulder while he took big gulps of air. "You're that guy from the newspaper office, aren't you?"

"Yeah . . . ," Don said, and tried to move away. He knew with utter certainty that Blasco should not be here. But Blasco's meaty hand tightened its grip.

"Look, I've been wandering in the woods since it got dark," Blasco said. "I got lost trying to find that goddamned town, and then I ran out of gas. I tried to go cross-country to a gas station, but once I got into the woods, I got all turned around, and couldn't get a signal on my cell." He opened his phone and scowled. "Still nothing. Dammit!" Then he saw the man beside the door. "Hi. Is there a working phone or a wireless connection here?"

"This-here's a barn," the old man said. "We don't let the cows have e-mail or long distance, as a rule."

The door opened, and two big young men, both with black hair, emerged in a blast of fiddle music. The door closed, silence returned, and one of them said, "Having a problem, Uncle Node?" They regarded both Don and Blasco with suspicion.

"This fella seems lost," the man called Uncle Node said with a nod at Blasco. "Can you help him find his way?"

"Wow, you're *all* Tufa People, aren't you?" Blasco said between wheezes. "Is this one of the places where you have your ceremonies? Any chance I could watch?"

"What's he talking about?" one of the young men asked.

"I think he's a little disoriented," Uncle Node said.

"We'll orient him right up, then," the other young man said. "Come on, friend."

The two of them guided Blasco down the gravel road into the night. Blasco protested, "Wait, fellas, really, I want to see what goes on. . . ." His voice quickly faded.

"Friend of yours?" Uncle Node asked Don.

Don shook his head. "He came by my office today. He's one of those Internet bloggers. Had some weird ideas about where the Tufa come from. I told him to go home."

"Good advice."

Don's eyes narrowed. "For me, too?"

Uncle Node laughed. "No, son, I'm sorry. We don't get too many people just wandering up here. No, you're Benji Oswald's great-grandson, you're family. Get on in there."

Don took a breath, mentally crossed his fingers, and opened the door.

The stage immediately drew his eye. A banjo picker, two fiddlers, and a girl hunched over an electric piano played a rip-snorting version of "The Queen of Argyll." The man singing was tall, thin, and dressed at least fifty years out of date. Along the wall lay a pile of instrument cases, some open and empty, others closed while their owners waited their turn. A girl in a cowboy hat and long denim skirt leaned against one of the old amplifier speakers and tuned her acoustic guitar, apparently oblivious of the music surging out around her.

He took in the rest of the room. The most striking thing about the crowd, he realized, was its amazing homogeneity: like him, everyone in sight had black hair and perfect white teeth. The room buzzed with energy, and with sudden urgency he wanted to be a part of it. He worked his way toward the stage.

A young man with a ponytail, his chin sporting a neat goatee, suddenly blocked his path. "Hey," he said over the music. "Don't believe we've met. Andy Silliphant."

"Don Swayback," he said as they shook hands. The music suddenly finished, and the two men awkwardly waited for the applause to end. When it did, Don added, "It's my first time here."

He expected some suspicion, maybe a question or two, but Andy merely grinned. "Well, then, let me show you around." He tapped the guitar case. "You here to play, I take it?"

"Maybe." He knew he should also ask about Bronwyn Hyatt, but at the moment it felt unbelievably rude. "I sure would like to try."

Andy laughed. "You'll be all right. Come on, let me introduce you to some folks."

He met a dozen musicians of all ages, all with the same Tufa look, all apparently without any suspicion of this stranger. The last was a slender woman with long braids, one upper arm wrapped with a snake tattoo. "We've met before," he said.

"We have?" Bliss Overbay said.

"You're an EMT, aren't you? Out of the Cloud County station?"

"Yes," Bliss said.

"I covered that train wreck last year, where it hit that truck full of people. I saw you there."

"Ah. Yes, that was a bad one."

It had been. A freight train plowed into a pickup truck carrying a load of Needsville people to a family picnic. Five people died at the scene, two later at the hospital, and only a toddler escaped unharmed. It had been one of those scenes that kept Don awake for weeks afterwards.

"You didn't want me to take your picture," Don continued. "That's why I remember you."

She nodded. "And you didn't. I remember *you* now. Thank you."

"This is getting kind of grim," Andy pointed out. "What's say Don comes up and plays with us a bit?"

"Sure," Bliss said. "Do you know 'Shady Grove'?"

He nodded.

Andy tapped Don's guitar case. "Then skin that song iron and let's throw down."

Bliss looked at him. "'Skin that song iron'?"

Andy shrugged. "One day I'll invent a catchphrase, you just wait and see."

They went onstage as an elderly lady clutching an autoharp said into the center stage microphone, "That's going to be it for me tonight, folks. I'll be turning things over to ol' Charlie Ray Bowles, and believe me, I wish I didn't have to." Good-natured laughter followed this teasing. "Here's the man himself, and y'all drive safely going home."

A squat little man in an enormous cowboy hat lumbered onstage and over to the microphone. "How's the wind tonight, folks?" he said, and there was some applause and cheering. "I figure we've had enough time for even the ladies to make it back from the facilities, so let's welcome Bliss Overbay, Andy Silliphant, and—" He looked at Don and frowned. "—and their special guest? . . ."

"Don Swayback," Don said as he put his guitar strap over his head.

"Don Stayback," Bowles said, then did an exaggerated double take. "Man, that's a weird name. You ever get any dates growing up?" He got a few more laughs than groans, which encouraged him. "I'd rather be called 'Don C'mon Over Here,' or 'Don Let's Be Friends.'"

"It's Swayback, not Stayback," Andy corrected. "Clean your ears with something other than your car keys, why don't you?"

"Oh, *Sway*back. That's a lot better." The look he gave the crowd conveyed the opposite opinion. "Well, let's welcome Mr. Swayback and his friends to our stage, why don't we?"

As the Tufas applauded, Bliss strapped on her guitar, Andy tucked his fiddle under his chin, and the three of them stepped up to the microphone. Bliss led them off and sang the first verse:

> *Shady Grove, my little love*
> *Shady Grove, my darling . . .*

Don had spent most of his musical life playing alone, in isolation, mastering chords he lacked the nerve to attempt before an audience. Yet suddenly here he was, strumming away on this obscure song he couldn't even recall learning, although he definitely knew it. His fingers found the changes with ease.

His eye was drawn to a young woman who stood in one of the open side doors, dancing by herself in slow, swaying contrast to the elaborate contra dancing around her. She looked familiar somehow, as if he'd known her once, long ago in his youth. But that wasn't possible, since she couldn't have been more than fifteen or sixteen now.

Suddenly he got chills as Bliss sang:

> *Well, I went to see my Shady Grove*
> *She was standing in the door,*
> *Flowers and braids all in her hair*
> *And little bare feet on the floor. . . .*

The lyric described the girl in the doorway precisely. She caught his eye and winked before turning away and fading into the night outside.

Don continued to play, but he felt disconnected, as if he'd somehow stepped into some parallel universe where songs came to life. Andy nudged him with a foot and nodded that they should join Bliss at the microphone for the final chorus.

Don was no shakes as a singer, let alone a harmony vocalist, but he somehow stayed on key as they finished the song. The applause was genuine and enthusiastic, and as it reached its crescendo Andy leaned close and said, "I bet you're related to Benji Oswald, aren't you?"

Too surprised to speak, Don just nodded. Andy laughed. And the whole purpose of this evening, to find Bronwyn Hyatt, was completely forgotten.

He had no idea how long he played. It seemed like hours, yet when he finally looked at his watch again, it was only ten thirty. The crowd had thinned a little, and he felt an inner certainty that it was time to leave. He said good-bye to the other musicians and put his guitar back in its case.

"Good show," Andy said as they shook hands. "Hope to see you back."

"Hope to *be* back," Don agreed.

"You know, you've got more Tufa in you than you think."

"Really?"

"Yeah. Your great-grandmother was a First Daughter. That carries some weight."

"In what way?"

Andy shrugged evasively. "We'll talk more if you come back."

"You said 'if,' not 'when.'"

"That's because it's entirely your call, man. If you want to feel like you did onstage again, come on back next week. If it was too weird for you . . ." He trailed off with another shrug.

Bliss joined them. "What sort of nonsense is Andy telling you now?"

"He invited me back next week," Don said.

"Well, shoot, that's what I was about to do," Bliss said. "You've got a nice sound."

Don smiled. "Thanks." He looked around at the departing crowd. "Listen I hate to ask this, but I don't suppose either of you know Bronwyn Hyatt, do you?"

"Why?" Andy asked.

"To tell you the truth, she's why I originally came here. Her father said I'd find her here, and I'm supposed to interview her for my newspaper if I want to keep my job. But . . ." He shrugged and smiled. "Guess I got carried away."

"That'll happen," Andy said.

"I know Bronwyn," Bliss said. "You just missed her tonight. She left about the same time you got here. I'll mention you to her when I see her."

"I appreciate that," Don said. "But don't put her on the spot or anything. She's been through enough."

Bliss cocked her head, as if this response pleasantly surprised her. "I'll remember you said that."

Still jovial, Don walked back to his car. He looked around for Shady Grove—no, he corrected himself, for the girl who'd reminded him of the song—but did not see her.

Don stopped his car at the end of the gravel road, looked both ways into the darkness, then pulled out onto the highway. The instant he did, bright headlights blinded him and a distinctive siren blared. He slammed on the brakes, stopped in the middle of the road, and held up his hand to block the light.

"You best put up both hands, boy," a man's voice said through a loudspeaker. Don recognized it, and did as instructed.

The headlights went out, and now he saw the flashing red and blue ones atop the state trooper car parked beside the intersection. Bob Pafford got out and switched on a flashlight, which he also shone right in Don's face. He took his time approaching the car.

Don felt the kind of dread that comes only from anticipating not death, but pain. Pafford tapped the huge flashlight on the window. Don rolled it down.

"You're parked in the middle of the road, boy," Pafford said with belittling patience. "That's a traffic hazard."

Don said nothing.

"Where you coming from?"

"Visiting some friends, sir." He hoped his tone was flat and noncommittal, but suspected that any answer would be the wrong one.

"You been drinking?"

The question took Don by surprise. Actually, he'd had nothing to drink, not even water, since he left home, and was suddenly aware of his own ravenous thirst. "No, sir," he said.

Pafford leaned down and shone the flashlight in Don's car. Then he blasted it into Don's face, studying him for a long moment. Finally he stood with a sigh and said, "I ain't getting paid to chat with you high-yellow Tufa bastards. Get on out of here, boy, before I decide you were resisting arrest."

Don was speechless. He put his car in gear and drove carefully away, watching the rearview mirror for any sign of pursuit. The cherry-top lights blinked out just before he topped the first hill, and he didn't feel truly safe until he was in his own driveway and five minutes had passed without Pafford roaring down the road toward him.

He sat alone in his living room, all the lights out, for a long time. Susie had pulled a double shift, so the house was empty. It seemed impossible, but had Pafford truly not recognized him? He clearly thought he was one of the local Tufas, not the reporter he'd chased away from the Hyatts; was he that stupid, or was something else at work? Fairies, he'd learned earlier that very day, could hide their true appearance behind something called *glamour*. And if he was a Tufa, and the Tufa were fairies . . .

"Oh, come on," he said aloud. That was as crazy as believing the real Shady Grove stood in the barn door, like a shade summoned by a song.

No, not a shade. Around here, they called them *haints*.

22

The First Daughters of the Tufa met irregularly, but always on the full moon. There was no arcane significance to this, only the practical: they convened deep in the forest and wanted to avoid flashlights or anything else that might allow them to be followed. There were those who resented the power of the First Daughters, especially among their opposite number in the Tufa clans led by Rockhouse Hicks.

Bronwyn's recovery would have astounded her grim army doctors. Less than a week after her surgery, she no longer needed the cast, and had replaced her crutches with a single walking stick loaned to her by Carvin' Ed Shill. The handle was shaped like a rattlesnake's head, complete with the little pits along its lips. The motif continued to the tip, which was a genuine rattle from a huge diamondback, shellacked and varnished to impenetrable hardness.

When Bliss arrived to pick her up, Brownwyn limped down the yard under her own power. Kell and Aiden flanked her but didn't actively help. With the setting sun flaring through the thin cotton dress, Bronwyn looked like she was edged with flame. Considering the topic of the upcoming meeting, that was truly a bad omen.

"You've come a long way, baby," Bliss said.

"This isn't Virginia," Bronwyn said, "and I ain't Slim." Up close the pain and effort tightened her face, but her determination kept her going.

Kell opened the passenger door and helped Bronwyn inside. Aiden watched with evident concern. "Be careful," he called to his sister.

Kell kissed her cheek and said, "Remember, that cane's for walking, not whacking people."

"I never whacked anyone who didn't need it," Bronwyn said. She turned to Aiden. "And don't look so serious, I'll be back before you go to bed." She glanced up at the house, but saw no sign of her mother. There wasn't much Chloe could say, but it still sent a pang through Bronwyn; the meeting was to prepare for Chloe's possible death.

"I'll take good care of her," Bliss said. Once they were on the road, she turned to Bronwyn. "I guess you know we're going to talk about your mother. Everyone will want to know if you're ready to learn her song."

"I'm doing my best."

"Show me."

Bronwyn closed her eyes, then began to sing:

> *Boys on the Cripple Creek 'bout half grown,*
> *Jump on a girl like a dog on a bone.*
> *Roll my britches up to my knees,*
> *I'll wade old Cripple Creek when I please.*

Bliss nodded. "That's good."

"Mom keeps after me. Says it won't take long to learn her song when I'm ready."

They reached the turnoff for the road that led to the meeting. Once they went behind a stand of trees, they would be invisible from the blacktop. They went down a hill until the headlights revealed five other cars parked along the road. Bliss parked her truck; then she and Bronwyn began the descent to the meeting place on foot.

It took longer than normal because of Bronwyn's injuries. She remembered her first time here, brought by her mother to meet the latest generation of First Daughters, all children like herself. Once a daughter reached what they called "the age of cognition," she was offered the chance to join her mother in the group, an honor few declined. Bronwyn had not, either, although she'd often wished she had. She suspected some of the others did as well.

There was no light to mark the way, only the cool overhead moon turning everything gray, and the shimmering fireflies that danced in the trees and grass. Here and there, a patch of foxfire glowed on a fallen limb. Bliss stayed close, ready to act if Bronwyn fell but otherwise content to let her struggle on.

They reached the clearing, where eleven other women waited for them. They ranged in apparent age from childhood to close to a century, but not even the oldest betrayed any sign of infirmity. Local legend had it that you could *kill* a Tufa, but they never did just *die*. That wasn't accurate, but it wasn't a total lie, either.

Bliss stopped. The other women stayed back, mere shapes in the darkness. Bliss raised her chin and sang:

I'll eat when I'm hungry,
I'll drink when I'm dry;
If the hard times don't kill me,
I'll live till I die.

Bronwyn cleared her throat and sang, in a considerably weaker voice:

I'll tune up my fiddle,
And I'll rosin my bow,
I'll make myself welcome,
Wherever I go.

Bronwyn fought the urge to roll her eyes as she and Bliss made the same elaborate sign with their left hands. She wanted to maintain the solemnity of the occasion, but couldn't shake both her annoyance at the pretentiousness and the sense that, in this day and age, these arcane convocations were just plain silly. Only the very real threat to her mother would ever have gotten her down in this valley again.

"Welcome, sisters," said Peggy Goins. She hugged Bliss, then kissed Bronwyn on the cheek. "Ain't had a chance to properly welcome you back yet. The last time I saw you, there were five thousand people in the way."

"I should've invited you out for some iced tea and pie," Bronwyn agreed. It was etiquette to say it, but she also meant it; she'd sat in her house and waited for everyone to come to her, like some queen bee. "Same for all of you. My mama would be ashamed of me."

Bliss turned suddenly and looked behind them up the hill,

toward their parked vehicles. She raised a hand for silence. "Someone's coming."

"No, someone's *here*." The voice was young and feminine, and as the girl stepped into the moonlight, they all recognized her. "Someone who's got as much right to be here as any of you." As if to prove it, she sang:

> *I've no man to quarrel*
> *No babies to bawl;*
> *The best way of living*
> *Is be no wife at all.*

"Carolanne," Bliss said. "I thought you and I had settled this."

"You mean you thought I agreed with you because I quit arguing," the girl said bitterly. She was seventeen, with black hair cut shoulder length and held back with pins. "I just know when to stop wasting my time. You say I can't be part of this, and I say I can. I *am* a First Daughter. I know my mother's song, and I've ridden the night wind."

"Yes, that's all true," Peggy said. "But you don't have full Tufa blood. That's nothing anyone can change, and it's no one's fault. It simply is what it is."

"Can all of you *prove* you have one hundred percent true blood? Is there a blood test they can do for this? You work with blood every day, Bliss Overbay, so tell us."

"We know," Bliss said. "And we also know you're *not*. You should go, Carolanne."

"Not before I tell you high-and-mighty First Daughters what I think about your little club." She held up her left hand and made a gesture they all knew, the first of the Four Signs of the First Daughters. Bronwyn heard someone gasp in surprise.

Bliss showed no emotion, and responded with the appropriate countersign. Then she made a sign herself, and Carolanne responded. "See?" the younger girl said defiantly. "I pay attention, I learn. I'm as good as any of you. You're lucky I don't take what I know over to Rockhouse's people. I bet they'd be just tickled to have this information."

"It's not a matter of learning," Bliss said. "It's all about the song in your blood. And threats just belittle us both."

Carolanne made another sign. "My song is as good as any of yours. And I know all your signs, see?"

"The song has to be as old as your blood, Carolanne. If it's not, you're not a First Daughter." Then she made a slow, careful final sign with her right hand.

Carolanne said nothing, and the darkness hid her expression. But her voice gave everything away. "What the hell is that? You just made that up right now, didn't you?"

"No," Bliss said with firm gentleness. "We're just doing what's always been done. This is not a sorority, Carolanne, we don't pick or exclude members. You either are one, or you're not. You can't *become* one. And as for telling Rockhouse's people—"

"Why not?" Bronwyn blurted. Even she was surprised by her words. Everyone turned to look at her.

Surprise far outweighed anger in Bliss's voice. "What?"

The words tumbled out. "Look, we all have this First Daughter pure-blood *thing* that none of us asked for, and that for the most part causes us nothing but aggravation. Carolanne here clearly wants to be part of this bad enough to figure out where and when we meet, and to learn almost all of our signs. The fact that she *hasn't* given them away says something about her, doesn't it? Maybe . . ."

She stopped, suddenly aware of the scrutiny. "Nothing," she finished abruptly, and turned away. For a long moment only the crickets and tree frogs were heard.

Finally Bliss said, "I'm sorry, Carolanne. But you really need to go. It isn't safe to be alone in these woods tonight."

"Is that a threat?" Carolanne snapped.

"Only as much as yours," Bliss replied evenly.

Carolanne started to reply, then turned on her heel and stomped petulantly into the night.

Now Bliss directed her attention at Bronwyn. With no malice, only puzzlement, she asked, "What was *that* all about?"

Bronwyn shook her head. "Hell if I know. It just popped out."

"Is that how you really feel?"

"I think so," she said. "I hadn't really thought about it before now. But . . . yeah, it is."

Bliss turned to another member of the circle. "Mandalay? Any thoughts?"

A small figure in a simple dress stepped forward. When the moonlight struck her serene face, it showed a child only ten years old. Yet she spoke with the calm authority of one who knew her power. "Some, but there's more important things to deal with right now. Y'all follow me?"

They fell into step behind her and walked down a short trail through thick trees. Each kept a hand lightly on the back of the woman in front of her, and the line moved slowly so Bronwyn could keep up. The sound of cicadas, wind, and the occasional owl filled the night, rendering it anything but silent.

Each time the owl hooted, Bronwyn shuddered. The owl was a bad omen, and its presence reminded her of the danger circling her family.

They emerged into a small clearing bathed in moonlight. At the center, a table-sized rock protruded from the ground. On one side an image had been chiseled deep enough that innumerable mountain winters had not worn it away. It was a crude line drawing of a human figure with large wings; lines indicated long hair, and the form had the unmistakable curves of a female. Its style was similar to the ancient images found in caves throughout Europe. The wings resembled those of a dragonfly.

The ten-year-old, Mandalay Harris, knelt and kissed the carving. One by one the others followed. Because of her leg, Bronwyn waited to go last.

When this ritual was done, Mandalay climbed onto the rock, sat cross-legged, and said, "Welcome back, Bronwyn. I saw you at your parade; you looked pretty in your uniform."

Bronwyn tried not to laugh. Despite her heritage and responsibility, Mandalay was still a little girl at heart. "Thanks," she said. "Glad to be shed of it and back in civilian clothes, though."

Mandalay nodded, then said firmly, "I guess there ain't no point in dancing around things. How's your mama?"

"Nothing so far. Daddy's got wards up, and we're all watching out. She ain't letting it slow her down."

"All you can do," she said sadly. "But what about the rest of us? We're here because Chloe Hyatt may be about to die. None of us want that, and the signs aren't certain, of course. But we'd be foolish not to be prepared."

A heavy woman with streaks of gray in her hair stepped forward. "I dreamed I lost one of my bottom teeth. Reckon that means someone in my family younger than me will die. Your mama fits that, Brownyn. I'm real sorry."

"That mantel clock Chloe gave me when I got married started working again," another woman said. "It ain't kept time in three years."

"And don't forget the sin eater," someone else said. "Chloe herself saw him. He don't come around unless he thinks there might be something left out for him."

Peggy Goins added, "I'd say we've gotten all the warning we're going to get."

"That means it could happen any day," one of the others said.

"Hey, this is my *mom* we're talking about," Bronwyn said. "I'm all for reading sign and all, but we have to be able to *do* something here. I mean, for how many generations have we been here? How many times have we watched someone die and done nothing but *sing* about it?"

"That's what we *do*," Mandalay said patiently. "It's what we *are*. The night wind blew us here, and keeps us here at her pleasure. We all know that. But no one lives forever."

"And," said a tall woman in her thirties, "none of us would *want* to."

Bronwyn turned to her, intending to refute her comment, but when she saw the distant, sad look in her eyes, she bit back the words. Delilah had spent longer than any of them alone, after her true love had died on their wedding day. She knew the weight of time more than any of them.

"Yeah, well," Bronwyn said at last, "I'm not ready to sing my mom's dirge just yet. And neither are Aiden or Kell. So you'll excuse me if I keep trying to find the song that will change things."

"It doesn't exist," Mandalay said patiently. "You're not the first to think it does. But all we can do, all we've ever done, is sing the songs we were given."

"You mean it doesn't exist *yet*," Bronwyn insisted. "A line came to me the other day. Maybe more will come. It could be a new song for her."

"That's a dream, Bronwyn. A beautiful one, one we've all had, but no more than a wisp of a thing. And you have a greater concern. You have to accept what the night wind has willed to you, and you *must* learn your mother's song."

"I will. But we don't know for certain we're reading the signs right, do we? I mean, the clock thing could mean *you're* going to die, Sandy, not my mama. Maybe it's all a coincidence."

"I've read plenty of signs, especially death signs," Peggy said sadly. "It ain't a coincidence."

Mandalay put her hand over her own heart. "And you must agree, you must *swear*, to pass the song on to your daughter."

It took a few seconds for the words to register. Bronwyn almost blurted out, "But I don't have a daughter," and then realized exactly *what* she was being asked to agree to. They wanted her solemn word that she would find a consort among the Tufa men, many of whom were already related to her. They wanted her promise to breed a daughter.

"Fuck that," she said. Her voice trembled not from fear, but from outrage. "I'm not swearing to *that*."

Mandalay climbed off the rock, walked over, and looked up at her. The girl's serious face, bathed in cold moonlight, gave Bronwyn the willies, and when she spoke, her voice bore no hint of childishness. "Bronwyn, listen to me. I know all the stories of you, how you hate to be told what to do, how to behave, who to be with. The Bronwynator was a legend here long before the rest of the world heard about you. But this is probably the most important thing anyone's ever asked of you. We, your sisters and mothers and daughters, all need you to promise this. We need the certainty that the song will be saved. You won't face this alone, you know, and it's not like we're choosing a mate for you."

"What do you know about mates, you still play with Barbie dolls," Bronwyn snapped. She looked at the others. "This is exactly the kind of crap that made me want to leave in the first place. Just because we're ancient doesn't mean we can't make new ways. Are we mud-stuck like the Christians or the Jews? Do we have to take our instructions from a book written for a culture that died two thousand years ago? Or do we write our own songs?"

None of the others responded. The shadows over their eyes made their impressions hard to judge. Even Bliss seemed implacable.

"Fine," Bronwyn said with a scowl. "Fuck y'all, anyway."

"Bronwyn," someone scolded.

She ignored it. "I'll learn the damn song because I said I would, and because I love my mama. But I'm *not* promising to add my daughter to this silly-ass girls' club. You can't just put me in a field and send a prize bull around to see if I'm in season."

Mandalay continued to gaze up at her. "Then there's nothing more to say."

"No," Bronwyn agreed, although the child's eminently reasonable tone made her even angrier.

Mandalay turned to the others. "Thank you all for coming, and for being true to our songs. And I include you in that, Bronwyn."

Bronwyn said nothing. She turned and began climbing the trail back toward the cars. The others passed her in silence, not out of disdain but simply because idle conversation seemed inappropriate. Only Bliss remained with her, and by the time they reached the vehicles, hers was the only one left.

23

When they reached the Hyatt residence, Bliss asked, "Are you all right?" It was the first time either had spoken for the entire ride.

"Yeah," Bronwyn said. "I'm just tired. And my leg hurts."

Bliss stopped the truck at the gate and looked up the hill. The house was completely dark except for the porch light, left on for Brownyn. "Want me to drive you to the front door?"

Bronwyn laughed. "Good Lord, no. Dwayne already tore up the yard when I sent him packing; Daddy would have a fit if somebody else drove all over it."

"Well . . . I'll check in with you tomorrow."

Bronwyn did not look back. "Sure. Thanks for the ride, Bliss."

As Bliss drove away, Bronwyn opened the gate enough to squeak through and slowly climbed the hill. By the time she reached the porch steps, she had to sit down and catch her breath. For a moment she watched things only a Tufa could see in the night, and smiled as they recognized her as well.

Why did she *care* about the First Daughters, anyway? She understood their purpose, but didn't share their belief in its importance. So what if the "true Tufa way" died out? The Tufa themselves would remain, maybe diluted into the general population but still there, ready to awaken when the music was right and the night wind called them to ride.

She slid the dress up her thigh and ran her hand along her injured leg, feeling the little bumps of scars. They would fade with time, but she didn't really mind them. She knew that if she wanted a man to find her attractive, he would.

She slowly opened the screen door, pausing just before it squeaked. She'd learned that trick as a preteen, and it had served her well all through high school. The inner door opened without a sound. She stood in the darkened living room and was about to move forward when something made her freeze.

She turned toward movement in the shadows off to her right. Something was on the couch, moving slowly, the fabric creaking as it did. Bronwyn stared, trying to resolve it into a shape she could recognize.

Then a head popped up, tossing black hair back from a face shiny with sweat and effort. A face she recognized as *her own*.

The face turned to her. It wasn't her, of course; it was her mother, naked and astride her father. They moved together as silently as they could, since Aiden and Kell were asleep in the house. Apparently her father had not heard Bronwyn enter, because he continued to nuzzle Chloe's breasts as his hands roamed over her skin.

Chloe's eyelids fluttered, and she gasped. Bronwyn wanted to look away, but couldn't. She watched her mother have an orgasm, silent except for a sharp exhalation, and then curl around Deacon like she was molding her limbs to him. She looked again at Bronwyn, and their eyes locked for a moment. *I am alive,* her mother's defiant gaze seemed to say. *See? I'm not dead by a damn sight yet.*

Bronwyn ran into her room, the first time in months she'd moved that quickly. She fell halfway onto the bed and began sobbing, clenching her teeth against the sound. She didn't want to wake either of her brothers, and she sure didn't want her father to know she'd seen anything. My God, what were they *thinking,* carrying on like teenagers? They were both in their *forties.*

She crawled onto the bed and curled up clutching her Dolly-wood souvenir pillow. Everything she'd counted on was changing into something else. The First Daughters, until now mainly a ceremonial thing that meant nothing, actually expected something from her. Her parents, those solid, reliable figures she'd always counted on even as a wild-child teenager, were humping in the front room. Even Aiden was on the verge of turning from a boy into a young man, and Kell would soon have to decide if his song led him away from Cloud County or back to it. And then there was Craig the minister, and Terry-Joe, and Dwayne. There was nothing left to hold on to, she thought grimly, except this stupid pillow with Dolly Parton's face embroidered on it.

Finally, long past midnight, she fell asleep.

Bronwyn's eyes snapped open. A sound had awakened her. She blinked into the darkness, and listened intently, hoping it wasn't more noises from the living room. It came again: a light tapping at her window. Her dream-fuddled brain's first thought was, *Dwayne?* Then she turned and saw the face beyond the glass.

The *haint*.

She blinked, and suddenly the ghost was in her room. She sat up and snapped, "This is a really bad night, Sally."

"It's time to remember," the haint said. "You can't avoid this."

Bronwyn started to fire something back, but instead she sat up, crawled to the edge of the bed, and without her cane, stood up to face the haint. "So what, then, is so goddamned important that I need to remember?"

"What happened to you."

Bronwyn's bad leg trembled with fury. "You think I didn't read what happened to me? I know what all those words mean, honey, especially the really good ones like 'sodomize.' I don't *need* to remember what that felt like."

"You'll face more challenges soon. Your strength will come from knowing you've endured these things."

"I *do* know it!" Bronwyn bellowed. She no longer cared who heard her. "I know that I was blown up, cut up, ass-fucked, and stitched back together. I know I took down nearly a dozen of those bastards before they got me. I know that if it wasn't for being a Tufa, I'd be dead by now, okay? *I know* all that! What I'm real fucking tired of is people, alive *or* dead, telling me what the fuck I *need*!"

She turned her back on the haint. "Go away, Sally. There's nothing for you here. I don't hear you anymore, and when I turn around I won't see you."

Before she could say anything, her bedroom door opened and Chloe entered. She was wrapped in a bathrobe, and her black hair was disheveled. "Are you all right? I heard shouting."

"Is there anyone behind me?"

"No."

"Then I'm fine," she said, and sat heavily on the edge of the bed. Then she scowled up at her mother. "And how are you?"

"You could've . . . I don't know, knocked or something."

"At my own front door? *You* could've stopped."

"Not at that moment, I couldn't."

Brownyn shook her head. "Man, that is *so* much more than I need to know."

Chloe closed the door and sat down beside her daughter. "I recall walking in on you and Dwayne once. Believe me, I had no desire to see *that,* either."

Bronwyn couldn't repress a smile. "Yeah, and he got stuck going out the window." She looked over at the glass, expecting to see Sally outside it, but there was nothing but darkness. "Everyone's telling me what I have to do. Not asking me, even, *telling* me. I'm not in the army anymore, I don't have to take orders."

"They want things to be safe if something happens to me."

"Things. They want a song to be safe. A stupid song."

"A song that's *ours.* That we brought across the water on the night wind. That's been kept as a treasure ever since."

"Just because something's old doesn't mean it's valuable."

"Spoken by the young."

"Yeah, yeah, whatever." She fell back on the bed. "I'll learn your damn song, Mom. I promised I would. But I won't have a damn baby just because people want me to, and I won't dig up things out of my own head just so a ghost can feel useful." She put the Dollywood pillow over her face.

"You'll do what you want, like you always have," Chloe said sadly. She stopped as she opened the door. "You should probably try to figure out why that is. You didn't get it from me, and I'm pretty sure your father's not like that. But there's a word for people who only care about what they want themselves."

"Sociopath?" Bronwyn said sarcastically.

"I was thinking 'asshole.' But whatever works for you."

Don Swayback found himself walking through a graveyard in the middle of the day. He knew it was a dream, but he couldn't help but admire the vision his subconscious presented. The cemetery was on a mountainside, and below it stretched a beautiful valley bisected by a meandering river. Except for the headstones, there was no sign of civilization. The valley was covered in unnaturally green grass, and the sky was wincingly blue. He leaned on one of the headstones and slowly took in the view.

"What you *really* want to see," a voice said, "is this way."

He turned. A beautiful young woman in desert-themed military clothes stood in the shade of a tree. Something about her was odd, and in a moment he spotted it: a gaping space in her side, as if her flesh had been scooped out with a giant ice cream dipper. She carried her helmet under the opposite arm, and her bangs fell into her eyes. Her skin was pale with death.

Before Don could respond, she nodded to one side. He turned and saw an old woman seated in a folding lawn chair, a guitar across her lap. Sun dappled across her as the branch shading her waved in the wind. She was heavyset, with black hair starting to turn gray. She said to him, "That's your cousin, Sally Olds. Died in Iraq back in the first Gulf War. She was my great-grandniece."

"Hi," Don said. He knew who she had to be. "So you're Grandma Benji."

She strummed the guitar. "Darn tootin'. You're close to the line on some things, and you and I need to talk before you step over it." She looked up at Sally. "Y'all go on, I know you got things to do. Me and Don just need to chew the fat for a tic."

Sally leaned down and kissed Grandma Benji on the cheek. The tatters of flesh and organs swayed with her movements. Then she was gone, although Don had not seen her actually leave. He said, "It's nice to finally meet you."

"You know this is a dream, right?"

"Yeah, I know."

"But you think you're really meeting me?"

He looked at her closely. There was a fixed quality to her that seemed at odds with the mutable details of everything else around him. "I figure it can't hurt to be polite either way."

She chortled. "Anyway, we need to talk about blood. You got more Tufa in you than you realize. It ain't always about quantity: you can have a man ninety-five percent pureblood, but if that missing five percent is the part that lets him ride the wind, he ain't a true Tufa. You know about riding the night wind?"

Don shook his head.

"You will, I reckon. I hope. One night you'll go outside, look up at the sky, and either hear the hum or feel the shiver. If it's the shiver . . . well, you're still kin and I love you, but it means you'll never be a real Tufa. If it's the hum, though, you'll feel the stirrin' of your wings."

"That sounds . . . dramatic."

She ran a riff down the guitar neck, her fingers nimble and sure. "That ain't what I want to straighten you out about, though. It's which side you're gonna be on."

"Which side of what?"

"Most folks think the Tufa are one big family. We ain't; we're two. One's no better than the other, and one can't go on without the other; like you can't have light without dark for it to show up against. Make sense?"

"Sure."

"Rockhouse Hicks runs one side. Mandalay Harris runs the other. You know either of them?"

"Nope."

"You will. I was one of Rockhouse's family. I was with him since the night wind first blew us here. But he turned sour. He's a mean, bitter fella, closing in on bein' evil. I'd hate to see you get involved with him."

"Then I'll join up with the other one. Mandalay, you said his name was?"

"*Her* name. But it ain't that easy. You should have someone to guide you in this, but this is the best I can do. I hope you remember all this when you wake up."

"I usually do."

"I know." She smiled. "Now, enough of this grim business. Let's play a little."

He was about to say he didn't have his guitar, when he noticed it propped beside him. Smiling, he took it out and followed his dead grandmother as she counted them into "Wicked Polly."

In the little frame house that counted as the church's parsonage, Craig Chess tossed in the big bed. Normally he slept peacefully, but tonight nothing was peaceful. His mind seethed with things that seemed to come from some other subconscious, presenting him with images that he'd never even considered.

The visions were intense, brutal, and terrifying. Soldiers dying in the desert, limbs and organs blown apart. Something wet and meaty lay beside a fallen gun, coated with sand and already attracting flies. A man held the stump of his right hand with his left, while blood oozed between his fingers. Another man stood with his arms wrapped around his abdomen to keep inside what seemed determined to fall out.

Craig felt the concussion of each explosion, his teeth rattling despite his attempts to clench them. The scent of burning fuel and meat filled the air. He looked wildly around, uncertain which way to run, unable to tell where the attack originated.

Suddenly a hand took his. He turned and saw a soldier, a young woman, looking at him in sympathy. "It's quieter this way," she said, and he heard her clearly despite the roaring chaos. He followed her around the end of a shredded troop carrier, and suddenly they stood beside the old catfish pond on his uncle's farm. As in most dreams, this transition was seamless and felt entirely reasonable.

"That's better," the woman said. She took off her helmet and shook her head. She had short black hair. "I have to tell you something."

"Okay," Craig said. He noticed that there was a huge chunk of flesh and bone missing from the woman's side; the ends of ribs poked through the tattered edges of her uniform. "You're hurt."

"I'm dead," she said easily. "But that's not the important thing. You need to know about Bronwyn."

"Bronwyn Hyatt?"

The woman nodded. "She's going to face the biggest challenge of her life soon."

"Worse than what happened in Iraq?"

"That was no challenge. She was a soldier, she was trained, and it was life or death. Decisions come easy that way. She survived, which was her purpose. What's next will be much harder, and much more important."

"Okay. What do I need to do?"

The woman tossed a stone across the water. It skipped several times. "To help her, you'll have to question everything you believe, and find a way to resolve it. Contradictions will appear where you never saw them, and it'll be easy to lose faith. But you can't."

"Never have," he assured her.

"It's never mattered this much. Bronwyn will need your help and, more important, your love."

"My *love*?"

The woman nodded. "It may seem far-fetched now. It won't before long."

"Okay," he said again. Truthfully, in the dream it *didn't* seem that far-fetched. He'd thought about her more than any other woman he'd ever known.

The woman stepped close. He could see the veins in her eyes, exploded with the impact of whatever killed her. "Be strong. Be honest. Be fearless."

"No one is really fearless."

"Sure they are. When they know they're right. Be right."

"That attitude tends to get preachers into trouble."

"You are more than your job. The preacher doesn't have to be right. *Craig* does."

He was about to say okay again when he opened his eyes and saw his bedroom ceiling in the gray dawn light.

He dressed quickly and went outside, across the still-damp lawn and up the concrete steps to the church's front door. The sanctuary first thing in the morning was the quietest, most relaxing place he knew, one of the few places he felt he could hear the whisper of God's voice. He reached for the handle, then realized he'd forgotten the key. He sat on the porch rail and watched the sky lighten in the east, pondering the dream.

24

Bronwyn opened her eyes and smiled.

She stretched on the bed, feeling the sheets slide against her body. There was no pain now, just stiffness from muscles not yet restored to full strength. She sat up with a yawn and swung her legs over the side of the bed. She went to the dresser and dug out an overlarge T-shirt. She pulled it on and suddenly realized she had not even thought of grabbing her cane.

She looked down at her leg. It was still considerably thinner than its mate, but that pasty hospital color was gone. The pink scars remained, but they no longer itched. She wiggled her toes and felt no numbness or tingling.

"You," she said to her leg, "are getting shaved today. Yes, you are."

She looked at herself in the mirror over her dresser. Something had changed in her face as well; the hard set of her eyes, the way her jaw cut a sharp line when she clenched her teeth, seemed to be gone. She looked younger than when she'd joined the army, she thought suddenly. Her sleep-tousled hair only added to the effect.

She pulled on some shorts and went into the bathroom. Later, following her shower, she sat on her bed combing her wet hair when there was a soft knock at the door. "Y'all decent?" a male voice said.

It was not her father or either of her brothers, so she quickly pulled on cut-offs and a tank top. "No, but now I'm dressed. Come on in."

Terry-Joe Gitterman opened the door. He wore jeans and a black T-shirt, and looked handsome as the sunrise. He smiled when he saw her. "You look like a million bucks."

"That's a lot of deer," she said, and winked. She put her comb aside and sat back on the bed, deliberately crossing her newly shorn bad leg over her good. "What do you think? Not bad for two weeks, is it?"

"Not bad at all," he said appreciatively, and propped his mandolin case against the wall. "Hope you don't mind me stopping by unannounced like this. Your daddy said it was okay to come on back."

"Heck, yeah. What brings you by this early?"

He tapped his mandolin case. "I figure you're doing pretty well with your playing now, so I thought we might jam out a little. If you feel up to it. I just want to hear you cut loose."

Bronwyn's eyes playfully narrowed. "Did Bliss Overbay send you to check on me?"

"She might've suggested it. But I wasn't hard to convince. What do you say?"

She grinned. "I say skin that song iron."

In a few moments she'd retrieved Magda and held the instrument ready against her chest. Terry-Joe sat on her desk chair, his own instrument across his lap. His foot eagerly tapped the floor. "What do you feel like playing today?"

"Hm. You know 'The White Cockade'?"

He nodded. They decided on a key, and he said, "You lead us off."

Bronwyn tapped her finger on the mandolin's body four times, then began to play.

After the first verse, Terry-Joe said, "Now sing."

"Oh, I can't *really* sing," she said with a shy smile.

"Sure you can."

She cleared her throat and began the verse.

My love was born in Aberdeen,
The prettiest lad that ever was seen,
But now he makes our hearts so sad,
He takes the Field with his White Cockade.

Terry-Joe leaned closer to harmonize on the chorus. She could feel his breath, warm and alive, on her cheek.

Oh, he's a ranting, roving lad,
He is a brisk and a bonny lad,
Come what may, I will be wed,
And follow the boy with the White Cockade.

He looked up, and their eyes met. She stopped playing. He continued, his shoulder muscles moving beneath his shirt. He gazed at her with unabashed desire. "You're the most beautiful girl I personally know," he said finally.

"You should get out more," she said, but her voice was a little raspy. She remembered that first day when she'd found him working on her wheelchair and later pressed against him as he held the door. The urge to press against him anew swelled in her.

Now he stopped playing. He looked down as he said, "Tell you the truth about something, Bronwyn. My brother may brag about his money and his wheels, but you're the only thing of Dwayne's I ever wanted."

"I'm not like his truck. He didn't hold the pink slip on me."

Still avoiding her gaze, he shrugged and said, "To him, you were."

"I'm not anymore."

Now he looked at her, and the heat in his eyes matched her own. "He'd kill me if he knew I was even thinking about this."

"Thinking about what?"

He leaned closer and their lips met.

She wasn't clear as to how exactly they got from that point to lying on the bed, their instruments safely on the floor. But there she was, on her back, Terry-Joe still kissing her as his hands roamed over her. His lips moved to her neck, then her cleavage, and she put up no resistance when his hands slid beneath her shirt and closed over her breasts. He was tentative, but as gentle with her as he'd been that first day with Magda and she felt everything that she'd denied herself since the attack flare back to life.

She whipped off the tank top and arched her back. His lips found her nipples, and she made a sound she couldn't hear over the blood roaring in her ears. Then he took off his own shirt, and she reciprocated, tonguing and biting his hard chest and tiny pink nipples.

She could not remember when another's skin against her own had felt so good. He was hot to the touch, and his muscles were well defined and not bulky like Dwayne's. He caressed her thighs and rear through her shorts while nuzzling her breasts, then her heaving belly. He kissed her navel, and when his lips moved beneath it and she felt his tongue along the top of her shorts, she was sure she screamed. He unsnapped her shorts and slid them down her thighs, leaving her clad only in her panties. He kissed along the lace edge of them, and she was infinitely glad she'd shaved and trimmed that morning. But then he was lifting the elastic and probing with his tongue, and suddenly nothing else mattered.

Until the voice in her head said, *He's seventeen, and he's never been out of the valley.*

She rose suddenly on her elbows and gasped, "Wait!"

He looked up. She had her good leg draped across his back, and quickly lowered it. "What?" he asked breathlessly. "Did I do something wrong?"

"Good God, no," she said, and scrambled away to sit on the edge of the bed. She quickly found her tank top and pulled up her shorts. "Believe me, you've got my motor racing like no one has in longer than I can remember, and that includes your no-account brother."

He looked confused. A red flush of arousal covered his shoulders and neck. "Then what's wrong?"

She trembled with the intensity of her feelings. It felt as if the last set of switches had been thrown, bringing some huge, powerful engine roaring to life. It had nothing really to do with sex, although she was certainly turned on. It was more an awareness of the world, as if she now saw in vivid color what had previously been pastel. Last night she had asserted her independence from Tufa expectations; now she broke free from the things that once ruled her in the past.

She reached over and touched his cheek, unable to repress a smile. "Nothing's wrong, baby. Whoever taught you did a fine job, because you sure know how to treat a girl. But . . ." And here she had to choke back a laugh at the absurdity, because she didn't want Terry-Joe to misinterpret it. "We're coming at this from two completely different directions, and they won't ever really meet up."

He took her hand and kissed her fingertips. "I think they will. Somewhere below the waist, maybe?"

Now she did laugh. She kissed him quick and soft. "Terry-Joe, I know you want to make love to me because you like me, or maybe even think you're in love with me, and not to get back at your brother, which is the thing that would motivate most boys your age." She saw his face fall at the use of the word "boy."

She continued, "But if *I* did it, it'd just be because . . . well, it's been a while since I wanted to, and now I do. Not for any other real reason. I like you, Terry-Joe, but if we went all the way, it'd mess that up."

He frowned. "So if we did it, you wouldn't like me anymore?"

"*I* wouldn't feel any different. *You* might, though, and that could lead to all sorts of mischief. Best we leave it where it is."

"But I was doing it the right way, wasn't I?"

She laughed again, and kissed him a final time. "You were sure enough doing it right. I'm so fired up, you could light a joint off me."

He smiled and reached for his own shirt. "Well, I reckon I can't be too upset, then."

She watched him pull the shirt down over his torso, recalling its touch beneath her fingertips. The morning sun through the window glinted off its sweaty contours. She had a brief twinge that perhaps she was making a mistake, that letting him have her might be good for them both. But she knew which parts of her body were talking, and it wasn't her head or heart. "You're really not mad?" she asked.

Now he kissed her, on the cheek. "If I leave you better than I found you, how can I be mad?"

She giggled. "You sure enough did that."

Bronwyn walked Terry-Joe to the front door and watched him amble down the hill to his bike. The buzz as it started echoed off the hills, and when he spun out and headed down the drive toward the road, its whine reminded Bronwyn of a sad, long wail. Yet he waved and grinned as he disappeared.

She leaned on the door until Chloe said behind her, "You're letting the flies in."

She closed the screen door and turned around. Chloe wore overalls and carried the big gloves she used for gardening. Her hair was tucked beneath one of Deacon's baseball caps, this one sporting a bass in midleap. "I heard you two playing, then you stopped. What happened?"

Brownyn nodded toward the boys' bedrooms. "Anyone else home?"

Chloe shook her head. "Kell and Aiden went fishing, your dad's out in the fields."

Bronwyn sat heavily at the kitchen table. "Terry-Joe and I almost . . . made out. All the way." She looked at her thumb as it moved back and forth across the wood.

Chloe said nothing for a long moment, then leaned against the counter and crossed her arms. "Why didn't you?"

Bronwyn shrugged. "I don't know, it just felt wrong."

Chloe sat opposite her, deliberately keeping the table between them. "'Cause of Dwayne?"

"No, because of *me*. And Terry-Joe. I could've . . . well . . . had a good time with him, and let it go as that. But he'd have fallen in love. It was three-quarters there in his eyes already."

"Was a time," Chloe said evenly, "when that wouldn't have mattered."

"Yeah, well, that time's past."

"And he's a Tufa. Not pure as us, but close. And what's there's true. That's the only reason I made your daddy put up with Dwayne for so long."

Bronwyn frowned; then her eyes opened wide. She recalled Mandalay's words, the promise they tried to exact from her, and jumped to her feet. "You gotta be kidding me," she rasped. "You mean you *pimped me out* to Dwayne Gitterman?"

Chloe laughed bitterly. "Don't be so dramatic. You found Dwayne all on your own, and we couldn't have pried you off him with a crowbar. But your daddy would've sung his dyin' dirge a long time ago if I'd let him. He knew exactly what Dwayne was about."

"Did *you*?"

"Bronwyn, you ain't the only woman in this family. Everything you feel, I've felt. Everything that you wanted, I've wanted. You think I don't know the appeal of someone like Dwayne? You think I didn't have someone like that when I was younger? I've been everywhere you have, girl. On my knees, on my back. And nobody had to force me there, I *enjoyed* it." Her eyes grew shiny and her words harsh. "I laughed at your daddy back then, wanting me to settle down and raise a family. I laughed at the First Daughters telling me he was the right man for me. How could any man so goddamned dull compete with the boys who'd take you off into the woods and show you the hum and the shiver?"

Bronwyn could hardly breathe. Who *was* this woman? "Holy shit, Mom," was all she could say.

"And here you are. It's like looking in a mirror some days, Bronwyn, and seeing myself twenty-five years ago. And you know what? I *hate* it. I don't want to know about the boys you chase, and especially the ones you catch. I don't want to imagine you with them, and you know why? Because when I'm lying awake at night staring at the ceiling, it makes me *jealous*. I'll never feel that way again, and some days it feels like I've already died."

She stood, went to the sink, and twisted the cold water tap. The running water covered any other sounds she made.

Bronwyn stood and put her hand on her mother's shoulder. "Mom, I—"

"Go away, Bronwyn," Chloe said.

Bronwyn felt the breath tight in her chest. "I don't want you to die, Mom."

Chloe said nothing.

Bronwyn's vision grew misty. "You still have to teach me your song."

Still nothing.

"All right. I'll be around when you're ready." She turned and went back down the hall to her room.

When she heard the door close, Chloe splashed cold water on her face and turned off the tap. Her eye fell on two pictures hanging on the wall beside the front door. One showed Bronwyn in her uniform, fresh out of basic, stern and straight and with her natural fire tamped down by military brainwashing.

The other showed Bronwyn and Kell, with baby Aiden in Kell's lap. Bronwyn had her older brother in a headlock and he was trying to resist and keep his smile at the same time. It showed their dynamic perfectly, which is why Chloe loved it.

She also hated it. Those three children represented the loss of her freedom and tied her to a man she dearly loved but who seldom excited her to a frenzy anymore. She felt a jolt deep inside at the memory of a young dark-haired brute of a man, her own Dwayne Gitterman, so handsome and masculine that just the rumble of his voice saying her name could make her knees wobble. But he was long gone, and she was no longer that girl. How had she allowed that to happen?

And now the threat of death hung over her. Signs that could be ignored individually, together hinted at an undeniable fate, and it took all her strength to pretend she wasn't scared.

She took off the baseball cap and shook her hair free. This was not the way to think, not the song she needed to sing. Deacon was the best thing that ever happened to her, and none of her children had asked to be born to her. They all deserved better than a mother who despised their existence. Especially Bronwyn, her baby girl, who'd endured such unimaginable torments. She suddenly realized that perhaps Bronwyn's selfishness as a child hadn't been an anomaly after all; maybe she actually *had* gotten it from Chloe. Only a selfish, bitter woman would've said the things she'd just told her daughter.

She closed her eyes. There was no time for bitterness, or selfishness. It was time for her to be strong, to be a true First Daughter.

She went to find her autoharp.

25

Susie Swayback looked across the plate of blueberry pancakes at her husband. It wasn't her imagination: there really *was* something different about him, a change that made him somehow more attractive and at the same time disconcerted her. She couldn't define it exactly, but his amorous attentions had certainly improved and she wasn't about to complain about that. She said playfully, "What are you thinking so hard about?"

Don blinked back to the moment. He'd been staring past his own reflection in the window, out into the twilight. He watched the treetops wave in the wind, and the sight mesmerized him. It was almost like a song he couldn't quite recall, hovering just beyond his consciousness. He'd experienced that a lot lately. He smiled and said, "Sorry. Just zoning out."

"Because of work?"

He shrugged. "Nah. Work was just work." In truth, the day had flown by, and even Sam seemed impressed with the column inches Don produced. It wasn't easy for two men and a handful of stringers to fill a weekly newspaper, and usually they ran more filler than any respectable journalist could stomach. But tomorrow's edition would be filled with real if not terribly exciting news stories, most of them rustled up and written by Don. From higher electrical rates to the construction of a new bridge on County Road K, he'd called his contacts until he got results. It was the way he'd been as a young reporter fresh out of college.

Sam hadn't even bugged him about missing the deadline for the Hyatt interview. He seemed to accept that Don was working on it, building trust in the Tufa community as he went.

Now Don and Susie sat at the Waffle House outside Unicorn. Their first date as freshmen had been to a Waffle House after a movie, and they considered any of these restaurants "their" special place. Susie was off work for the whole weekend, so it seemed an appropriate way to celebrate a free Friday night. They were overdressed for the place, but that also echoed their first date.

"Well, you certainly seem to be in a better mood lately," Susie said.

He scowled. "Wow. Was it that bad before?"

"Let's just say I didn't mind working extra shifts. But now I'm actually looking forward to seeing you again." She waggled her eyebrows for emphasis.

He smiled and winked. "I've been feeling the same way about you."

She reached across the booth table and squeezed his hand. Her wedding ring caught the light. "If I'd known getting your guitar out would've done this, you'd have been picking and grinning years ago. Think I could come with you the next time you go play somewhere?"

Don was about to reply when suddenly the front door opened with a slam. A tall young man with black hair and a cowboy hat strode inside with a loud, "Don't nobody drop your pancakes!"

He laughed at the sound of silverware and crockery. People turned to glare at him, then quickly looked away. Intimidation radiated from him with no discernible effort. He took a french fry from a man's plate, ate it, and went behind the counter where he pressed himself against the waitress. "Hey, sweet thang, I drove all the way out here just to stare at them fine titties. You glad to see me?"

The lone waitress, whose name tag read ALSIE, did not look at him. She continued to refill the ketchup bottles, although her hands now shook. "Dwayne Gitterman, you're drunk and you're behaving like an ass. I think we'd all appreciate it if you'd just leave."

He blatantly ground his hips against her behind. "Aw, Alsie, don't be that way. You know you're the prettiest girl in the Waffle House. Take the rest of the night off and let me show you what this big ass of yours can do." He slapped one buttock for emphasis.

Alsie squirmed away, her face red. She had blond hair with artificial streaks piled into a bun on top of her head, and her eyes shone with tears of humiliation. "Dwayne, *leave*. Please. I don't want any trouble."

Don looked at the half dozen other patrons, all men, none of whom seemed inclined to stand up for the waitress. Not even the cook, a stout Mexican with a wispy mustache, looked up from his grill. Alsie was clearly terrified, and just as clearly Dwayne was enjoying her fear.

Softly Don said, "Hey, Sue? Got your cell phone with you?"

"Yes," Susie replied quietly. "Why?"

"Get ready to call 911, will you?"

Her eyes opened wide. "What are you going to do?"

He shrugged. "Ask him to leave."

He stood, avoiding Susie's grab at his arm, and walked to the counter. He was no fighter, and there was no way he could intimidate the younger, larger, no doubt stronger man. But something in him just couldn't let this happen. He leaned across the battered Formica and tugged on Dwayne's sleeve. When he looked around, Don said, "'Scuse me, son, I think I heard the lady ask you to leave? Might be the best thing to do."

Dwayne's eyes took a moment to focus on him. "Who the fuck are you, her daddy?"

Don smiled. "No, just a guy who'd like to finish his dinner in peace. I'm not trying to start anything."

"Well, that's too bad," Dwayne said. With a sudden explosive move, he shoved Alsie aside and grabbed Don's shirt. He yanked Don up onto the edge of the counter, holding him there so that Don's feet almost left the floor. "'Cause it looks you *have* started something, big man. I don't imagine your ass can cash the check your mouth just wrote, now, can it?"

The other men stopped eating and sat still and silent. Amazingly, Don was completely calm. He had no idea where the words came from, but he said softly, so that only Dwayne could hear: "I know your dirge, pal. Want me to sing it for you?"

Dwayne laughed, but it was thin, and the amusement drained from his face.

Don began to hum. Out of nowhere the words, *"The arms that hold you are not those of love, you cannot see down nor anything above. . . ."* came to him, bursting out in a tune he neither knew nor recognized.

Dwayne turned pale, shoved Don away, and banged his way out the door. In a moment his truck started and roared off into the dusk.

Don stared after him, then looked at Susie. She was speechless, and shook her head in both wonder and confusion. He shrugged.

"That's it!" Alsie screeched, and slapped the counter for emphasis. "Y'all get out of here, right *now*! I mean it!"

It took Don a moment to realize she was referring to him. "Me?"

"Yes, you and your dang gook wife over there! Get your trailer-trash Tufa asses out of here or I'll call the cops."

Don looked at the others for some kind of help, but met their cold, suspicious stares. Alsie had out her cell phone and said, "I mean it, I've already dialed the nine and the one."

Don tossed a twenty on the table and pulled Susie out the door after him. When they were in the car she said, "That little skank called me a gook, did you hear that?"

"I did."

"And they called you a Tufa. What was that about?"

"Guess that's what we look like to them."

"Well, we won't be coming back here again, that's for sure." She glared through the windshield at the restaurant. "And their corporate headquarters will be getting one nasty e-mail."

Don put the car in gear and backed out of the lot. He turned toward Needsville, then caught himself and headed instead toward home. After a few moments of silence Susie said, "Okay, now that I'm past the whole 'gook' thing, I have to ask. If I was seeing things correctly, you sang a song to that boy and he freaked out."

"Yeah. It just popped into my head. Weird, huh?"

"Weird, huh," she agreed. She watched him drive for a while and said, "It's like you're turning into a different person."

"Really?"

"Yeah."

"In a bad way?"

"I don't know. Not yet. I guess it depends on where it stops." She reached over and took his hand. "I'm proud of you for standing up to that guy, though. There was a time you wouldn't have done that."

"You could still make a case that it wasn't terribly smart."

"Oh, it was completely idiotic. He could've mopped the floor with you, and dusted the shelves with what was left over. But it was still a brave thing to do."

He smiled and squeezed her hand back. But inside he felt a little jolt of fear. Who *was* he turning into? Or what?

The Pair-A-Dice roadhouse was, and always had been, neutral territory. Tufa from either side could eat, drink, and play with no fear of reprisal or confrontation. It allowed musicians to jam who never played together anywhere else. Those rare outsiders who stumbled onto the place swore it was the best music they'd *ever* heard, played by beat-up old men who looked like they'd just walked in out of the fields.

Kell Hyatt desperately wanted a drink, a song, and some time away from the drama at home. The tension between Bronwyn and their mother made the air around them crackle, and their father certainly wasn't going to intercede. Most of the time Kell admired Deacon, but on days like this he really wondered what the old man considered important. He seemed blithely unconcerned with Chloe's impending death or Bronwyn's shifting personality, content to attribute both to the will of the night wind.

"Well, if it ain't the prodigal Hyatt," the bartender said. "I guess you didn't get a parade like your sister, did you?"

Kell knew there was no harm intended in the joke, but it annoyed him just the same. "Parades ain't for the people on the floats, they're for the ones watching it go by."

The bartender whistled, mock impressed. He was one of Rockhouse's people, but at the Pair-A-Dice he usually he didn't go out of his way to be obnoxious. "I should write that one down."

"Write it on my ass while you're kissing it," Kell said, took his beer, and moved away. The bartender laughed behind him.

He sipped his beer and looked for a place to sit. Benches ran along three of the big room's four sides, leaving gaps for the bandstand and bar. The walls were lined with wood paneling that should have ruined the acoustics but somehow didn't. The tables and chairs were an eclectic mismatched lot, as were the glasses and utensils. Torn, stained posters and faded photos lined the walls; they depicted the greats and also-rans of Southern music. Some of the posters went back more than sixty years, to a time when giants like Hank Williams walked the earth in a haze of whiskey-drenched loneliness.

He sat on one of the benches that ran along the bar. He drank half his beer in one swallow, then leaned back and closed his eyes. Not for the first time, he was glad he wasn't a Tufa woman. Being a full-blooded Tufa male had its own baggage, but it involved contests and hierarchies that were simple, if intense. Tufa women always seemed to be nursing secrets and deciding who was worthy to know them. To Kell, that sounded exhausting.

When he opened eyes, Terry-Joe Gitterman stood before him.

"Hey," Kell said guardedly. "What's up?"

Terry-Joe nervously stuck his hands in his pockets, then pulled them back out. "Mind if I sit down?"

"Nope."

Terry-Joe took a chair from a nearby table and straddled it, his arms across the back. "Can I ask you a question and have it just be between you and me?"

Kell frowned. "I don't know. Is this about Bronwyn?"

Terry-Joe nodded.

"I reckon, then."

Terry-Joe paused to muster the words. "Do you think . . . Is Bronwyn still hung up on my brother?"

"Dwayne?" Kell almost barked out the name. He laughed and shook his head. "Honestly, I don't think Bronwyn would piss on him if he was on fire. It took her a while, but she finally sees him for what he is. No offense."

"None taken; I know what he is, too."

Kell was about to ask why Terry-Joe wanted to know, when suddenly he comprehended. Unrequited love was written in the lines of emotional anguish on the younger man's face. Kell had seen it before, on nice boys who thought they could win Bronwyn away from her own hell-bent desires. None of them had fared well at all.

He chose his words carefully. "Terry-Joe, I should tell you, her leg may be a lot better, but Bronwyn ain't exactly all there yet. I don't know if you read about what happened to her—"

"Sure I did."

"Well, you don't come back from that in a hurry, no matter

how much the music helps. Sometimes you don't come all the way back at all."

"She will," Terry-Joe said with certainty. "I've heard her play."

"I hope you're right," Kell said. "But even if she does—"

They both jumped as the front door slammed against the wall. Dwayne Gitterman strode through with a loud, high shout of arrival. He was flushed red with drink and possibly more, and nearly stumbled over someone who couldn't step aside fast enough. He yelled, "God*damn,* you old fart, can't you see me comin'?" and slapped the man with his cowboy hat. He looked around and spotted Terry-Joe and Kell; a slow, mean smile split his face.

"Shit," Terry-Joe said.

"Pretty much," Kell agreed.

26

Bronwyn was asleep. There were no nightmares in her head, no dreams of fire, or explosions, or heat. She did not taste sand or the salty tang of her own blood. No one screamed her name, or the first syllable of her name before ending in a wet gurgle.

Instead, she wandered through fields and forests, flew over lakes and mossy rocks, and harmonized with the songs that whispered in the wind. She recognized others doing the same, but kept to herself. She would dance and sing and fly with them later.

I am like them, she realized calmly, *but also different. I have tasks no one else can do.* She felt the calm certainty of that, even if the tasks themselves were a little vague.

Then something tapped at her window.

She opened her eyes in the darkness, instantly wide awake. The dream dissipated, along with the knowledge it held. She lay with her back to the window, facing the closed door to her room. The tapping came again, rapid and insistent.

Had Sally Olds returned? Every tale, every song said that a haint could be sent away by someone who no longer needed its presence, and Bronwyn certainly didn't need the poor dead girl hanging around. *She* would decide what memories she wanted, and if they came back, it would be in their own good time, not at the behest of some supernatural nanny trying to force her into a role she had no intention of assuming.

She took a deep breath, exhaled, and rolled over, intending to confront the haint once and for all. She wished she'd remembered to return the protective blue glass to the windowsill. "Goddammit, Sally, I *told* you—"

She stopped. It wasn't the haint, or at least not the haint she expected. A slender, definitely masculine shape stood silhouetted beyond the window. She could tell instantly that it wasn't Dwayne, or either of her brothers. Bronwyn drew the covers up to her chest.

The tapping came again.

"Who is it?" she hissed.

"It's me, Terry-Joe," he said in a soft, urgent voice. "I have to tell you something, Bronwyn."

She sighed. With a chuckle at the absurdity of the situation, she swung her legs off the bed and pulled on a T-shirt. "Terry-Joe, I thought we settled—"

"No, it's not that. Something bad's happened."

She frowned. The intensity in his voice was not lust, she realized. It was fear. She went to the window and opened it. "What's wrong?"

His hair was mussed, and he was out of breath with panic and anxiety. He looked off to the side, mustering his courage. "Bronwyn . . . Dwayne stabbed Kell."

The words took several moments to process. *"What?"*

The words rushed out. "Kell was at the Pair-A-Dice. Dwayne came in and started talking trash about you. Kell took it as long as he could, then smacked him. He was winning the fight when Dwayne pulled a knife and stabbed him."

Bronwyn couldn't breathe. "Is he—?"

"No, he's at the hospital over in Unicorn, they say he'll be fine. I drove him there; he wouldn't let me call an ambulance or the police. Said it was just something between him and my brother that they needed to settle. And he made me promise I wouldn't call you or let anyone else call. Swore me on my word. So I drove out here as quick as I could. You probably want to get your folks out of bed and head down there, to make sure he doesn't walk off before they finish stitching him up."

Bronwyn's hands tightened on the windowsill. Her nails bent painfully against the wood. Rage like she'd never felt built in her chest, crushing more air from her lungs.

"Bronwyn?" Terry-Joe asked.

She reached for her jeans, then stopped in midmotion. "Terry-Joe, how'd you get here?"

"Kell's car. I still had the keys from driving him to the emergency room. Figured it might keep him at the hospital a while longer."

She quickly pulled on her pants, then grabbed her tennis shoes and went to the window. She pushed him back and wriggled out. "What are you doing?" Terry-Joe gasped as she nimbly dropped to the ground. Her leg sent a little warning twinge up her spine, but held firm.

"Take me to the hospital," she said. "I need to know what happened before my parents find out. He won't tell them the whole truth, I know him. He'll make it sound like it was all his fault." She looked up at the boy, and even in the darkness he could see the rage and certainty boiling in her eyes. "Your brother's gone too far this time, Terry-Joe. *Way* too far. Now let's go."

Terry-Joe hesitated. Bronwyn grabbed the front of his shirt. "*Listen* to me," she said, softly but with earth-shaking fervor. "That's *my* brother. I will go to him one way or the other, but if you don't want to help me, then you're singing harmony with Dwayne."

"So 'if you're not with us, you're against us,' is that it?" he snapped back.

She released him. "Tonight, yeah, that's it exactly."

He sighed. "Come on, then."

The highway was deserted between Needsville and Unicorn, except for Trooper Bob Pafford watching from his usual hiding place. It had been a good night so far: two speeding tickets for well over a hundred dollars, and the chance to slap one smart-ass teenager out of sight of the dashboard video camera. Those monitoring devices had made his job much harder, but they also meant each time he outsmarted them, the rush was that much more intense. At his age, it saved him from complacency.

Some nights he looked at himself in the visor mirror, his skin bluish green in the dashboard light, and wondered if somehow he was off the track. He knew his conduct was considered reprehensible, yet he was secure enough not to care; as long as there were punks and smart-asses, he would continue to treat them the way they deserved. It wasn't about law or ticket quotas, it was about holding the line against disrespect and chaos. Once a society lost its manners, once it flagrantly disregarded its own most basic rules of conduct, it was doomed. And if he had to sting a few cheeks to accomplish this, he would do it and sleep the sleep of the just afterwards.

He recalled his ex-wife, her own cheek bright red from a blow, as she left him for the final time. "If you come near me again," she'd said in that cold voice of hers, "I'll kill you. I mean it. You've taught me how to get away with it, too. You're through intimidating me."

He shook his head at the memory. A few slaps to keep a wife in line were not "beatings." Choice words to express his righteous displeasure were not "abuse." It was that therapist of hers, telling her things that directly contradicted everything Pafford knew to be true. If the man hadn't moved his practice out of state, Pafford would've made sure he couldn't turn around in his driveway without getting a moving violation.

He got the tingle on the back of his neck before he saw the approaching headlights. He watched them grow larger, and experience told him they were well past the posted speed limit of forty-five miles per hour. He smiled, sat up straight, and watched the radar gun's readout. As the vehicle passed through the beam, the numbers read *72*.

He flipped the switches for lights and siren, and spun gravel as he tore out of the roadside park onto the blacktop.

"Shit," Terry-Joe muttered when he saw the lights. He immediately pulled over. The shoulder sloped precariously down toward the ditch, tilting the car sideways.

The state trooper pulled in behind them. Terry-Joe sat still, his heart pounding, hands on the steering wheel. He had no doubt who would soon appear at his window. Only one trooper worked off the interstate in Cloud County.

Pafford heaved himself out of his car and walked slowly toward the other vehicle, one hand on the butt of his pistol. He reached the car and tapped on the glass with his flashlight. Terry-Joe rolled it down and was immediately blinded. "Terry-Joe Gitterman," he drawled. "I'd have expected your brother."

"You'd be wrong," Terry-Joe mumbled.

"In kind of a hurry, wasn't you, son? Where's the fire?"

"Her brother got took to the hosp—"

Pafford shoved the flashlight slightly, so that the edge around the lens struck Terry-Joe in the temple. The flashlight's weight did all the work, and the move was invisible to the dashboard camera.

"You need to learn the meaning of 'ree-torical,' son. I don't give a rat's ass where you Tufa trash were going."

Terry-Joe's eyes watered from the blow, and he felt himself turn red with fury. He gingerly touched the side of his head. "Yes, sir," he said tightly.

Pafford looked into the backseat. "This your car, boy?"

"No, sir. It belongs to Kell Hyatt."

"Does he know you have it?"

"Yes, sir."

Pafford shone the light onto his passenger. "And who's this little piece of ass you're toting around? Hope she's over eighteen, for your sake."

Bronwyn turned and looked straight and steady into the light, willing her eyes not to blink. She heard Pafford gasp in surprise. "Well, I'll be a goddamned monkey in the zoo. If it ain't the Bronwynator. Now, I happen to know you're over eighteen, but I can't quite recall Mr. Gitterman's age here. You wouldn't be out corruptin' a minor in your big brother's car, would you?"

"My brother," she said quietly, "is in the hospital in Unicorn. He got stabbed tonight."

He snorted. "I bet he did. Probably some blonde's boyfriend did it. You Tufa boys love chasing white women, don't you?" He withdrew the flashlight and slapped the roof of the car. "I smell marijuana," he said loudly, for the camera's benefit. "Both of you, step out of the car now. Keep your hands where I can see them."

Terry-Joe and Bronwyn did as instructed. They put their hands on the edge of the car's roof, and Pafford quickly patted Terry-Joe down. Then he turned to Bronwyn.

He took a moment to savor this. Leaned forward, tight jeans hugging her firm ass, she was a sight, and he made sure to take his time. She wore no bra under her T-shirt, and he let his thick fingers caress the sides of her breasts through the cotton. He moved to her waist, then down the sides of her thighs. He grunted as he knelt to continue down.

He stopped suddenly. "How come one of your legs is so much bigger than the other one?"

"I just got one out of a cast," Bronwyn said through clenched teeth. "The muscle's all—"

She gasped with agony as he dug one huge iron-fingered hand into the tender skin of her injured calf. Her leg collapsed, and she fell to the ground. Her vision went hazy, and little sparks swirled around the edges.

Terry-Joe jumped back and said, "What the *hell,* man! You know she was hurt in the war!"

Pafford's gun was in his hand without a conscious thought. He pointed it at the center of Terry-Joe's chest and hissed, "You make another sound, and whatever you had for dinner will be splattered all over the pavement." More loudly he said, "Miss, this behavior won't help at your trial."

Bronwyn looked up at him with hatred stronger than anything Pafford had ever encountered. She was breathing hard and quick through her teeth, and spittle collected at the corners of her mouth. "All right," she whispered, and then more loudly said, "All right! I'll suck you off, just don't shoot him!"

Pafford blinked in confusion. Before he could reply, Bronwyn got to her knees and whipped off her T-shirt, exposing her breasts to both the night and the dashboard video camera. "Yes, sir, anything you say," she cried. "You can come on my tits. Do you want my pants off, too?"

Pafford stared, speechless. Bronwyn Hyatt half-naked was a sight to make any man pause, and the utter incongruity of it froze him in place. It was only belatedly, after she'd said, "Yes, sir, I remember what you told me to do the last time, when I was sixteen," that he understood what she was doing.

He got to his feet and backed away, the gun still pointed at them. "You goddamned *whore*," he huffed.

She stayed on her knees, chin high. "Yes, sir, I'm a whore, whatever you say. Do you want me to lick your balls again, too?"

He scuttled backward to the driver's door of his car. "I'm letting you off with a warning!" he yelled, his voice higher than normal. He got behind the wheel and spun burning tires backward as he pulled onto the deserted road.

Bronwyn winced as the tiny rocks stung her bare skin. Then she laughed as Pafford awkwardly turned around, nearly going rear-bumper-first into the opposite ditch, and roared off into the night the way he'd come. In moments, the only sounds were the normal ones.

27

Kell looked up from the gurney as Bronwyn pushed the plastic curtain aside. His black hair was tangled, and the fluorescent light gave his skin a deathly pallor. The sheet was pulled down to his waist, exposing a swath of bandages around his ribs. On one side, two tiny red spots soaked through the gauze. He sighed and closed his eyes guiltily. "Don't say it," he said.

"You *moron*," she wanted to yell. Her whisper was somehow worse.

"Good to see you, too, sis."

She stepped into the enclosed area and yanked the curtain shut behind her. A woman with one of the other patients hummed "Amazing Grace," and a child coughed laboriously. She put her hands on her hips. "I don't know where to even start on the list of things about this that piss me off."

He pressed the button that raised the bed beneath his upper body. "You'll pick one."

"You picked a fight with Dwayne. Over *me*. Who

are you and what did you do with my sensible, level-headed brother, the one who's never been in a fight in his life?"

"That's not true, I got in a fight with Hobart Tilling."

"That was in *grade school*."

He sighed helplessly. "I can't explain it, Bronwyn. He just made me mad."

"Mom's going to kill you," Bronwyn said.

"I know. Is she with you?"

"No, they don't know yet. Terry-Joe came and got me first, and you better be glad he did because it gives us both time to think up something to tell Mom and Dad."

"Look, I didn't go there *looking* for Dwayne. I was there first, even. Things just . . ."

"What did he say that was so bad? That you haven't heard people say about me before?"

He looked away. "I don't want to talk about it."

She stepped closed and grabbed the hair on the back of his head. "Well, I do. What was it?"

He slapped her hand away. "Stop it. It was bad enough."

"What?" she insisted.

"You really want to know? Okay. He said the only reason the Iraqis didn't kill you was because you . . . gave them all great oral sex. I'm paraphrasing."

Bronwyn was silent. The woman now sang "Shall We Gather at the River." The child continued to cough. "Well," Bronwyn said at last.

"There were a lot of people around who heard him say it," Kell added. "A lot of Rockhouse's people. They started laughing. I just couldn't let it go."

She looked down at her feet for a moment, waiting for the

blush to fade. It was no secret among Cloud County's males that the old Bronwyn Hyatt, the Bronwynator, enjoyed giving oral sex as much as they enjoyed getting it. The sense of power, of reducing these posturing overgrown child-men to moaning helplessness, was better than any drug she'd found. Most of the time the men were appropriately grateful, and both parties were satisfied and discreet about it afterwards.

But Dwayne had never been able to climax that way, and became resentful of the stories of Bronwyn's skill. Of course he would say something like that to get a rise out of her brother. Still . . .

"It was the grin, really," Kell continued. "I could've ignored him saying it and everyone laughing about it. But his god-damned, shit-eating, smug-ass *grin*—"

"Mr. Hyatt?" a firm new voice said. They turned to see a sheriff's deputy standing at the foot of the bed. He was tall, lean, and had the steady gaze of a man with a clear moral compass, the opposite in every way of Bob Pafford. He held his hat and nodded to Bronwyn. "Excuse me, ma'am, I need to speak to the gentleman."

"This is my sister," Kell said. "You can talk in front of her."

The deputy looked at her as if he knew her, but couldn't quite place it. Then with mild astonishment he said, "Aren't you Bronwyn Hyatt?"

She nodded, too tired to be sarcastic.

"It's an honor to meet you, ma'am. We said a prayer for you at church every Sunday while you were in the hospital."

Bronwyn managed a smile. "That's nice. It must've worked. Thank everyone there for me."

"I will do. And thank you for serving our country."

He turned his attention back to Kell. "Now, about your little altercation. I talked to folks at the Pair-A-Dice and they all pretty much agree Mr. Gitterman started it. Add to that use of a deadly weapon by a fellow on parole, and he's in some pretty deep shit, pardon my language, ma'am. Do you want to press charges?"

"Yes," Bronwyn said before Kell could answer.

Kell glared at her. "I was *going* to say yes."

"No, you were going to be all tough-guy and noble and say, 'It was all a misunderstanding.'" She deepened her voice in mocking imitation of his. To the deputy she said, "But he *will* press charges."

"Yes," Kell agreed, still scowling.

"All right, I reckon that's all I need right now. We will need a statement from you as soon as you're up and about. In the meantime, you don't worry. We'll find him. Fellows like that, they always mess up. Especially when they're scared." He nodded to Bronwyn again. "Ma'am."

When he was gone, Kell mimicked, "Ma'am."

"Shut up, rest, and let the police do their job," Bronwyn said. "I'm going to go break the news to Mom and Dad." She kissed him on the forehead. "I love you, you know. Jackass."

"Bitch," he replied with a smile.

In the waiting room, Terry-Joe sat wriggling uncomfortably in one of the ancient vinyl chairs. He stood as Bronwyn strode over and said, "You know where Dwayne is, don't you?"

Terry-Joe tried to change the subject. "How's Kell?"

Bronwyn stepped close and her voice was tight, soft, and vicious. "Don't *fuck* with me, Terry-Joe. I know him better than you do. He's wherever he's got his pot patch now, isn't he?"

Terry-Joe started to dissemble, then gave up with a sigh. "Probably."

"Do you know where that is?"

He nodded.

"Then let's go." She grabbed his arm and dragged him toward the door.

"Wait, wait," he said, wrenching free. "I talked to that deputy. They'll find him."

"Did you tell them where he was?"

Terry-Joe shook his head; no matter what, Dwayne was his brother, and he wouldn't rat him out to that degree. "But he has to come out eventually, and they'll get him then."

She spoke with a cold certainty he'd never heard her use before. "I'm not in the mood to wait."

"He didn't do this just to get back at you, you know," Terry-Joe said defensively. "I was there, it just *happened*."

"The hell it did. Picking a fight with my brother, with you right there? He knows damn well I'll come after him, and he'll be waiting for me."

"Then why are you going to do it?"

"Because . . ." She suddenly found it hard to breathe, and realized she was sweating. The dream came back to her, the certainty that some things only she could do. Was this one of them? "Because . . ."

Suddenly the doors opened and Craig Chess walked in out of the night. He was unshaven, his hair matted from sleep, and he wore shoes with no socks. He stopped dead when he saw Bronwyn. He ran a quick, useless hand through his hair. "Well. Hello, Ms. Hyatt."

She stared in surprise. "Hi."

He took in her lack of cast, bandage, or crutches. "Wow. You've really mended."

"Yeah, it's . . ." She went blank. Her anger seemed somehow childish in Craig's presence, which made her ashamed. And she hated that. "Clean mountain air," she finished with a nervous little laugh.

He looked at Terry-Joe. "Hi, Craig Chess, pastor of the Triple Springs Methodist Church." He offered his hand.

"Terry-Joe Gitterman," he said as they shook. He jealously noted the way Bronwyn stared at this man. "Nice to meet you."

"Likewise." Craig turned back to Bronwyn. "So are you all right?"

She frowned. "Why wouldn't I be?"

"You're in the hospital emergency room in the middle of the night."

"Oh. No, it's . . . my brother had an accident."

"I'm sorry to hear that. Was it Aiden?"

"No, Kell. I don't think you've met him. He's my older brother."

"How is he?"

"He should be fine. Nothing too serious."

Their eyes met. Neither knew what held them there, but for a long moment they could not look away. Something passed between them, and a link that had been a mere thread grew more substantial and important.

Bronwyn blinked back to the present and said, "And what brings you here?"

"One of my elderly parishioners had a heart attack. Her family can't be here until tomorrow, so I said I'd sit with her while they do their tests."

"Is that part of your job?"

He smiled. "I always figured that *is* my job. The sermons are what I do to keep busy when no one has any immediate need."

"Never thought of it that way."

"Lots of people don't. Lots of *preachers* don't."

She impulsively reached out and ran her fingers down his arm, brushing the fabric of his sleeve; she wanted more than anything to wrap her arms around him, but that would surely freak him out. Hell, it freaked *her* out, because she had no idea why she felt it so strongly. "I have to go," she blurted.

"Okay. I'm glad you're feeling better, and I hope your brother recovers."

"He will. Hyatts are tough."

"So I've noticed."

She firmly took Terry-Joe's arm. "Good seeing you again, Reverend Chess."

"Likewise. And nice to meet you, Terry-Joe."

Terry-Joe said nothing, but looked down sullenly as she pulled him toward the exit. He risked a *she's mine* glare back at Craig, but the preacher's confused expression made it pointless. It seemed none of them knew exactly what had just happened.

Hidden in the shadows at the far end of the empty hospital parking lot, Bob Pafford watched Bronwyn and Terry-Joe climb into Kell Hyatt's car. The dispatcher had confirmed both the car's ownership and that the elder Hyatt had, in fact, been stabbed by Dwayne Gitterman at the Pair-A-Dice outside Needsville.

Pafford's fingers tapped nervously on his polyester-uniformed knee. When the night's dashboard video was finally seen, he would have a hard time getting around what it showed. The truth was so outlandish that no one would believe it, and he had far too many enemies just waiting for a misstep like this one. He could come up with no other explanation, *unless* he could claim it was all part of his plan to get the younger Gitterman boy and Hyatt girl to lead him to Dwayne. It was a long shot, but it was all he had, and it hinged on him apprehending the fugitive. So he watched the car drive off, started his engine, and followed them out of Unicorn and into the Cloud County night.

28

The car rumbled through the night, traveling up and down the uneven gravel roads far into the hills above Needsville. Terry-Joe—so tense, his chest hurt—skidded and nearly missed curves he normally handled easily. Bronwyn braced herself against the dash and passenger door, ignoring the seat belt.

Occasionally he thought he saw headlights far behind him, and wondered who else would be out at this time of night, on these isolated roads. But the lights always failed to appear when he slowed a bit to let them catch up, so he wrote them off as just other folks going about their own nocturnal business.

Bronwyn said nothing, simply staring ahead into the dark. Once Terry-Joe turned on the radio to break the silence, and she immediately turned it off. He took the hint.

Finally, forty-five minutes after leaving the hospital, he slowed and stopped at the side of a gravel road. The dust from their passage drifted past them and gave the

headlight beams sharp outlines in the darkness. Insects almos
immediately appeared, drawn from the surrounding forest.

He killed the engine, then the light. The thick old-growt
forest blocked out most of the moon's illumination. The nois
of the summer woods quickly filled the silence. He glanced i
the mirror, but saw no sign of their intermittent pursuer; per
haps he'd been imagining things.

He nodded at Dwayne's pickup, its shape barely visible be
hind some thick bushes. Only reflection from the obsessivel
polished chrome gave it away. "His truck's blocking the road
We'll have to walk."

"He'll be drunk off his ass by now," Bronwyn said with cer
tainty. "Might even be passed out."

"He's scared, Bronwyn. He told me about jail once, abou
some of the things that happened. Stuff he did, stuff that go
done to him. He doesn't want to go back."

"Should've thought of that before he stabbed Kell," she sai
coldly.

Terry-Joe turned in the seat to face her in the darkness. "Mayb
we should talk to Bliss Overbay or Mandalay Harris or some
body. One Tufa stabbing another might be something the
should know about."

"They know," she snapped. "They *always* know. I'm surprise
Bliss wasn't at the hospital before we were. But this has nothin
to do with them, this is between Dwayne and me."

He put his hands on her shoulders. It was the first time h
had touched her with any real assertiveness. "*Why*, Bronwyn?"

"I need to look into his eyes and see what's there," she said
"I want to know if the Dwayne I remember ever existed for rea
or was just something I made up in my head." *I did love hir
once, didn't I?* she asked herself.

"He's just another hillbilly fuckup. Being Tufa doesn't change that."

She shrugged out of his grip. "Don't pretend you know what I'm thinking, Terry-Joe. The only thing you can do is help me, and if you can't do that, you'd best wait in the car. Which is it?"

He felt his own anger rise, then quickly subside. Wearily he said, "You know which it is."

"Then let's get going."

Dwayne's truck blocked a wide path that followed the land's contours. Their eyes had adjusted enough they could see by the patches of intermittent moonlight. Ahead, a dim glow grew stronger as they approached.

They topped a ridge and immediately knew they were in the right place: Nickelback blared out at them from the darkness. "My God," Bronwyn muttered, "that's the same shit he was listening to when I left for the army."

She descended into the gully, no longer needing Terry-Joe's help. The light from a battery-powered lantern guided her into the clearing, where marijuana plants nearly five feet tall grew packed together in the half acre of open space. The trees around them provided ideal cover, hiding them both from the ground and from overhead, yet still allowing enough sunlight for them to flourish. Within his limited area of expertise, Dwayne was a gardening genius.

He sat in a canvas camp chair, smoking a joint amid a scatter of beer cans. His old CD boom box rested beside his feet. Mosquitoes and midges drawn to the lantern swirled around it. With the light blinding him, he did not notice his visitors until Terry-Joe shut off the music and Bronwyn kicked his boot to break through his daze.

His red, heavy-lidded eyes blinked. Then he snapped wide awake and jumped to his feet. "How the fuck did you find me?" he screeched, his voice panicky. Then he saw Terry-Joe. "Why, you backstabbing little pissant—"

Bronwyn jabbed him in the chest with her finger. "You best stay focused on your immediate problem, fuckhead. You stabbed my brother."

Dwayne shook his head, tried to back up, but tripped over the chair. "I ain't going back to jail, Bronwyn. That ain't happening. I'll kill so many cops, they'll have to shoot me down."

Bronwyn laughed, a sound so cold and heartless, it made Terry-Joe freeze in midstep. "You couldn't kill anybody, Dwayne. You've hurt some people, because behind that Tim McGraw smile you're stupid and mean. But you've never killed anybody." She dropped her voice so only he could hear. "I have."

Dwayne scurried around the chair, keeping it between them. "Stay away from me, Bronwyn."

She rushed forward and shoved him so hard that he tripped over his own feet and landed on his back. He jumped to his feet, glazed eyes blazing, one fist cocked.

Terry-Joe jumped in between them. "Whoa, there, big bro. This won't help anything." His voice shook a little.

Dwayne grabbed him by the shirt. "You been bird-dogging after me, you little faggot. That's why you were sucking up to her asshole brother, wasn't it?"

"Back off, Dwayne," Bronwyn said. "This has nothing to do with him."

Dwayne continued to stare at Terry-Joe. Then slowly he smiled, the smile that caused girls all over the mountains to sigh and drop their panties. "Aw, ain't no thang, little brother," he drawled, then with his free hand grabbed Terry-Joe's genitals and crushed with all his strength. Terry-Joe screamed but could do nothing.

Bronwyn reached past Terry-Joe, shoved two fingers up Dwayne's nose and pulled as hard as she could. She heard cartilage give way.

"Fuck!" he yelled, and released his brother. Terry-Joe collapsed. Dwayne swung wildly at Bronwyn, and she couldn't step aside fast enough. His huge fist connected with her side, lifting her feet momentarily off the ground.

Something snapped. They all heard it.

Dwayne stepped back, eyes wide, buzz completely gone.

Bronwyn dropped to her knees. "Oh, shit," she whispered, gingerly covering her ribs. There was that awful moment of anticipation before the pain hit, when she had time to think, *This is really going to hurt.* Then it washed over her with an intensity she never imagined. She had no memory of her battlefield injuries, which she rationally assumed must've been worse, so the agony ripped through her like an angry cat tearing through tissue paper.

"Goddammit, Dwayne," Terry-Joe croaked, and crawled to Bronwyn. She coughed, gagged, then spit out a mouthful of blood that hung stringy between her lips and the ground, sparkling in the lantern light.

When she saw the blood, something more intangible also snapped. She glared up at Dwayne with fury that was pure Tufa, and despite the pain keened, *"The arms that hold you are not those of love. . . ."*

"Oh, fuck this," Dwayne whispered. That was twice in one night someone had begun singing his dying dirge, and even his gummy brain understood the implications. He turned and ran off into the woods, tearing clumsily through the undergrowth.

His footsteps quickly faded, leaving only the sound of labored breathing from the other two.

Bronwyn's vision blurred, and she felt a chill settle in her body. She knew she was going into shock. "Terry-Joe," Bronwyn gurgled, trying to stay calm, "I think this might be serious." Tears of pain trickled down her cheek. "Oh, God . . ."

Terry-Joe got to his feet despite his throbbing testicles. When she looked up at him, the blood on her mouth shone like black lipstick. She took his hand, nearly pulling him down on top of her. They staggered slowly, leaning together, back up the hill toward the car.

They did not notice Bob Pafford hidden in the shadows just off the trail. When they were out of sight, he emerged, switched on his flashlight, and headed down the gully after Dwayne. His held his cocked gun in his other hand.

Bronwyn had serious trouble breathing by the time Kell's car left gravel and hit pavement. Terry-Joe floored it across the valley, merged onto the interstate with horn blaring and emergency flashers on, and finally stood on the brakes to leave smoking trails of rubber in front of the emergency room door. He'd managed the whole trip in less than half an hour.

As they drove, Bronwyn rode waves of pain that seemed to incrementally crush her lungs, making each breath harder to draw and impossible to hang on to. She had a sudden epiphany: What if all the death signs had applied to *her,* not her mother? Everyone assumed that if she'd been marked for death, it would've happened in Iraq; but what if the night wind was just waiting for her to return home before snatching her away?

The nurses and orderlies took Bronwyn immediately to triage; they knew who she was, and none of them wanted a hero's death on their shift. Terry-Joe asked for a bag of ice, which he applied to his crotch with an utter lack of self-consciousness. He settled into another of the waiting room's plastic chairs and waited for his crushed balls to grow numb.

He looked up as Craig Chess suddenly came out of the examination area, saw him, and did a double take. The minister looked worried and grim. "Terry-Joe, right? Didn't you leave with Bronwyn Hyatt a while back?"

Terry-Joe was too tired and sore to argue. "Yeah."

Craig looked around. "Where is she?"

Terry-Joe nodded at the double doors that led back to the actual treatment area. "She had an accident. She's in there."

"What kind of accident?"

"You'll have to ask her."

Craig gazed at the doors, then at the entrance. He seemed preoccupied, and made no mention of the ice Terry-Joe held between his legs. At last he said, "Okay, listen. I need your help with something really important. I need you to watch out for her parents. You know them, right?"

"Sure."

"Well, they're on their way here. Should get here any minute."

He nodded. Eventually Kell would've had to call them. Now, he thought wryly, they'd get double good news. At least Aiden was too young to also go off and try to seek vengeance. "Okay. I'll send them back as soon as—"

"*No.* Please. Keep them here. I'll keep checking back, okay?

Thanks." Craig turned and went back into the treatment room. Terry-Joe tried to find a more comfortable position, but realized that at the moment there wasn't one.

Craig quickly found Bronwyn, who lay flat on her back on a stretcher behind a curtain. An IV had been set up, and she had an oxygen tube beneath her nose. "Ms. Hyatt," he said. "Are you all right?"

Her voice was tight and thin. "Don't make me laugh, Reverend, it hurts. And for God's sake, call me Bronwyn."

There was still dried blood on her lips and chin. He asked, "What happened to you?"

"Cracked a rib, maybe poked a lung. Waiting for the X-rays to see how serious it is."

"How did you crack a rib in the middle of the night?"

She managed a smile. "I'm the Bronwynator."

"Excuse me just a second," he said, and stepped out to check the waiting room. He returned a moment later.

"Where'd you go?" she asked.

"I'm expecting someone," he said. He touched her hand where it lay on the bed rail. "I sure hope you didn't do anything too serious."

She laughed, then winced. "I think, after everything else, I can handle this. It was scary for a bit, though; amazing how you get used to breathing."

He closed his fingers around hers. The room was chilly, and the warmth of their flesh made both tingle. Their gazes met, and held.

She saw something disturbing in his eyes. "Are *you* okay, Reverend?"

Before he could answer, they heard a loud, wailing scream of such despair that it seemed to burrow into the hearts of everyone within earshot. It emanated from the waiting room; the doors and curtains did little to muffle its intensity. Despite the pain, Bronwyn rose on her elbows, eyes wide, because she recognized the voice.

Her mother, Chloe. In agony.

29

Craig rushed out of the treatment area knowing what he'd find. *Dammit*! He'd done everything he could to prevent this, and at the last moment he'd been distracted by the touch of a pretty girl.

In the middle of the waiting room, Deacon Hyatt knelt beside his wife. Chloe sprawled on the floor, screaming with an abandon only sudden bone-deep grief inspires. She wore denim shorts and a T-shirt, and as she thrashed, her flip-flops shot across the room. A doctor, middle-aged and tired-looking, stood beside them, his hands extended in useless, unwanted sympathy. Terry-Joe stood as well, his jeans wet from the melted ice, his expression anguished.

The door opened behind Craig, and Bronwyn pushed past him, cradling her ribs and unconcerned with the way her hospital gown gapped open. Blood trickled from her arm where she'd torn out the IV. She slid down beside her mother, brushing Chloe's hair back from her face.

"Mom, what's wrong?" she shouted over the woman's cries. Chloe only screamed again, alternately tearing at her hair and beating hands and feet against the floor.

Bronwyn looked at her father. "Daddy?"

Deacon, his face stoic, said simply, "Kell's gone."

"Gone where?" she asked in a small voice.

Deacon's face darkened. "He's *dead*!" he yelled at his daughter.

At those words, Chloe screamed again. By now, more doctors and nurses had gathered around them, looking uncertainly at one another. Many were part Tufa, so they knew the Hyatts and their status in the community; but they couldn't just leave the woman screaming on the floor.

Finally Craig pushed through them and knelt beside Deacon. "Mr. Hyatt," he said gently, "let's get her off the floor and onto a bed." Deacon nodded, and together they lifted Chloe, who put up no resistance. Bronwyn had seen her mother cry before, but never like this; she felt her own tears battling with confusion, rage, and pain as they sought escape.

She saw Terry-Joe standing in the door to the lobby, almost comical with the wet stain from the icepack. She rushed to him and threw her arms around him. Words rushed out, tight and thin because of her injury. "Kell's dead, I don't know what happened, they said he's dead, Daddy said he's dead. . . ."

Terry-Joe held her close, careful not to squeeze too tight. Her choked, breathless sobs cut through him, and he felt his own tears boiling free. He stroked her hair, and despite everything thought happily that she'd run to *him* when she needed comfort.

Craig returned from getting Chloe onto a gurney, where her cries continued to ring out. He took Bronwyn by the arm, holding her hospital gown closed with one hand. "Come with me," he said firmly. To Terry-Joe he said, "Could you get her a robe from one of the nurses?"

Terry-Joe started to ask Craig why *he* couldn't get the robe, but the older man's authority stopped him. "Yes, sir," he mumbled, and released the girl he now knew he loved.

Craig took Bronwyn into the little side room where doctors delivered bad news. It was cold, bright, and inhuman. Terry-Joe knocked softly and handed in the thin robe. She sat numbly as Craig draped the robe around her.

She began to shake. She looked up at him, suddenly conscious of their different ages and positions in life, seeing him as an elder, as someone she should respect. "What happened, Reverend?" she whimpered. "I just saw him an hour and a half ago, he was fine. We were joking, he . . . The last thing he said to me was, 'bitch.'" She laughed despite everything, but it was momentary. "They said it was nothing serious."

Craig knelt beside the chair and put his hand on her shoulder. He'd never wanted to hold and comfort someone more in his life, and yet he knew that was not his role, not what she and her family needed. As gently as he could, he said, "Apparently the knife nicked a blood vessel that didn't start bleeding until after they'd treated his injuries. By the time they noticed, it was too late. They did all they could, Bronwyn, I promise."

"Did he say anything else?" she asked in a tiny child's voice.

Craig shook his head. "They'd sedated him for the pain, so he never woke up. He never felt a thing."

She nodded slowly. "Then Dwayne murdered him."

Craig said nothing.

She blinked, rubbed her head, and said, "I didn't see Aiden. Did Mom and Dad leave him at home?"

"Yes. They didn't know how bad it was when they left. It all happened while they were on their way here. I'm sure they thought there was no need to wake him up."

"Then he's home all alone."

Craig reached over and took her hand. "I'll go see about him, and bring him down here to be with everyone else. If you think that's where he should be."

She stared at him. "Why do *you* care?"

He was used to the brusqueness of grief, and it didn't faze him. "Partly because it's my nature, partly because it's my job."

She took a deep breath, winced at the pain, and said, "I'm sorry, that was rude. It would be very nice of you to go get him, and I would be very grateful."

"Will you go back to bed?"

She shook her head and got to her feet. "I have to be with Mom and Dad. And before you say anything, you'll have to accept that that's *my* nature."

"Fair enough."

A doctor knocked on the door and said Bronwyn could, if she wished, view the body before it was taken "downstairs." She leaned on Craig as they joined her parents behind the omnipresent privacy curtain. Chloe, her sobs reduced to choking gulps, clung to Deacon the way Bronwyn did to Craig. Terry-Joe stood off to one side. They all gazed down at the form on the gurney.

Kell Hyatt's eyes were closed and his face impassive; he looked young and untroubled. His black hair was brushed back from his face, in a style wholly unlike him. Chloe reached down and tugged his bangs down onto his forehead.

Bronwyn pulled away and stood beside Chloe. Craig moved back a bit, observing. Deacon had his arm tightly across Chloe's shoulders, and his chin trembled with the effort of holding back his own tears. Bronwyn silently held her mother's hand, her injuries forgotten. Only Chloe felt free to truly express what they all felt.

Craig caught Terry-Joe's eye and nodded for the young man to follow. They left the Hyatts and returned to the waiting room.

"Aiden Hyatt is still back at his house," Craig said. "He doesn't know what's happened, and I sure don't want him to find out by a phone call. Will you take a ride out there with me to pick him up? You're his friend, and he might need one tonight."

Terry-Joe nodded.

As they prepared to leave, a voice came from behind the double doors, loud and pure and unconcerned with propriety. It broke through Craig's professional distance and training, and he felt hot tears well in his own eyes. He recognized it as Chloe Hyatt.

> *My baby is so tired tonight,*
> *He does not like the candlelight.*
> *His little head will soon be pressed*
> *Against his mama's loving breast,*
> *And mama's song will sound the best. . . .*

"What song is that?" Craig asked, his voice catching in his throat.

Terry-Joe was too weary to be circumspect. "Kell's dyin' dirge. Every Tufa has one. It comes to the people around him when it's time for it."

Now there was harmony, from the husband and daughter beside her.

So sing, sigh, little boy sleep.
So sing, sigh, the wind her watch will keep.
Oh baby mine, how fondly I love you.
Oh son of mine, a family's love is true.

Craig wiped at his eyes. The sound was so plaintive, so touching, that its sorrow was irresistible. A nurse emerged from the treatment area sobbing into a tissue.

"We should go," Craig said.

Aiden came to the door rubbing his eyes, clad in sweatpants and a Transformers T-shirt. "What?" he said, drawing the word out into several syllables.

"It's me, Terry-Joe. Can you open the door?"

"Ain't supposed to."

"This is important, Aiden. I've got Reverend Chess with me. We need to talk to you."

"To me?"

Terry-Joe was tired, and his balls ached. *"Aiden, open the goddamned door!"*

"All right, all right," the boy said. Craig put a calming hand on Terry-Joe's shoulder, but the younger man shrugged it off. He pulled the screen door open as soon as Aiden unhooked it and went inside.

Aiden looked askance at Terry-Joe's wet spot. "Did you pee your pants?"

"Never mind. Listen, something bad's happened," Terry-Joe said. He couldn't look directly at the boy, so he gazed at the floor.

"Is Bronwyn hurt?"

"No. I mean, yes, but that's not the bad thing. The bad thing is . . ." And Terry-Joe froze. He simply couldn't say the words.

Craig stepped up. "Son, I'm afraid your brother, Kell, has passed on."

Aiden blinked, and the last of the sleep cleared from his eyes. "Wha . . . Kell's *dead*?"

"I'm afraid so."

"Well, then *say* dead!" Aiden yelled, making them both jump. He turned to Terry-Joe. "What happened?"

"Ah . . . he got in a fight with my brother."

Aiden stared at Terry-Joe with the kind of betrayal only a child can feel when his idol topples from the pedestal. Dwayne Gitterman had been the epitome of cool when Aiden was a small boy, always showing off and bringing treats. "*Dwayne* killed him?"

Terry-Joe nodded, still looking at the floor.

"Your mom, dad, and sister asked us to come bring you to the hospital," Craig said. "You should probably get dressed first."

Aiden swallowed hard. He was too overwhelmed to cry. He turned and went into his room, and they heard dresser drawers opening and closing.

Craig looked around at the family pictures. He saw photos of Deacon and Chloe as young newlyweds, then with their gradually increasing brood. He was impressed with how little they had visibly aged; Chloe, especially, was as vibrant now as she'd been as a young woman in the eighties and nineties.

There were three pictures of only Kell; in one he was a toddler, in another an adolescent proudly holding a stringer of fish, and finally his high school graduation picture. Craig had never met Kell, and he realized now he'd never see him alive. The boy holding those fish was gone forever.

Another picture drew his eye. Bronwyn, fourteen or fifteen in a halter top and shorts, making a muscle for her father, who felt it and feigned terror. Even though the picture was only a few years old—when it had been taken, Craig was probably finishing his undergraduate degree—there seemed ages of difference between the girl in the photo and the one he'd met. It wasn't just the trauma of her experience, although that was part of it. There was a power within Bronwyn now that was entirely missing from this earlier girl.

Then he was yanked back to the present when Aiden strode from his room, dressed and carrying his hunting rifle. "Y'all lock up behind yourselves," he said without looking at them.

With cries of alarm, Terry-Joe jumped at Aiden, while Craig rushed to block the door. Terry-Joe grabbed the rifle by the barrel, but Aiden wasn't letting it go. Craig held up his hands in a *calm down* gesture. "Aiden, I think you need to take a deep breath."

"I think y'all need to step back," Aiden said.

"You're not leaving with that gun," Craig said seriously.

"The hell I'm not," he said, and began tugging to get it away from Terry-Joe. Craig jumped forward to intercede just as a loud crack filled the room. Terry-Joe jumped back, and Aiden dropped the gun.

Craig put his foot on the barrel to keep anyone else from grabbing it. For a moment no one moved. Then he asked, "Are you two hurt?"

Terry-Joe shook his head. Aiden stared wide eyed at the wall. The bullet had passed through a framed picture, shattering the brittle glass. Craig glanced at it, then looked more closely; it appeared to be a piece of sandpaper. He tentatively touched it and confirmed this, then saw an *X* drawn with a

Sharpie. The words, *I'm going here* were written beside it, and the signature, *Love, Pvt. Bronwyn Hyatt.*

Craig picked up the gun, unscrewed the tube, and poured the little gold cartridges out into his hand. He worked the bolt action several times to make sure nothing was left in the chamber. Then he tossed the weapon onto the couch. "That wasn't real bright," he said through his teeth, forcing his anger down. The boy had just gotten terrible news, after all.

Aiden turned to Terry-Joe. "Sorry, Terry-Joe, I wasn't trying to hurt you," he said flatly, as if discussing a ball game. "But I reckon I have to kill your brother, either tonight or eventually."

Craig turned Aiden's face to him. "Aiden, listen to me. Right now the living need you more than the dead. Your mom, dad, and sister are at the hospital, and they want us to take you there. Unarmed. Okay?"

Aiden nodded. Then his lower lip began to tremble.

Craig managed a wry, sad smile. "I don't blame you, I'd cry, too."

Aiden burst out with a sob, splattering saliva and mucus in Craig's face. He ignored it, dropped to his knees, and wrapped the boy in a big hug.

Terry-Joe, still shaken by the gunshot, suddenly had a thought. He ran into Bronwyn's bedroom and grabbed her mandolin from under the bed.

Craig picked Aiden up and carried him outside. The boy cried all the way to the hospital.

30

At the hospital, Bronwyn was back in her bed, her parents seated in chairs beside her. Kell's body was now in the morgue, evidence of a capital crime. The police had been notified, and the search for Dwayne Gitterman went from casual to much more serious.

None of the Hyatts spoke. They knew that, in the lobby, members of the Tufa community had begun to gather, but none of them felt like making an appearance.

The wrapping around Bronwyn's chest had begun to pinch and itch, and the artificial weariness of the pain medication kept her mind fuzzy. She fought the drowsiness, though; she couldn't imagine sleeping through a time like this.

Kell. Was. Dead. The certainty of that encircled her and cinched far worse than the bandages. The older brother who'd taught her to shoot and drive, who'd helped her hide from her parents the first time she came in drunk, who'd advised her repeatedly not to hang out with that no-account Dwayne Gitterman, was now gone.

Dwayne. The bad boy with the good heart. Except he didn't have a good heart, or it had gone bad while she was away in Iraq. Whatever the cause, he couldn't be allowed to roam free anymore.

Suddenly her mind cleared. The dream returned, its meaning suddenly obvious.

Dwayne hadn't turned to petty crime out of a desire for wealth or power, but from simple laziness; it was easier to steal something than work for the money to buy it. Now that he'd killed someone, he'd apply the same logic. From this point on, it would be easier to just eliminate someone than try to deal with them. That meant others would, sooner or later, die. Like an animal that had tasted human blood, Dwayne now knew what he'd been missing.

The police would arrest him. He would stand trial, probably be convicted, probably sent away for life. He had enough Tufa in him to understand how torturous that would be, separated from the night wind. So he would fight.

He would run.

He was running now.

And only she could catch him. Only she *should* catch him.

She started to throw back the sheet when a hand gently touched her wrist, startling her. She winced at the jolts of pain through her side, and glared at Bliss Overbay. "A little warning next time."

"Sorry. But you're in no shape to be leaving."

Chloe, who had spent an hour simply staring into space, blinked back to the moment. "You're leaving?"

"She's not leaving," Deacon said simply. It was the voice he used when he wanted no discussion from his children.

Bronwyn glared at all of them now. "First off, none of y'all can tell me what I'm going to do anymore. Second, you're all assuming I don't have sense enough to make a good decision. Granted that's been true in the past, and might even be true now, but it's nobody's business or trouble but mine."

Deacon stood, his face dark with rage. She knew its source; the urge to hunt down Dwayne must be eating him up, too, yet he had the control to sit quietly with the surviving members of his family, those who needed him most right now. "I *said*, you're not leaving. For once in your whiny little spit of a life, think of something besides yourself."

No one spoke for a long moment. Deacon's eyes burned with suppressed fury; then he looked away and sat again, staring at the space between his feet.

Bronwyn swallowed hard. Her face simmered in the cold hospital air, bright red with emotions she couldn't sort. She was about to speak when Bliss began to sing, so softly, her voice was a whisper that broke on the higher notes:

> *Near yonder stream that flows so free,*
> *Where storms can never rave,*
> *Beneath a drooping willow tree,*
> *Is gentle Annie's grave.*
> *My heart is sad for Annie dear,*
> *She's left me here alone,*
> *And over her grave I weep a tear,*
> *For Annie's lost and gone.*

Bronwyn began to tremble. Without conscious intent, she came in on the chorus, singing harmony, her voice shaky and thin:

She's gone, she's gone, we'll shed a tear,
Over gentle Annie's grave,
We'll never forget in memory dear,
Who sleeps where flowers wave.

Chloe stood and came to the bed. She put one hand on Bliss's shoulder, and the other stroked her daughter's hair. She sang the next verse alone:

Alas, my gentle Annie's gone,
She'll ride the wind no more,
We never can wander here alone,
As we have done before,
Where I have plucked the flowers of spring
And placed them in her hair,
The little birds still sweetly sing
But Annie is not there.

Deacon continued to stare at the floor between his shoes, his arms tightly folded. This was a woman's song; his own, the song of a man seeking justice, would come later.

The three women harmonized on the final chorus. It was something Bronwyn hadn't fully experienced since childhood: the Tufa bonding over song. All three of them were purebloods, their connection strongest to the night wind that brought them here and still guided their lives. And in music, they connected even more, their emotions surging into the other and finding balance as they were smoothed out and redistributed.

When they finished, Chloe wiped her eyes and said calmly, "Thank you, Bliss."

"Yeah, thank you," Bronwyn agreed. Then she pushed the sheet aside and swung her legs over the edge. "But I'm still going."

She turned to her father, and her rage matched his own. "And right now I don't give a fuck what you think, old man. Something has to be done, and I'm the one who has to do it. And if you try to stop me, you'll learn what other songs I know."

That was the greatest single threat one Tufa could make to another, the promise to sing their personal dirge and hasten—or even cause—their death. As a pureblood, Bronwyn could certainly carry it out. And the steady gaze in her eyes told Deacon she was close to doing so.

Yet he was a pureblood, too, and her father. After a long moment he said with chilling calm, "You left home as my daughter. You came back as a stranger. *Now* I know you, though. You're nothing but the killer the army made you. You're worse than Dwayne, because you *enjoy* it." He paused. "Now get out of my sight, Bronwyn," he added, then resumed staring at the floor.

Bliss said nothing. Chloe seemed not to have noticed.

"I'm sorry, Daddy," Bronwyn said softly. Then she added, "Now, where are my goddamned pants?"

Bronwyn strode into the waiting room, arm curled protectively around her side, and stopped as nearly two dozen people stood to greet her. They were frighteningly, ridiculously similar: black hair, dark skin, perfect white teeth, all gazing at her with the kind of sympathy that normally would've made her roll her eyes. Yet there was no pity to them, just genuine shared grief.

Kell had been a pureblood, too, one of their elite. They felt his loss as well.

She found she could not move. There was no way to get to the exit without pushing through the crowd, yet how could she do that? They needed her now, her guidance and her strength. They needed, in a different way, the Bronwynator.

Mrs. Chandler stepped toward Bronwyn, autoharp clutched to her chest. A nurse passed between them, frowned at the gathering, and continued on. Bronwyn smiled at Mrs. Chandler, who began to play and sing:

> *I dreamed that over my soul there came,*
> *A grief that moved my stricken heart;*
> *And as I mourned, the earthbound world*
> *Did taunt me with its wicked art. . . .*

The others didn't hesitate, but began to sing along, taking harmony parts by instinct and experience. Mrs. Chandler strummed her autoharp, and someone joined in with a banjo. A guitar's strum came from the back. Her own fingers ached for Magda, but the song now had its own life, and bore them along like the night wind did its riders.

She sang as she moved through the crowd, touching shoulders and feeling hands on her own arms. This was the Tufa community forming around whoever most needed them, and she felt the connection through the music and song. She also knew that at this moment, it wasn't for her.

Then she saw Terry-Joe standing beside the door, her mandolin case in his hand. He wasn't smiling, because that would be inappropriate, but she saw the pleasure in his eyes that said he'd read the signs correctly and knew she'd want her instrument. He put down the case, opened it, and offered Magda to her.

She reached for it, then stopped. Although the song continued around her, she felt herself separate from it, withdrawing into isolation. She closed her hand into a fist and pulled it back. Then before her resolve faltered, she ran out through the sliding glass doors. She would explain later. If there was a later.

She stopped beneath the weather overhang, feeling the night's heat and rawness. A storm was brewing in the sky, the kind that brought violence and change. She waited to see if anyone would pursue and try to bring her back, but no one did. She stepped out into the open and looked up at the stars, already blurring as the clouds coalesced. The wind would be vicious up there, slapping back and forth as it built toward release. Only the strongest of Tufa could ride it.

"You really have to tell me how you manage to heal so quickly," a voice said.

She turned. Craig Chess leaned against one of the brick pillars supporting the overhang. In the dim light he looked mysterious, like a detective in an old movie.

"What are you doing lurking out here?" she asked.

"I didn't want to intrude. It looked like a Tufa-only thing."

Through the glass doors, she saw the others still singing. "It is," she agreed. "Where's Aiden?"

He nodded toward his car, parked at the curb. "He cried himself to sleep on the way. I'll bring him in when he wakes up. He was pretty upset, and there was a little bit of a scene. He wanted to take his squirrel gun and go shoot Dwayne Gitterman."

She felt a jolt through her heart. "Yeah, well, he may have to take a number. Dad's spitting nails, too."

"I imagine. And how are *you*?"

"Set."

"Set?"

"In what I need to do." She looked at him closely. "Like you. You always know what to do, in every situation. You know what people need you to be. I just figured that out for myself tonight."

Their eyes met. Then their hands touched, fingers threading together. She had no sense of moving closer, but then they were face-to-face, him looking down at her.

"You take this minister thing seriously, don't you?" she said quietly.

"I do."

"So you'd never sleep with me just to see what it was like? Just to see if we got along that way, before we made any more serious plans?"

He shook his head. "I knew the rules when I took the job."

"What about kissing?"

Suddenly his mouth was on hers, his other hand tangled in her black hair and holding her close to him. She rose on her tiptoes to reach him. She could not recall a kiss that sent shivers through her like this since her very first one, at age ten.

When the kiss broke she stayed on her toes, her lips brushing his. "That's been coming for a while," she whispered.

"I think so," he agreed.

"You think your God brought us together?"

"He's everyone's God. And yes."

She patted his broad chest. "I have to go. I have to do something, but . . ."

He recalled the haint's words: *Be strong. Be honest. Be fearless.* He looked deep into her dark eyes and said, "Do what you have to, Bronwyn. I'll take care of things here. I'll be here when you finish."

She held his gaze for a long time. He heard a faint, tuneless humming in his ears. At last she said, "I believe you will."

"I will," he said. "But I need to ask you something first."

"What?"

"What *are* you? What are the Tufa?"

She kissed him again. The trees planted along the edge of the parking lot began to sigh in the wind. "Go to the Library."

"Beg pardon?"

"Go to the library over in Cricket. Ask to see the painting."

"What painting?"

"They'll know." She stepped away. "And don't look for me. When I'm done, I'll find you."

"Done?" he repeated. "I don't understand."

"That's okay. Look behind you."

He did, and saw nothing. When he turned back, she had vanished.

31

Don Swayback stared up at the stars. He could never recall doing that before, although he must've stargazed as a child. Yet now the vista above him seemed the most beautiful, amazing thing ever, and he wondered how he'd lived this long without noticing it.

The sky had been clear when he started, but now clouds began to edge in from the southwest. Wind made the tops of the trees wave in growing animation. And it was that wind that held his attention, that seemed to be whispering, humming, *singing* something he just couldn't quite catch.

He glanced back at his house. Susie was home but asleep, after more vigorous lovemaking that caused her to wonder aloud, "You're not stockpiling a certain little blue pill, are you?" He was exhausted, too, but ever since meeting the little girl earlier that day, he knew he'd end up outside looking up at the stars. He'd intended to tell Susie about it at dinner, but the altercation at the Waffle House made it slip his mind, and she was peacefully snoring by the time he remembered.

He'd met the girl when he drove through Needsville again. He'd taken to doing it at least once a day, spending his entire lunch hour in the car listening to CDs of the Carter Family and other bluegrass pioneers. The first few times he told himself it was to build up familiarity with the area for his eventual interview with Bronwyn Hyatt, but it had become its own reward, a kind of rolling meditation on the nature of his *own* nature.

This time, as he drove slowly down the main street, he recalled suddenly Susie asking him to pick up postage stamps. He parked outside the new brick post office building, and as he climbed the steps to the porch a voice said, "Hello."

He turned. An old man sat in the far rocking chair, but he hadn't spoken. Instead it had been the young girl in the chair beside him. She wore green cotton shorts, a sleeveless jersey, and flip-flops. Her black hair was in two braids. She held an old-fashioned bottled Coke with a bendy straw poking from the top.

"Hi," Don said.

"You were at the barn dance the other night, weren't you?"

Don smiled. "Yeah, I was. Were you there?"

She shook her head. "I just heard about it."

"You heard about *me*?"

She patted the arm of the third rocking chair. "Sit down."

The girl had an odd demeanor, nothing like a normal child, and he was a little disconcerted. The old man in the chair on her other side just looked at him, saying nothing. His eyes were narrow, squinting slits.

Don settled into the rocker and said, "Did you want to ask me something, Miss—?"

She shook her head. "My name is Mandalay. And I want to

tell you something." The seriousness in her words was belied by the way she slurped the last of the Coke through the straw.

"Okay," he said. "What?"

She burped lightly, then said, "You've come awake inside, and it's probably messing with you a little bit. You've been knowing things you didn't think you were supposed to know, singing songs you'd never heard before. Am I right?"

Don stared and nodded.

She spoke as if discussing Barbies with another child. "You'll have a choice pretty soon. Your Grandma Benji wasn't one of my people, but we all loved her anyway. You can go either way. With me, or with Rockhouse here, who's head of her people." She nodded at the old man, who said nothing. "You don't have to choose right now. But you will have to choose pretty soon."

He couldn't stop gazing into her eyes. They weren't those of a child.

"He done chose," Rockhouse finally said. "He went to your barn dance, not our hootenanny."

"A man can't choose if he don't know both sides," Mandalay snapped, and the old man fell silent. To Don she said, "You have to pick which one of us you want to join."

"Like the Seelie or the Unseelie?"

She shrugged. "Call it what you want."

"What do you call it?" Don asked.

"The Tufa. The Tufa blood in you is singing now. You can either sing along, or wait for it to go quiet again. Or . . ."

She motioned him closer and spoke softly. "Go outside tonight. Look up at the sky. Listen to the wind. See what it says to you."

"Hey!" Rockhouse said. "He ain't got no right—"

"He's got every right," the girl fired back, and the old man again fell silent. Then she returned her attention to Don. "Listen for the wind. Listen for the riders. Listen for what calls in your own blood. Then go to Cricket and look at the painting in their library. Then decide."

He could think of nothing to say. Mandalay smiled, wizened and old now like a Tibetan lama. He nodded, turned, and went back to his car. He was almost to the county line before realizing he'd forgotten the stamps. He wasn't about to go back for them.

That night he and Susie picked up ice cream on their way home from the Waffle House, and as they sat on the couch eating and flirting, Don said, "Can I ask you something about your work?"

"Is this for *your* work?"

"No, I'm just curious."

She nodded as she provocatively licked chocolate syrup from her spoon. "As long as it's not about a specific patient."

"You guys get a lot of Tufas in there, right? So they get the usual tests done, I assume. Tell me, is there anything different about them? I mean, different from . . ." He waved at the air with his own spoon.

"Different from what?" she asked.

"You know . . . human beings."

She laughed. "The Tufa *are* human beings. Just like black people, or Eskimos, or Asians."

"So, like, blood tests and stuff never come back . . . weird?"

"No, they come back with all the same things you'd find in anybody's blood." She touched the tip of his nose with her spoon, depositing a bit of vanilla ice cream on it. "I think you're spending too much time dwelling on this."

He wiped his nose and was hit anew by her attractiveness. "Well," he said throatily, "I can think of one thing that might take my mind off it."

"We haven't finished our ice cream," she pointed out.

He reached for her hand. "Bring it along."

Now he looked up at the sky, the wind, the night, and felt something impending within him, a change he both dreaded and desperately longed for. He spread his arms like wings and whispered, "Okay, if anybody's up there riding the night wind, I'm ready for a ride, too."

If Susie had looked outside a moment later, she would've found the backyard empty.

Mandalay Harris sat beside the stream, her feet in the water. Even at night the air was humid and warm, and she felt mosquitoes approach, alight on her skin and then buzz away, repelled by something in her nature. A strange but welcome perk of being a trueblood Tufa. She plucked idly at her autoharp, sending random notes out on the wind.

The porch light came on, and her stepmother, Leshell, stuck her head out the trailer door. "Mandy? Y'all out here?"

"Yes, ma'am," Mandalay called. She kicked the water and watched it twinkle in the moonlight. The stream was barely a foot deep, and the rock on which she sat bisected its yard-wide channel.

"It's past midnight," Leshell said.

"I know."

Leshell, in a long yellow T-shirt with a deer's head drawn on it, walked across the wet grass to the edge of the stream. "I think you're going to have company."

Mandalay looked at her stepmother and nodded. "I heard. I'll be in when I'm done."

When she turned back to the stream, Bronwyn Hyatt stood beside it.

"Hey," Mandalay said, as if the woman's sudden appearance was the most normal thing in the world.

"Hey, Mandalay," Bronwyn said, a little breathless. "Leshell."

"Bronwyn." Leshell nodded and went back inside.

Bronwyn's hair was windblown, and big sweat circles spread from under her arms. "Got a minute?"

The girl shrugged. At moments like this, her reality as a ten-year-old seemed strongest. She played a few bars of "Will the Circle Be Unbroken." "Not much happens this time of night."

Favoring her ribs, Bronwyn pulled up an old milk crate that lay in the weeds beside the creek and sat. She took long, deep breaths until she could speak without gasping. "You know what happened tonight, I suppose."

The girl nodded. "I'm real sorry. We all read the signs wrong. Some days it seems like the only sign that's clear is red and says *top*. The night wind was there for him, though."

"Is it there for me?"

Mandalay kicked at the water again. A distant rumble of thunder came over the mountains. "If you want it. You're a true-blood, and a First Daughter. If you call the wind, it'll answer."

"Even if I call it for something selfish and wrong?"

Mandalay giggled. "Listen to you. What's selfish and wrong? You want revenge for Kell's dying. Who can blame you?"

"I don't want *revenge*, Mandalay, I want Dwayne to be stopped. If he's not, somebody else will suffer like I am, like my parents and little brother are. And . . ."

"And what?"

"I think I'm the one who's supposed to stop him. It has to be

me because I've killed people before. It won't change my son
like it would my daddy's, or Aiden's, or Terry Joe's."

"So you remembered what happened to you, then?"

"No. I *know* what happened, and that's enough. If I *remembered* what happened, then the next time I tried to do it, it'd ge
all tangled up with those memories." She recalled the cliff-to
conversation with Bliss. "The night wind's been preparing m
for this, Mandalay. There's a need out there, and I can fill i
But it'll be on my terms."

"And what're those?"

Bronwyn smiled coldly. "Whatever I say they are."

"And how's that different from how you used to be? Th
Bronwynator, doing whatever she wants?"

"Maybe the 'how' ain't any different. But the 'why' is. You an
the First Daughters wanted me back, didn't you? Now you'v
got me. And if it means you got the hum you wanted but th
shiver's different, well, that's tough."

Mandalay looked down at the silver wakes caused by he
dangling feet. "Is this one of those times when we should'v
been careful what we wished for?"

Bronwyn laughed. "Maybe so."

Mandalay kicked at the water. "Then why are you here askin
me? I'm just a kid. It sounds like you've made up your mind."

"Yeah," Bronwyn said sadly.

Mandalay shook her head in that smug way children hav
when they know something their parents don't. The collec
tive wisdom and history of the Tufa was bound in this little gi
who could talk before she was a year old and pick out tunes o
a piano by age two. She had the history, but not the experience
so often her pronouncements and warnings would come out i
little-girl metaphors or childish descriptions. Now that she wa

lder this happened less often, but the dichotomy was both
disconcerting and sad. "That's not right, you know. I'm *not* a
kid."

"I know you're not, sweetie."

Mandalay leaned down and let the current play over her
fingers. "What was the desert like? I always wanted to see it."

Bronwyn laughed. "You want to talk about it now?"

"Might not get another chance."

Bronwyn caught the warning, but let it go. It didn't matter
anyway. "Well, it's all space. There's no trees, no mountains. It
rattles you at first, makes you feel even more exposed than you
do ordinarily."

"Did you know the Tufa were called Yellowbacks for a long
time because we never fought in any of the wars, even when we
were drafted?"

"Yeah, I know."

"But you fought."

"Daddy thinks it's because the war over there was easier to
fight than the one here."

"Was it?"

She shrugged. "It was different. It took a lot of nerve just to
stand there, knowing a bullet or a bomb could come from anywhere. But you also didn't know the people shooting at you or
blowing you up. Here . . . well . . . they're family."

She laughed at her own joke, then looked up at the sky. The
clouds were creeping in, and the wind tore at the trees higher
on the slopes. With calm certainty she said, "I'm also going to
marry that preacher, Mandalay. Not Terry-Joe Gitterman."

"Because that's what the Bronwynator wants?"

She shook her head. She felt serene, as if this were all reasoned out and decided even though it was literally coming to

her as she spoke. "Nope. Because just when I thought I was a
alone, he showed me I wasn't. I had every intention of this be
ing my last flight on the wind in this world."

"You'd do that to your parents? Two of their children gone?

"Hell, they ain't sure I'm back yet anyway. But it's beside th
point. I'm gonna marry the preacher, but I'm still going to hav
Terry-Joe's baby. Probably a girl. Next year, or the year after
Another First Daughter."

"She won't be a pureblood."

"No. We have to get past that idea anyway. Her blood wil
be true, and that's enough."

"How will the preacher take that?"

"Between now and then, I'll have to get both him and Terry
Joe ready to understand it."

"If you survive the night."

Bronwyn smiled wryly. "Mandalay, you've been watchin
too much TV. You sound like the bad guy in a spy movie."

"I can't see you in the morning, though. I can't hear you
song."

Bronwyn was silent for a moment. At last she said quietly
"Maybe that's because I'll have a new one by then." Sh
stood, suddenly feeling stronger than ever before in her life
"Thanks, Mandalay. You take care."

"You, too," the girl said.

She watched as Bronwyn opened herself to her full Tufa na
ture, spread her wings, and once again caught the night wind.

32

Dwayne slammed face-first into a tree. He felt—and worse, *heard*—the bridge of his already-broken nose crack again from the impact. He staggered back, slammed into another tree, and fell awkwardly to the forest floor. His whole face was numb, and his skull rang.

He raised his hands to his face, convinced he would find his nose completely flattened. It was still in place, although when he touched it, the formerly strong upper line now felt mushy. He whimpered in anticipation of the pain.

He was totally lost. After the realization that he'd seriously injured Bronwyn penetrated his dope-fogged brain, he'd tried to return to his truck, but could not find his way. Then he remembered that he'd also knifed Bronwyn's brother. The law would be after him now, to send him back to prison. He had to get out of Cloud County, out of Tennessee, maybe even out of the country somehow. But first he had to get out of these goddamned woods.

He tried to orient himself. It didn't matter which way he went, he reasoned, as long as it was downhill. Just as he was about to start walking, a new sound reached him and stopped him dead. Somewhere nearby, someone was *crying*.

He followed the sound and emerged into a clearing where a lone figure lay curled up on the ground. As Dwayne approached, the man raised his head and stared up at him.

"Thank God," Fred Blasco said. He crawled to him, holding his laptop computer to his chest, and clutched Dwayne's legs with his free hand. "Oh, sweet Jesus, thank you. You've got to help me, I can't find my way out of these woods, I've been wandering for days, I need help, I'm lost, I'm starving—"

Dwayne kicked the man away. "Get the fuck *off* me!"

"No, please, don't leave me!" Blasco begged. "I can pay you, really, you can have my credit cards, anything you want."

"Fuck you!" Dwayne said, and ran off into the night. Blasco began to cry again, a sound so forlorn, only the hardest, coldest of hearts could ignore it. Dwayne did.

He stumbled up a ridge and down into a gully. He tripped over a root, slid in the wet leaves, and rolled downhill until he slammed, again face-first, into a half-buried boulder. He turned slowly onto his back, groaning, wondering if his nose would ever look right again.

"That must've hurt," a voice said from the dark.

He sat up and looked wildly around. The forest was so thick, there were only little shafts of moonlight visible, like blue gray splinters piercing the blackness. Nothing moved in them.

"Fuck!" Dwayne bellowed into the night. Could the cops have already found him? Or someone worse? "Who the fuck is out there?"

The voice began to laugh. A shape emerged from the darkness as if exuded from it. "You don't know me, Dwayne Gitterman. But I know you."

The gathering clouds parted enough to let one wide, clear beam of moonlight reveal a shambling figure with a long beard and baggy clothes. *The sin eater,* Dwayne thought in terror: the man who waits outside the homes of the recently dead. Those inside take a plate of food from the corpse's chest and leave it at the back door; when the sin eater consumes the food, he also consumes the bad deeds of the deceased. No one knew his name, only that he did his job without complaint or fuss. And, of course, that it was a monumentally bad omen to meet him.

"What do you want?" Dwayne said, scooting back against a tree. "You following me?"

"I'm not looking for you, Dwayne. You crossed *my* path, remember?"

Blood ran both down his face and throat, coating his senses in its warm, salty taste. "Fuck you, then."

The sin eater laughed again. "Your old standby, eh? Don't you hear what's on the wind tonight? Hear the song?"

"Shut the fuck up."

The sin eater sang, his voice surprisingly clear and true:

> My baby is so tired tonight,
> He does not like the candlelight.
> His little head will soon be pressed
> Against his mama's loving breast,
> And mama's song will sound the best. . . .

When he finished he coughed a little, then said, "That's someone's dying dirge. Now who you reckon could be dead tonight?"

Dwayne almost gagged on his own blood as he said, "Not Bronwyn. I didn't hit her that fucking hard, it was just a tap, a fucking *shove*."

The sin eater smiled, and laughed again. "If you were smart, you'd *wish* Bronwyn Hyatt was dead, son. No, that's the song of *Kell* Hyatt, who's dancing in the wind tonight."

The memory of the fight, of the pure satisfaction of burying his knife in the other man's flesh, came back to him as he comprehended. "Wait, wha . . . Kell's *dead*? But he . . ."

The sin eater came closer, so that his charnel odor washed over Dwayne. "You got so far away from yourself that you started to think all those Tufa stories about riding the night winds and songs with the power of life or death were just dumb-ass superstitions, didn't you? But you can hear the wind tonight, can't you? And baby, it can hear you."

Dwayne's laugh turned into a gag, and he spit blood on the ground. "You been smoking what I been growing, old man."

"That's true," the sin eater agreed. "And you do grow a nice crop, I'll grant you. But it doesn't change anything. I won't be eating *your* sins; you'll tote them with you. I know what'll happen to the Tufa part of you; as for the rest, well . . . send me a postcard from Hell."

He did not move, but the shadows seemed to pull him back and reabsorb him. Dwayne threw the first rock his hand found after the sin eater, but it bounced harmlessly off a tree. He stuffed the front of his T-shirt against his face to stanch the blood and resumed moving forward. If he kept going downhill in a straight line, eventually he had to cross a road where he could flag a ride and get home. There he had guns, money, and transportation.

But he emerged from the trees and saw, stretched before him, the entire Needsville valley and realized with a start that

e'd been *climbing,* not descending. The terrain ended at the
dge of a cliff, and far below he saw the dark tops of trees wav-
ng slightly in the wind. The moon hung full and clear in the
cloudless half of the sky; the other half was dark and shimmery
with the approaching thunderstorm.

"Thanks," a familiar voice said. "You saved me the trouble
of tracking your sorry ass down."

33

For a moment, Bronwyn appeared to have *wings,* the kind Tufa stories told of: big, diaphanous structures, double lobed like a butterfly's, shimmery with rainbow-hued textures. It was how the real Tufas, the total pure-bloods and the ones who worked to maximize their Tufa nature, rode the night winds. As a child, Dwayne had been told he was one of them, but the world's tempta-tions drew him away. He finally stopped believing in their literal truth.

But now, when Bronwyn hovered in the air just past the edge of the cliff, held steady by those enormous wings made of something other than earthly matter, he could not deny the reality he'd once mocked.

Then Dwayne blinked, and she was human again, her feet on the ground. Surely she'd just used some shortcut. Man, he needed to stop smoking so much of his own stuff.

Thunder boomed in the clouds. "Kell's dead, Dwayne," Bronwyn said. "As a doornail. As a skunk n the road. As disco. That makes you a murderer. How does that feel?"

Dwayne backed away from her, away from the cliff's edge, toward the safety of the forest. He raised his hands in supplication. "Aw, baby, please, it was all a mistake, I never *meant* to kill him."

She put her hands on her hips. She looked tall, powerful, almost goddesslike. The air around her shimmered as if invisible wings fluttered there. "You stuck a knife in him, Dwayne."

"Yeah, but . . ."

She sighed. "The saddest part is, I believe you. I believe that you really could stab somebody without intending to kill them. You're messed up enough to think that way. But it doesn't change the ending. My big brother is dead, my parents have lost their first child—because of you. And if you get away with it, you'll just do it again."

Another rumble from the storm clouds shivered through the air. He tried his best smile. "C'mon, Bronnie, you know I didn't do it on purpose. We were just fucking around. I said something that he took wrong, and it got out of hand. I'm real sorry." He shrugged dismissively. "It was kind of his own fault, anyway. He should've known better than to pick a fight with *me.*"

He never saw Bronwyn actually move, but suddenly one of her hands closed around his throat and she yanked him back toward the edge of the cliff.

Bob Pafford burst from the forest just in time to see Bronwyn and Dwayne vanish over the edge. He yelled, "Hey!" and rushed forward, but they were already gone.

He stared down into the abyss. A lightning flash illuminated the whole valley below, and its accompanying thunder boomed almost immediately. The storm would be here in no time.

He heard the first big splat of raindrops on the brim of his hat. He couldn't believe what he'd just seen: Bronwyn Hyatt and Dwayne Gitterman leaping to their deaths. He moved away from the edge, his heart pounding, feeling both cheated of his prize and, oddly, frightened. He'd have to hurry back to the road, then locate the two bodies that had to be shredded among the trees below. He could use the time to fine-tune the story he'd tell to explain both the video in his car and the murder-suicide he'd just witnessed.

He refused to give any thought to the fact that, at the last moment before the doomed lovers vanished into the darkness, they seemed to suddenly fly upward.

Dwayne clutched at Bronwyn's arm, trying to dislodge the choking hold at his neck. She was stronger than he'd ever imagined possible. He kicked madly to find purchase, but there was no ground beneath them. They were in the sky, the stars above them and the great wide valley below, and the rushing night wind filled his ears.

He could not see her face clearly, but her eyes looked different somehow, larger and wider and utterly black. He tried to scream, but the fingers digging into his larynx silenced him.

Now he heard something else: She was *singing*. But her voice sounded both loud and whisperish, with a melody that seemed to touch feelings in him that had been deadened since childhood.

> *The arms that hold you are not those of love*
> *You cannot see down nor anything above*
> *You snatch what you want, leaving hot blood and tears*

Until the day when all of your fears
Come home to roost, come home to see
Come home to find, no one but thee
Cares for your heart, cares for your strife
Cares if you live another minute of life. . . .

Tears ran from his eyes, only to be snatched away by the wind. With abrupt, terrifying clarity he saw himself as everyone else did, saw the swath of harm he'd inflicted, and realized the song was true. No one would miss him: not Bronwyn, not Terry-Joe, not his family or his friends. To most of them he'd long outlived his welcome presence. The knowledge that he was hated, despised, and feared, that no love for him existed in the world, wrenched a cry that could've drowned out the very wind if it wasn't choked to silence by Bronwyn's grip.

He felt her lips against his ear. At first he thought she was kissing him; then he heard the faint words:

"Good-bye, Dwayne."

She took his earlobe in her teeth, then said, "If you can sing, you can fly. If you can't, you'll die. Which is it, Dwayne: the hum or the shiver?"

Then she was gone, and a clap of thunder rattled his teeth. The air around him seemed to glow, and he realized he was now *inside* the storm clouds.

Movement caught his eye, and he turned to see another human form in the air beside him. He squinted into the dimness until another flash of lightning illuminated the newcomer. This man had wings as well, and he watched Dwayne with the curiosity a child might have for an insect. It took a moment, but Dwayne recognized him: it was the man who'd challenged him at the Waffle House.

Dwayne desperately reached out and tried to scream for help, but the wind ate his words. Then the other man was gone.

Dwayne continued to scream. The wind seemed to lift him, raising him above the clouds toward the stars. Something writhed within him, like a tapeworm suddenly desperate to escape its host, as his long-ignored Tufa blood attempted to save him. He tried to think of a song, *any* song. But he'd long ago burned the music out of himself.

The wind sighed its disappointment and released him back to the world. He screamed all the way to the ground.

When Chloe, Deacon, and Aiden returned home the next morning, they found Bronwyn curled up asleep on the porch swing. Deacon picked her up and carried her inside to her bedroom. Chloe took down Deacon's charm against death; it was no longer needed, since death had already come.

Then they prepared for their visitors.

34

The irony made the national news for a day.

Dwayne Gitterman, wanted for the murder of war hero Bronwyn Hyatt's brother, committed suicide by jumping from a bluff that overlooked a Cloud County highway. In a gigantic fluke, he landed on Tennessee State Trooper Robert Pafford, who'd been urinating beside his car. Both were killed instantly. The long combined history of the two—Pafford first arrested Dwayne when he was ten—added to the weirdness. It was too much to be coincidence, some said, yet what else could it be? It was a dark and stormy night; Gitterman could not possibly have seen Pafford before he jumped.

In a week, the national news forgot about it. In a month, no one in Cloud County even spoke the names Dwayne Gitterman or Bob Pafford. None of the old songs were sung for him.

But a new one was written.

———

There were old songs for Kell Hyatt, though. Many of them. His body was released for burial, and Bliss brought it back home for a traditional "sitting." The practice was technically illegal, since the body had not been embalmed, but folks tended to let the Tufa care for their own, even in death.

Chloe, Bliss, Bronwyn, and several other ladies washed Kell thoroughly and dressed him in his best suit. Chloe had broken down only once, when she saw the stitched wound where he'd been stabbed. But it passed, and she and the others worked in what passed for musical silence, humming or singing but seldom speaking.

The men gathered as well, on the porch and in the yard. Deacon led them through the woods to the Hyatt family cemetery. It was on a hillside, with little horizontal outbuildings over some of the graves. They took turns digging, using pickaxes on the rocky soil and hauling the stones aside. They sang as well, bawdy songs of men and women, tales of prowess and exaggeration. By midday, the grave was ready.

Major Dan Maitland called Bronwyn as she was about to put on her black mourning dress. "I'm very sorry to hear about your brother, Private Hyatt."

"*Miss* Hyatt. Unless you're planning to stop-loss me."

"I don't think that would be good for either the image of the military, or for you as a person. Do you?"

"That may be the first thing we've entirely agreed on, Major."

Her new assertiveness made him pause and regroup. When he spoke again, it was with the voice of an equal, not a superior.

'Well, whatever the case, please express my sympathy to your family. They've certainly been through the wringer this year. How are you holding up?"

She looked at her lingerie-clad reflection in the full-length mirror. Her legs were more symmetrical and the scars were slowly fading. Only the elastic bandage around her ribs spoke of any recent trauma. "Wall to wall and treetop tall. Looking for love in all the wrong places."

"Any plans for the future?"

"Lots."

When she did not elaborate, he said, "Well, I won't keep you, Bronwyn. I know this is a tough time for you. Please know you're in my thoughts and prayers."

"Thanks, Dan. For everything." And she meant it. When she hung up, she added his number to the blocked list on her cell phone.

That afternoon, Craig parked at the end of a long line of vehicles and walked half a mile up the road to get to the Hyatts' house. The afternoon sun was murderous through his suit coat. He was stopped at the gate by Aiden and two other preteen boys, all dressed uncomfortably in jackets and clip-on ties. They gave him a serious, challenging group stare.

"I'd like permission to go up to the house," he said, playing along, "and offer my respects."

"You haven't passed the test," Aiden said grimly.

"What's the test?"

Aiden and the others huddled together, whispering. Craig tried to keep a straight face. Up the hill, he saw a woman dressed in black step out onto the porch and look toward them.

Was it Bronwyn? The distance and the sun made it impossible to tell.

Finally Aiden emerged from the confab and again faced him. "You have to answer a riddle."

"Okay."

"How many cats does it take to change a lightbulb?"

"None. Cats can see in the dark."

Aiden's face fell. He sighed and, without looking at Craig, said, "You can go up."

Craig resisted the urge to tousle the boy's hair as he climbed the hill toward the house. The woman on the porch *was* Bronwyn, and she watched him until he reached the bottom of the porch steps.

"Hot enough for you?" she asked.

"It'll do 'til hotter comes along," he said. "How are the ribs?"

"Sore. But they'll mend pretty quick."

"For you, that's saying something."

She smiled wryly. "I'm surprised to see you."

"Really?"

She looked down, shook her head, and grinned. "No, not really. Come on inside, I'll get you some tea."

Indoors all the women stepped aside for Bronwyn as if she was some sort of royalty. In fact, only Chloe met her daughter's gaze; the rest looked respectfully away. Bronwyn did not acknowledge this, but there was a different bearing to her now, something regal that made the deference appropriate.

She poured Craig some tea and then nodded for him to follow. They went past the coffin where Kell lay in state, and down the short hall to her bedroom. When they stepped inside, she quietly closed the door behind them.

He faced her as she settled her shoulders back against the

door. It might've been seductive except for the sadness in her eyes. "I'm glad you came, Reverend."

"Craig."

"Craig. I suppose we should talk about what happened outside the hospital."

"If you'd like."

She rattled the ice in her tea. "I've been pulled in several different directions since I got home. No, that's not true, it's been all my life. Some people wanted me to be one thing, some another. I've never taken well to that kind of thing."

He merely nodded.

"But I think I know what I want now. It's not what everyone else wants for me. Hell, it's not what *anyone* else wants for me. But it's what I'm meant to do."

"That's exceptionally vague, you know. Is that why everyone bowed and curtseyed to you in there?"

She smiled. "Yes. Some things have changed, besides Kell's death. I guess the best comparison I can make right now is that I'm as certain of my calling as you are, except I can have sex if I want to."

"That's a big difference."

"True," she agreed, then stepped closer and looked up at him.

He leaned down and kissed her, tenderly. She responded in kind. When they broke the kiss, he said, "I can't cross some lines, you know."

"I know," she said in a voice barely louder than a whisper. "And honestly, I may try to get you as close to them as possible. I'm like that. But I'll do my best to respect them."

"So are you asking me to be your boyfriend?" he said with a grin.

She laughed. "I'm asking you to dinner in Johnson City Monday night. You drive, I'll pay. But only after . . ."

"What?"

"Did you go and look at that painting in Cricket?"

"No, not yet."

"Do that. Then decide."

"Look at the painting, then decide if I want to go out with you?"

"Yes."

"What's so important about the painting?"

She smiled knowingly, teasingly. "If I told you that, it'd be cheating. And that'd be a terrible start to our relationship."

He stepped closer and kissed her again. This time she leaned up, her lips parted, and it became the kind of kiss that was as much promise as gratification. When they separated, she said, "That was the hum. If you're good, later I'll show you the shiver."

They rejoined the mourners. Craig thought about offering to speak, but figured that would be both rude and unwelcome. He realized he was the only male in the room just before the other men arrived, dirty and tired from grave-digging. With no comment they closed the casket and carried it outside. The women followed, their voices mixing in a song Craig had never before heard.

Bronwyn walked directly behind the casket, playing her mandolin. Chloe clutched her autoharp, and Deacon played long, mournful notes on his fiddle. A few others had instruments, but most simply sang. Craig knew none of the songs, and they seemed to vanish from his memory as soon as he heard them.

After the service, Brownyn and the other women went off together into the woods. Craig started to go with the men, but Aiden suddenly took his hand, the same grim look on his face.

"I'm supposed to walk you back to your car."

"You are."

He nodded. "Bronwyn said to tell you this part was private. She said you'd understand."

"Okay," he said. He looked back toward the woods, but everyone had vanished into its shadows.

As he drove away, he kept thinking he saw movement along the tops of the trees, as if things flew up from the forest and into the evening's purple sky. He finally put it down to a trick of the light.

35

Craig visited the town of Cricket on the Monday following Kell Hyatt's funeral. When he looked up the directions online, he found a link to the town's official Web site, and read its history with wonder.

The world watched in 1875 as famous British author, statesman, and social reformer Roy Howard dedicated the new town of Cricket. It was to be a cooperative, class-free society, a Utopia where artisans, tradesmen, and farming families could build a new community through agriculture, temperance, and high moral principles. Today, in a gentle mountain setting little changed by twenty-first-century technology, this would-be Shangri-la survives. More than two dozen of its decorative, gabled buildings remain, and Cricket's dual Victorian and Appalachian heritage is everywhere visible.

The Roy Howard Library in Cricket had one door and a spire like a church, only with no cross atop it. The roof was plated with metal sheets stained to look like the original copper. It stood in a little grove of trees next to the visitors' center, with no connection to the sidewalk.

Inside, the library consisted of one big room, with ten-foot-high shelves along every available bit of the walls. Two standing shelf units took up the middle of the floor, along with a table covered with elaborate first editions.

The librarian, a tall freckled woman with short hair and glasses, stood as he entered. "Welcome to the Howard Library. I have to tell you not to touch anything without putting on these." She tapped a box of disposable cotton gloves.

"Why?" Craig asked.

"Almost every book in here is a rare first edition over a hundred years old. The oil from your fingers can damage the paper. Were you looking for anything in particular?"

"I'm supposed to ask to see the painting."

She gestured at the walls above the shelves, where several old-fashioned paintings hung in the dimness. "Which painting?"

"I'm not sure. I was told just to ask to see *the* painting."

"By whom?"

"Bronwyn Hyatt, actually."

The librarian's expression turned skeptical. "The war hero? Well, she *is* a Cloud County Tufa, I've heard."

"She is," Craig assured her.

"Then I know the one she means."

"Wait for me," said another voice.

Craig turned. Don Swayback had entered silently, and now offered his hand. "Hey there, Reverend. Good to see you again."

"Don," Craig said as they shook. "Missed you in church yesterday."

"Stayed out in the wind too long," he said, and grinned as if it were a private joke.

"What brings you here?"

"From what I just overheard, the same thing as you. Somebody told me to come check out the painting."

The librarian led them to the back of one of the freestanding shelf units. There, hanging on the end piece, was a painting two feet high by a foot wide, displayed in an elaborate wooden frame that made it appear much larger. It depicted a score of diminutive European storybook fairies gathered around a dominant central figure. This main subject faced away from the viewer and held what looked like an ax above his head. He seemed about to bring it down on a hickory nut at his feet. Stems of grass and flower blossoms laced through the image gave it both scale and depth. The style was a kind of hyperrealism, in which the characters' proportions seemed slightly distorted beneath the wealth of surface detail.

"The Fairy Feller's Master Stroke," the librarian said. "It's one of our most prized pieces. And it's not the watercolor copy, either. That's in the Tate Gallery in London. This," she said with pride, "is the original."

Don noted its location. "You don't exactly show it off."

"We've left it exactly where the charter residents of Cricket placed it," the librarian said. "Would you like to see something especially impressive about it?"

She took out her keychain and switched on a tiny flashlight. "Watch this." She slowly moved the circle of light across the surface.

It was astounding. The painting was almost done in three

dimensions, with layer upon layer of paint creating a depth hidden by flat illumination. The librarian continued, "The artist worked on this one canvas for eight years, from 1855 to 1864, while confined in an asylum after he killed his father."

Craig barely heard her words. To the left of center the figure of a woman, looking away as if distracted by her friend behind her, bore an uncanny resemblance to Bronwyn despite the artist's stylization. The similarity was so strong, he couldn't believe it was mere coincidence, yet how could it be otherwise?

"They all look like Tufas," Don said softly.

Craig slowly nodded. "Wow. Who told you to come see this?"

"A little Tufa girl I met. You?" But before Craig could answer, Don looked at his watch and exclaimed, "Oh, hell, I've got to go, I'm going to be late. Good to see you again, Reverend."

"Where are you off to?" Craig asked.

"I've got my exclusive interview this afternoon with Bronwyn Hyatt. What about you?"

He smiled. "I have to finish some work early to get ready for a date tonight." He deliberately didn't mention Bronwyn's name.

"A date?" Don teased. "Are preachers *allowed* to date?"

"Yes," Craig deadpanned. "We're not priests."

Don laughed. "I reckon not. Well, hope my interview and your date both work out."

"Same here."

The two men thanked the librarian and went outside. Don stopped as he opened his car door. "Oh, and if you're looking for something to do on your date, I'm playing at a local barn dance. Bronwyn knows where it is. I've got a new song about all the recent trouble, you know with Dwayne Gitterman and that patrolman."

"You wrote a song about it?"

SONG CREDITS

*All song lyrics are original except the following,
which are all public domain:*

CHAPTER SEVEN
"When Love Gets You Fast in Her Clutches" (composed
1795; words by Thomas Morton, music by Dr. Samuel
Arnold [1742–1802])

CHAPTER THIRTEEN
"On My Journey Home" by Isaac Watts (July 17, 1674–
November 25, 1748)

CHAPTER SIXTEEN
"John Barleycorn" (traditional English folk song)
A version of the song is included in the Bannatyne
Manuscript of 1568.
http://www.pdmusic.org/folk/John_Barleycorn.txt

CHAPTER TWENTY
"Wildwood Flower," aka "I'll Twine 'Mid the Ringlets" (composed approximately 1860; words by Maud Irving,

music by Joseph Philbrick Webster)
http://www.pdmusic.org/webster/jpw60itmtr.txt
Final verse modified from the traditional by the author

CHAPTER TWENTY-ONE
"Shady Grove" (traditional; eighteenth-century American variation
of the seventeenth-century English ballad "Matty Groves")
http://en.wikipedia.org/wiki/Shady_Grove_(song)

CHAPTER TWENTY-TWO
"Cripple Creek" (melody, lyrics, and chords from p. 232
[#118] from *The Folk Songs of North America: In the English
Language* by Alan Lomax)
http://www.pdmusic.org/folk/Cripple_Creek.txt
Modified from the traditional by the author

"Rye Whisky" (traditional folksong)
Mentioned in *American Ballads and Folk Songs* by John A.
Lomax and Alan Lomax (Dover, 1994; originally Macmillan
1934)
http://www.pdmusic.org/folk/Rye_Whisky.txt
Modified from the traditional by the author

CHAPTER TWENTY-FOUR
"The White Cockade" by Robert Burns (1759–1796)
http://www2.bc.edu/~hafner/lmm/music-articles/
white_cockade_ryan.html
http://www.contemplator.com/scotland/whitcock.html

CHAPTER TWENTY-SEVEN
"The Bird Song" by Carrie Jacobs Bond (composed 1899)
http://www.pdmusic.org/bond/cjb99tbs.txt
Modified from the original by the author

CHAPTER TWENTY-EIGHT
"The Grave of Gentle Annie" written by William Shakespeare
Hays (1837–1907) (composed 1858)
http://www.pdmusic.org/hays/wsh58tgoga.txt
Modified from the original by the author

"Mercy's Dream" by Septimus Winner (1827–1902) (composed
1854)
http://www.pdmusic.org/winner/sw54md.txt
Modified from the original by the author